ADRIFT

Ariboslia Book II

J. F. Rogers

*Trust in the Lord with all your heart
and lean not on your own understanding;
in all your ways acknowledge Him,
and He will set your paths straight.
-Proverbs 3:5-6*

Pronunciation Guide

People

Achaius \ ah-key-us \ Rescues babies and elderly from the Treasach

Aodan Tuama \ ay-den Too-ah-ma \ Fallon's uncle and leader of the fasgadair

Be'Norr* \ beh-norr \ Evan's fasgadair name

Cahal Fidhne \ kah-hal Feen \ Accompanies Fallon on her quest

Cataleen \ Cat-ah-lean \ Fallon's mother

Cairbre \ kar-bruh \ A legendary hero

Declan Cael \ deck-lan Kayl

Deirdra \ deer-drah \ The love of legendary hero Cairbre

De'Mere \ deh-meer \ Faolan's fasgadair name

Fallon \ fal-lawn \ The main character

Faolan \ fway-lawn \ A friend of Fallon's mother (also known as Wolf)

Fiona \ fee-own-ah \ Fallon's paternal grandmother

Hreidmar \ hreyd-mar \ Leader of the dark pech

Jacobus Durnin \ jay-koh-bus duhr-nin \ Rowan's old friend

Jorge Durnin \ jorj duhr-nin \ Rowan's old friend's father

Kai \ keye \ An exile

Maili \ may-lee \ Declan's betrothed

Miloslsv \ mee-los-slaf \ A dark pech who forged the zpět

Mirna \ Meer-nah \ Fallon's maternal grandmother

Morrigan \ More-ih-gahn \ The original fasgadair

Pepin \ pep-in \ The pech who made Drochaid

Sandor \ san-door \ A guard for Bandia

General Seung \ say-ung \ A selkie general

Sully \ sull-ee \ A seer
Tyge \ teeg \ A guard for Bandia

Clans
Ain-Dìleas \ ahn dill-ay-ahs \ from Bandia
Arlen \ are-luhn \ from Kylemore
Cael \ kayl \ from Notirr
Dosne \ Dohs-nee \ from Fàsach
Olwen \ Ohl-ven \ from Reòdh
Treasach \ treh-zack \ from Gnuatthara

Races
Fasgadair \ faz-geh-deer \ Vampires (means "blood drinker")
Gachen \ gah-chen \ Shape-shifters (anagram for "change")
Pech \ peck \ Small, strong people with abilities with stone
Selkie \ sell-key \ Gachen who turn into seals

Places
Ariboslia \ air-eh-bows-lia \ The realm
Ardara \ ahr-dahr-ah \ A gachen village
Bandia \ ban-dee-ah \ Occupied by the Ain-Dìleas
Bàthadh Sea \ bah-thach \ The sea leading to the land to the east
Ceas Croi* \ kase kree \ A city in a mountain created by the pech occupied by the fasgadair
Cnatan Mountains \ crah-dan \ The mountains that make Bandia difficult to reach by land
Diabalta \ dee-ah-ball-tah \ A formerly great city now under Morrigan's control
Fàsach \ fah-zack \ A village in the dessert occupied by the Dosne
Gnuatthara \ new-tara \ A fortified city occupied by the Treasach
Kylemore \ kyle-more \ A village in the trees occupied by the Arlen
Notirr* \ no-tear \ A village of mounds in hills occupied by the Cael
Reòdh* \ ray-och \ A village in the ice lands occupied by the Olwen
Saltinat \ salt-in-at \ An underwater city occupied by the selkie

Taobh Na Mara \ toov nah mah-rah \ A seaside village occupied by the selkie
Tower of Galore \ ga-lore \ A large tower rumored to be occupied by giants

Things
Bian \ bee-ahn \ The time when gachen or selkie come of age and shapeshift for the first time
Buille cridhe \ bool-yah kree \ A potion
Cianese \ see-ahn-eese \ A foreign language (most speak Ariboslian)
Co-Cheangail \ ko-kang-gale \ A committee of United Clans
Drochaid* \ dro-hach \ The amulet Pepin created
Feamainn \ fee-min \ Seaweed
Glemmestein \ glem-eh-stine \ A mineral that results in memory loss
Ionraic* \ on-eh-rick \ The committee of believers after the Co-Cheangail fell apart
Rác \ rack \ Kai's dog
Sàl samhanach \ Sahl Sam-ann-ack \ A giant octopus-like sea creature
Sirist \ see-rist \ A small, green pitted fruit
torman-ciùil* \ tor-man kyohl \ A stringed instrument that sits on your lap
Turnering av Stryke* \ turn-ay-eh-ring ahv streek \ An annual pech competition of strength
Uilebheist \ oo-deh-bish \ A monster the pech use as a death penalty
Uisge bàs \ oosh-geh bahs \ Poison
Zpĕt \ sp-yet \ The amulet that resurrected Morrigan

False Gods
Aine \ awn-yah \ god of love and fertility
Aoibhell \ ee-vell \ her harp is a premonition of death
Camalus \ cam-al-is \ god of war
Druantia \ drew-ahn-tia \ god of protection, knowledge, creativity

*trill the r

PROLOGUE

B E'THORR PERCHED IN THE trees—trapped. Wind parted the leaves, threatening to expose him. If Fallon caught him now…

Fallon sat in her bedroom window seat. Her black hair hung down, concealing her face. She appeared to be reading, sometimes writing. Was she doing schoolwork? From what he understood of her world, her formal education should be complete.

What was she doing?

He ruffled his feathers, eager to escape.

Why wouldn't she leave?

Fallon glanced out the window, the tip of her writing utensil in her mouth, her purple eyes shifted his way. Be'Thorr ducked, then shook his head at his paranoia. She'd never spot him in this tree. As long as he stayed put.

She resumed her writing. Should he risk fleeing now? No. She'd look up the moment he took flight.

That would be his luck.

What a fool he'd been. What else did he expect her to do today of all days? Sleep it away? Go out somewhere? No. She'd be up waiting for someone to take her back to Ariboslia. How could he be so daft? He should have left hours ago. But he lingered, both eager for and dreading what was to come. And Fallon had risen earlier than expected and planted herself in that blasted window. And now her friend was awake too.

He wished *he* could take her back to Ariboslia. But that wasn't possible. Not now.

The sun was rising. Birds began their morning chatter. As they flew near his perch, they scattered, chirping warnings to others who might venture too close. But they needn't have worried. Be'Thorr wouldn't risk exposing himself for a meal. Despite his growing hunger.

A cool summer breeze rustled the leaves, exposing him. He held his breath. His cover settled back into place, and he breathed easier. Somewhat.

His stomach felt heavy and uneasy, like a thick sludge churned within.

Ah, Fallon. So clueless as to the truth about to be revealed. How much could her heart take? He wanted to protect her. But he needed his distance. And she was tough. Tougher than she realized.

His heart ached, to the extent his heart could hurt in its present condition. There she sat. So anxious she never left that spot…or went longer than five seconds without peering out the window. Waiting. How many hours would she sit there?

Something grunted below him. A huge boulder moved along the ground, through the woods, and into Fallon's backyard. The stone pitched forward, slamming one end into the ground with a loud thud, shaking everything within earshot. Be'Thorr shifted his grip and unfurled his wings to regain his balance, staring at whatever had thrown the rock. A small person with a red braid brushed his hands. Pepin.

Fallon and her friend pressed their faces against the window. A finger pointed at Pepin strolling down the path, probably to fetch another boulder. The girls disappeared from the window.

This was his chance.

Be'Thorr secured the amulet cord with his beak, careful not to snip it. He flew deeper into the woods, landed high in the trees, and listened for footsteps. Nothing followed. No shouts. He relaxed.

Was Pepin building a new megalith?

No matter. Be'Thorr leaped from his perch and flew toward the megalith from which he'd come. He'd catch up with them in Kylemore.

CHAPTER ONE

PROPPED IN THE WINDOW seat, clutching my journal, I stared into the backyard where I'd sometimes glimpse Wolf watching over me. He was gone now. Nothing but the overgrown lawn, the dilapidated tree house, and the woods.

Today was the day.

Stacy flopped on my bed, flipped a page in her magazine, and gasped. Instead of taking the bait, I browsed earlier entries in my journal.

October 29. My memories of Ariboslia dim with the ever-darkening New England days. So depressing. Nothing compares with those heart-elevating, adrenaline-pumping months. This world is so bland. Like a plain, over-boiled potato. Going to school and pretending all I experienced hadn't happened is like watching television in black and white, trying to convince myself color never existed. However boring this world seemed before my adventures was now multiplied a hundredfold. School: a jail full of immature, shallow students who live for themselves, raising themselves above all others, and ignorant teachers who speak with authority on subjects they don't understand.

I've seen an invisible world! What I've seen would awaken people to unimaginable possibilities beyond their nearsightedness. But I'm denied, forced to answer science exams incorrectly for a decent grade. Muted. Unable to speak about reality for fear of being imprisoned, trapped in a padded cell, wrapped in a love-me jacket.

Stacy let out another gasp. Louder. I flipped ahead a few pages.

January 17. Stacy, our church, periodic visits from Wolf, brief trips to the sky in falcon form (when I dare), and the promise of returning to Ariboslia sustain me during these dark days. The new calendar and increasing sunlight renew my hope. The day is growing closer.

I returned to my latest entry.

June 21. My eighteenth birthday has finally arrived. A year ago today, I was dragged to Ariboslia. Was it all a dream? I have nothing to prove it. Only this journal…something the world would assume to be the ramblings of a psychopath.

But there was Wolf. And I'm able to transform into a falcon and fly. There is no doubt about that…. Today, if I'm given the choice to return as promised, I'll know.

My heart flipped. I glanced down at Drochaid for the gazillionth time, hoping for one of the arrows to light up, showing me where to go. My mother's amulet guided me every step of the way last year. Still, I kept checking. But who was I kidding? I'd feel its warmth first. I pulled my pencil from my mouth and continued writing.

This day, more than any other, I expect Drochaid's glow.

But I'm torn. On one hand, I want nothing more than to return to the mysterious, untamed land where I received new life. I want to do God's will and save lives…my family. I don't want to waste my life in this house with my grandmother. On the other hand, I hate to leave Stacy. But more than that, I'm afraid. My life will be in constant danger. I won't know who to help. Those I'm meant to save and those who want me dead are the same—the fasgadair.

Then there's Declan….

Ah, Declan. Was it wrong that my heart did a little somersault? He's betrothed. Unavailable. And yet…those eyes. Those intense green eyes always penetrated my soul. So many memories of Ariboslia had faded, but those eyes were burned into my psyche.

I took a deep breath. This wasn't about Declan. It was about God's plans and my part in them. I must remember….

I tapped the pencil against the notebook, unsure what to add.

Didn't I have to do what God called me to do? How else would I live with myself? And how could I stay here? Bored out of my mind. I would regret it forever. I crisscrossed my legs and glanced in irritation at the dull amulet around my neck.

"You're obsessing, Fal. Stop thinking about it." Stacy peeked out over the magazine as she lounged on my pillows and a few overly loved stuffed animals from Bumpah.

"I can't help it." The notebook slid off my lap. "It's supposed to be today. What if Pepin was wrong? What if they decide they don't want me to return? What if something happened to them?"

Stacy lowered the magazine onto her chest and raised an eyebrow. "Are you serious right now? It's only six a.m. What time do you expect this to happen?"

Okay. She had me there.

"Wasn't it much later last time?"

Another good point.

"You still have the entire day. Besides, would it be so bad if you stayed a little longer? You have me. And it's not so bad to live with your grandmother anymore, right?"

"That's because *I've* changed." It started with little things: cleaning dishes left sitting in the sink, taking out the overflowing trash, and responding in a pleasant tone.

"That's all it takes. One person to take the high road." Stacy rolled the magazine into a log. "And I'm telling you. She was a wreck when you were gone."

"Yeah. She seemed happy to see me…. For a few minutes anyway." I bent to pick up the journal. "The scrapbook made a huge difference too." What a project—sorting through the massive piles of postcards from Bumpah stashed all over the house, mapping them in a scrapbook with the few pictures I found of him.

"I so wish I'd seen her face when you gave it to her." She drummed the magazine against her leg. "You got her to stop sending herself more postcards."

"True. I curbed the insanity a bit."

"And she likes you a lot more now. So…I repeat: Would it be so bad if you stayed?"

Yes, yes, it would be. "It's funny. I keep thinking I have a choice. But I never applied to any colleges. I've never considered staying."

Stacy gripped the magazine and bit her lip.

"I'm not eager to leave *you*, ya know."

She fiddled with something invisible on her right knee.

"I don't belong here."

"None of us do, Fal."

"It's more than what awaits us after this life. There's unfinished business in Ariboslia. There's so much more I need to do—to learn."

"Well, I'm in no hurry for you to leave." Her frown deepened. Then she smiled, her eyes mischievous. "And I don't think Jeremy is either."

I rolled my eyes and groaned. "Oh please." There was one guy for me, and it wasn't any high-school boy…or recent grad. Not from this realm.

"What? He likes you."

Her singsong, teasing tone invoked my pillow-throwing reflex.

"Hey." She laughed, peeling the pillow from her face.

High-school boys. Nothing brought forth a more pronounced groan than their mention. Stacy knew this…and that I'd take the bait. "I would rather—"

She bolted upright and shushed me.

"What?"

"Shhh!" She held her hand up to silence me as she leaned her ear toward the left. "Did you hear that?"

"Hear what?" My un-hushed voice met more shushing. Her hand, still upright, waved at me.

A heavy thud shook the house. I twisted to peer outside. She slammed into me and pressed her face against the window.

"Dude, a *dwarf!*

Chapter Two

A SMALL MAN WITH a stout body strolled down the path into the woods, red braid swinging to his waddle.

"Pepin!" I banged on the window. Why was he heading toward the woods?

Stacy's face lit up. We sprinted through the bedroom door, jostling each other in our haste. Decorative plates displayed in the hutch and on the walls rattled as we rushed to the kitchen. Breathless, we reached the door and fought to get out first.

I won the battle and flung the door open. "Pepin!"

My stomach sank. Where was he? He wouldn't leave without coming to the house. Would he?

I ran across the yard. Pepin stood on the path, a ginormous stone braced overhead. *Thank God.* I ran to the little man. "Pepin!"

Startled, he stepped back, the rock tipped. Pepin righted the slab and sighted me. Recognition crinkled his face into a smile. Or a grimace? "Fallon." His voice strained.

"I see you grew your beard." I rubbed my chin to illustrate my point.

He grunted something resembling assent. Sweat moistened his sideburns. His typical ruddy complexion a bit redder than usual, almost matching his hair, he trudged forward with the monstrous rock. I followed him to two more. One lay on the ground, another planted on its end. So that's what shook the house. Veins popping, he slammed the slab into the soil, standing it perpendicular to the first. Stacy and I splayed our arms to keep our balance as the world shook.

Her eyes bulged. "How'd he do that?"

"I told you, Stace. The pech are strong. They have abilities with stone I still don't understand."

Pepin brushed his hands. Not that it did any good. Grime caked his stubby hands.

"I remember. But wow." She trailed her fingers over a planted rock, then nudged it. When it didn't fall, she pushed harder.

"Why are you building a megalith here?" I folded my arms across my chest, covering the BTS logo on my T-shirt. "What's wrong with the one in the woods?"

"Not safe. Need new."

"But it's not far away. If it isn't safe, how could this one be?"

"Far enough. Move quick."

His response wasn't right. "Stacy, do you understand him?"

"Yeah. Shouldn't I?"

Gripping myself tighter, I faced Pepin. "You speak English?"

A twinkle brightened his amber eyes. He pinched his plump fingers together. "Little."

"How?"

"I travel. Remember?"

"To my realm?" Hadn't he said he traveled all over Ariboslia? He said nothing about visiting here.

"Yes." He planted his feet and picked up the last rock. Like a professional weightlifter, he grunted, his face distorted. He heaved the thing overhead and carried it toward the other two, sinking into the soil with each step. When he reached the others, he lowered the stone on their upright ends and left it balancing there, reminding me of faulty structures I'd created with blocks as a child. He pointed to the hole in its center. "Time. We go."

"Now? That's so quick. Drochaid isn't glowing."

He shrugged. "Sully sent. For you."

Sully. The seer? He sent Pepin? "Why you? Why not Cahal or…" Or Declan.

He aimed a stubby thumb at himself. "Little pech. No one care."

So, this was how it would be.

Why was I dragging my feet?

****

I stood at the back door, my stomach twisted like a misused slinky. Last time I didn't get to say goodbye. Perhaps it was better. Despite the scrapbook, Fiona and I weren't close. Saying goodbye was odd, but not hard. Stacy. Stacy would be hard.

The screen door slammed against the house as I strolled into the backyard. I adjusted the pack I'd been stuffing since my first paycheck and hoisted it over my shoulders. "I'm ready."

"How was Fiona?" Stacy stood and wiped her hands on her jeans.

"She told me not to get lost."

She chuckled. "Gotta love her."

My old self wanted to rise and ask, "Do I?" But I knew the answer. Yes. I had to love her.

I stared at the megalith. Rocks. A bizarre pile of rocks. Without Drochaid or another amulet that allowed travel through the realms, they *were* just rocks. But to me, they were more. A gateway to an alternate reality. I gazed into the center—the blank space that was my future.

My last visit nearly killed me, physically and mentally. I wasn't human. Not fully. I was half human and half gachen. A shape-shifter. I could turn into a falcon, for Pete's sake. And my mother. She was still alive.

But the fasgadair. This time, they'll know me. If they discovered what my blood can do, I'll be a human pincushion. Or they'll kill me. Or use me as a pincushion *then* kill me. I dropped to my knees as the weight pressed on me. I'd had an entire school year to process all I'd learned, all I'd experienced. Wasn't that enough? Was I ready to deal with whatever this trip might bring?

God, help me.

Stacy rushed to my side. "Are you okay?" She snugged an arm around me.

I took a deep breath. This was more difficult than I expected. I forced a smile. "I'll be okay."

"I'm going to miss you, Fal." Tears streamed down her face. "At least this time, you're not disappearing without a trace. We won't think you ran away and get the police involved." Tears dripped onto her shirt. She waved toward Pepin, his arms crossed, his foot tapping. "And now I *know* you're not insane."

I choked out a laugh. "That's a plus." My eyes welled up as I hugged her. "I'm gonna miss you, Stace." I squeaked out her name. My stomach dipped as if I'd taken a dive on a roller coaster. I gave her a weak hug. When she released me from her vice grip, I wiped the dirt from my jeans and zombie shuffled toward the megalith.

"Where's Wolf?" We couldn't leave without him.

"Other side. I check. Safe. You wait."

Pepin crawled under the rock. His head disappeared, then his torso. Only his bottom-half remained. Where his upper half should have poked through the other side was nothing but dirt, grass, and air. He shuffled forward and disappeared.

Stacy gasped, her wet eyes wide, hands covering her gaping mouth.

"How'd you think it worked?" I laughed.

"It's just so weird to see."

I knelt to follow when Pepin's head nearly collided with mine. His furry eyebrows rose, then closed in as he backed up, bumping the stone above him. "I say wait. Why you no wait?"

"Well, I—"

"I say wait. You wait." He pointed a chubby digit in my face as his caterpillar uni-brow danced across his forehead.

"Okay, okay." I pushed back onto my knees.

"'Tis safe. Come." His face disappeared, followed by his beckoning sausage fingers.

"Bye, Stace. You are loved." I gave a final wave, took a mental picture of her tear-streaked face, then crawled through the megalith to whatever lay on the other side.

CHAPTER THREE

LIGHT DAZZLED ME. I swatted away tears, but everything remained blurry. My contacts. I plucked them out, and my surroundings came into focus. Ah. No more contacts. One benefit of Ariboslia. And now, it was certain—I wasn't crazy.

I breathed in the sweet air and memories of my visit. As before, everything appeared brighter and sharper, even from a considerable distance—without corrective lenses. Sunlight bounced off a rippling lake. Multicolored small birds fluttered over its surface. Each snatched a water bug and landed on a bare tree nearby, twittering as they went, then repeated the process like a dancing rainbow.

This was the Ariboslia view of my backyard? If I had my bearings, my house would be underwater. The first megalith should be in the woods to the left. There must be a clearing beyond the trees. In this realm, the first megalith was in a field.

Rocks crashed behind me. I swung around. Pepin wiped his hands next to a pile of rocks that had once been the megalith. "Does that pile look like this in my realm too?"

He nodded. "The only constants between the realms are megaliths and time…that I know of."

"I hope Stacy wasn't standing too close when they fell." I imagined her face, wet with tears, staring at the felled rocks. "You should have warned her."

Pepin shrugged.

The image of Stacy crying out, crushed under rocks chilled me. Knowing her, she might've tried crawling through. I shook it off. No. If she'd been too close, she would've jumped away when they moved. Right? Yes. She was fine. No sense worrying. I couldn't do anything anyway. And she was quick.

Beyond Pepin stood a forest of dead trees with spindly, bare branches. "It's the beginning of summer. Why are the trees all dead?" So strange. In one direction, the place reminded me of heaven. On the other, Halloween.

The birds' playful twittering turned to alarmed squeaks. They banded together and darted off, disappearing into the horizon. Had I scared them, or had something else?

"Lower your voice. Let's not attract unwanted attention."

"But you…" I motioned to the rocks. Like knocking those over wouldn't attract attention.

He grabbed a satchel resting against the rocks. "They're not dead. They're fur trees."

"*Fur* trees?" He couldn't mean fir trees.

"Yes. Do you not have them in your realm?" He shifted the weight over his shoulder. "I don't recall seeing any in my travels."

"I don't think so."

"They shed their fur in the summer when it gets hot. You should see them in the winter. Beautiful."

Yup. I was in Ariboslia. Time to stop trying to make sense of things.

"You're not speaking English anymore, are you?" So much for not bothering to seek understanding. That lasted one nanosecond.

"No. You have Drochaid and Stacy is gone. There's no need. This way." He pointed to the right of the lake, toward the fur trees. "We must reach Kylemore before dark. Grab your pack."

I slipped my arm through one loop and fumbled with the other. Something flew at me and knocked me down. "Ow."

Wolf nudged my face with his muzzle.

"Wolf!"

"Shhh!" Pepin bulged his eyes as if to say, "Didn't I tell you to be quiet?"

I righted myself and threw my arms around Wolf, burying my face in his fur, savoring the moment.

Pepin cleared his throat in a less-than-subtle manner. I released Wolf and scanned the woods. Without leaves, there wasn't much privacy. "Do you need to change?"

Wolf shook his head.

"Don't you have a lot to tell me? Plans? Where we're going?"

Wolf blew air out his nose and shook his head again. His shaggy mane billowed. He circled me, cinched my pack in his teeth, and tugged.

I grasped the straps. "What are you doing?"

He refused to release, so I did. "Fine." My belongings thudded to the ground. "What do you want with it? Or do you want to wear *my* clothes?"

Wolf drooped, his eyes half-lidded, unimpressed. He snorted and shifted his attention to the pack for a couple seconds, then tilted his head at Pepin.

Pepin snatched my bag. "He wants me to carry it."

"Why?"

"Ariboslia has changed. It's more dangerous. Especially at night. We must reach Kylemore before sundown. We'll take shelter there, then travel to Bandia. If I ride Wolf and you fly, we might make it. Be on the lookout for danger. Warn us before we meet it on the ground."

I gulped. That's what we did when Ryann was killed.

No. I couldn't think that way. The past was the past. Everything happened for a reason. Time to move forward. "Which way?"

"Southeast." Pepin aimed through the dead forest. "Kylemore is a village in the trees. You won't find it. Keep your eye on us and potential danger."

Tiny bubbles burst in my stomach, sending ripples throughout my body. Fear of getting caught shape-shifting in my world stopped me from doing it often. Here I hoped to have many opportunities. The mere thought of soaring above the tree line made my fingers and feet tingle.

I changed. My wings flapped to disentangle myself from my clothing. Once I found an opening, I folded my wings and hopped to freedom. Pepin picked up the pile and shoved it into my bag. "How much did you pack?" He removed his own, more modest satchel and heaved my pack onto his back. Good thing he was strong. Otherwise, he might topple. He draped the strap of his own over his head, then settled upon Wolf's back. Wolf's legs buckled a second under the weight. Pepin, sandwiched between two packs, didn't have wiggle room. Guess I shouldn't have packed so much.

Wolf gave me a quick nod and bolted into the dead forest. I took to the sky like a kid bounding downstairs on Christmas morning.

It required fancy maneuvering to navigate the branches, and I was out of practice. But I made it to the blue sky. The wind rushed through my feathers. The creepy trees weren't gloomy from these heights. It would be easier to spot danger and keep track of Wolf and Pepin without the foliage.

How I had missed this! Peace filled my soul. In the sky, I felt closer to God. I cut through the air and breathed in the sweet fragrance of wildflowers. A cool breeze pushed my feathers, lifting me higher into the quiet sky where the sounds below failed to travel. So peaceful.

The sky darkened in the distance. But nothing would sway my joy.

I circled back for Pepin and Wolf. Had they fallen behind? I probably flew faster than Wolf could run carrying his load. Pepin seemed solid, like the rocks he so loved. He must weigh a ton.

I located them and flew ahead again, circling like a buzzard who'd spotted roadkill.

Evergreens infiltrated the fur trees. Wolf disappeared beneath their needles, then reemerged. The sky darkened as storm clouds advanced.

A prickly sensation swept over me like someone was watching me. My eyesight was better in this form. I could track anything chipmunk-sized or larger moving on the ground …assuming it was unobscured by the greenery. A few rodents and a rabbit scrambled into hiding at Wolf's approach. But that was all. Nothing suspicious.

Was it following me? I couldn't turn my head without flying in that direction, so I circled around. Nothing.

But that feeling—that ice-cube-on-the-back-of-the-neck feeling—wouldn't go away. Something was following us. Did Morrigan have spies? I flew ahead of my friends as if nothing was wrong, then tucked into a dive and spun in the air.

A bird swooped behind a tall pine.

CHAPTER FOUR

I FLEW TOWARD THE pine. A raindrop pelted me. More followed. The clouds let loose, pouring in sheets, soaking my feathers. I shivered.

Seriously, God? Rain? Again? Don't You want us to succeed?

The pine blurred in the torrential downpour. I started through the storm clouds to rise above them, then stopped. What was I thinking? I wouldn't see anything through the clouds. There'd be no way to keep an eye on Wolf and Pepin. I turned back to my friends. A gray mist blanketed the ground. My breath caught. Every nerve sent the same terrifying message—*You'll never find your friends in this.* But getting separated wasn't an option. Too bad I couldn't text them. Ariboslia seriously needed cell service. I didn't know where I was going. Why hadn't they told me where Kylemore was, so I could meet them? Not that I'd find it on my own without a compass...or Drochaid.

Oh no! Without Drochaid, I wouldn't even be able to communicate with anyone. I had to find them. I. Had. To.

Thick fog obscured my vision. I dropped altitude. I only saw a couple of feet in front of me. A tree emerged from the blur. I swooped to avoid it.

God, help me!

I banked left. A branch scraped my wing. I maneuvered between trees, above and below branches, with nothing but a few seconds to choose each course of action to avoid a collision. My heart raced with each near miss. This was no good. I'd kill myself flying through these trees. And I'd never find Wolf and Pepin.

I swooped down a few feet above the ground and transfigured. Too low. I fell on my knees in a puddle. Mud splashed me as I pitched forward, catching my fall with my palms.

"Wolf!" I righted myself and spun. Rain matted my hair and washed away the mud. "Pepin!"

I shivered and ran. "Wolf! Pepin!" The shower slowed somewhat. I still couldn't see much. Or hear. The rain was too loud. I strained to listen, desperate for any evidence of my friends.

My heart beat like an overly caffeinated drummer. I fought the urge to cry, clenched my fists, and screamed with all my lungpower, "Wooooooooolf!"

I fell to my knees. But no sound rose above my heavy breathing and the pounding rain.

Please help me find Wolf and Pepin.

Something crunched to my right. I jolted.

A low growl sounded. A furry face appeared, half obscured by a tree.

"Wolf?" I backed away.

The thing snarled and snapped its jaw.

Not Wolf. A coyote.

I ran, jumped with all my strength, and transfigured midair. My heavy wings fought to gain altitude. Teeth gnashing, the coyote leapt. My talon scratched something. His nose? He fell back to the ground as I retreated to the sky. The coyote snuffed, then took off running.

I hadn't become the coyote's meal. My heartbeat returned to normal. But my situation hadn't improved. If I didn't find my friends, I wouldn't have a way to communicate or protect myself. Or clothes.

The rain was now a mist. The patchy fog had lessened. So, I circled. And circled. And circled.

Please…please…please show me where they are.

A smoke tendril spiraled, acting as a beacon through the trees. Hope escalated like a deep-sea diver running out of air. I flew toward the smoke, praying I'd find my friends at the other end and not something else.

CHAPTER FIVE

I FLAPPED WITH ALL my strength. The smoke rose from under a felled tree. I landed on a nearby branch. Pepin bent over a pitiful fire, more smoke than flames. I wanted to cry, laugh, and yell as I hopped next to him, screeching. "Kak! Kak! Kak!"

Pepin shouted something I couldn't understand without Drochaid. He dropped my pack on the other side of the tree, by the upended roots. I changed and hurried back before my clothes got soaked. I already felt like a used mop.

"A coyote tried to attack me. And there's a bird following us. I'm sure it's a fasgadair."

Pepin's eyes darted in every direction, then scanned the sky.

"The coyote took off. And the bird is probably holed up somewhere." I hugged myself and smoothed my goosebumps. "Trust me, it's not fun to fly in the rain."

"A gift from God." Pepin's cheeks puffed as he blew the smoke.

"The rain? You hate to get wet."

"As do the fasgadair, even in animal form. And the rain covers our sound and makes us harder to spot. Should give us time for a safe meal." He gestured to his pathetic fire. "Can you get those sticks to ignite? They're wet."

It had been a while since I'd started a fire. And I'd never tried to start one in the rain. I stared at the twigs, and they erupted into flames. Just like flying. Once you learned, you never forgot.

"Won't the smoke give away our location?"

"Did you see a pack of strange animals while you were up there?"

"Just the coyote."

"Then we should be all right. A lone coyote would be a fool to attack three."

"Where's Wolf?"

"Hunting." Pepin threw more sticks on the fire.

"Do we have time for this?" I sat on a rock and stretched my shoulders, cursing myself for not practicing flying as I had hiking and running.

"We need to keep up our strength." He huddled underneath the tree. "Besides, birds get cold and hungry. And you'd slow us down as a human."

Something crunched behind me. I jumped to my feet.

Wolf chuckled and sauntered over, a rabbit in each hand. "A wee bit jumpy are ye?"

"Faolan!" I rushed into him and squeezed though he was wet. He held his arms out to keep the rabbits from touching me.

"You're strong," he said in a falsetto voice.

Laughing, I let him go. He looked the same as when I left. Only wet. His black hair hung in wet clumps, sticking to his face and the back of his neck.

"And call me Wolf. Faolan is too similar to Fallon. It gets confusing."

"Okay…Wolf." Calling a grown man Wolf was odd. Although he looked much younger, closer to my age, he carried himself like an older man. And he was. A middle-aged man trapped in a young guy's body from his years of stunted growth in fasgadair form. Such news would be dangerous in my realm. The next antiaging fad and get-rich-quick scheme.

But he was right. And Wolf was better than De'Mere, his

fasgadair name. I shuddered to think he'd ever been one. "I can't believe I'm here, and you're serving me rabbit…again."

"Ye weren't so trusting the first time." He winked.

"You were chasing me." I gave his shoulder a gentle shove. "I thought you were going to kill me."

"Aye." He shrugged and handed Pepin the rabbits. "There was that. But then I remember ye screaming that ye couldn't prepare a rabbit."

"I thought you were just a wolf. If I knew I'd hear about it later…" I returned to my seat. "So, what did I miss?"

Wolf massaged his lower back, then settled on a dry spot under our meager roof while Pepin set to work on the rabbits. "I was in your world, watching over ye. But Pepin's been about. He shared whilst I carried him and both your loads." Wolf groaned and rubbed his back again. "He's quite the windbag, blathering on. 'Tis time *ye* got to work, chum."

Pepin rolled his eyes. "You try riding an overstuffed animal…" He continued mumbling something as he fashioned a spit for the fire. He walked bowlegged with more of a waddle than usual.

"Talk about overstuffed…" Wolf's hazel eyes dulled. "Ariboslia has gotten worse than I'd imagined."

"Worse?" I hugged my cold arms tight about my middle. "Didn't Aodan's death make things better?"

"Aodan's death 'twas only the beginning. He was kind compared to his replacement, Na'Rycha. Not one clan has remained unaffected except the Ain-Dìleas in the city of Bandia in the Cnatan Mountains."

Pepin snorted. "If you consider becoming an overrun military outpost unaffected. Survivors are taking refuge there now. They're training all able-bodied males to fight."

"What about my mother and the rest of the Ceas Croi escapees? What about the Cael?" Pepin had sent a warning before I returned home.

Pepin skinned a rabbit with skilled precision. "Everyone made it to Bandia before Na'Rycha burned Notirr down."

Notirr? My Ariboslian home. The homes in the hills, the tent where we gathered for meals, the barns and stables…the animals. Was it all gone? The pier where I'd first talked to Declan must still be there. Thank God, the people survived. I hoped the animals did too.

"But the Ain-Dìleas's alliance is shaky." Pepin hacked at our dinner. "Since they worship false gods, they see the Cael and many other clans who believe in the one true God as intolerant fools. They're waiting for your arrival to decide how to proceed. They've heard rumors about you."

"What rumors?" Clan leaders were talking about me?

Pepin stilled, his chunky arms lowering one rabbit to his side as he met my gaze in the firelight. Part of me didn't want to hear his answers. Part of me wanted him to hurry up and say it.

"Some want you to join the fight, believing you're the key to winning. Others fear harboring you will make them a target."

"Aye." Wolf scrunched his face and shook out his hair, flinging droplets my way. He needed to spend less time as a wolf. "Morrigan wants to avenge Aodan's death. She's sent troops of armies under Na'Rycha's ruthless charge, destroying everything in their path, seeking you."

"Avenge Aodan? *She* killed him."

Wolf threw me his are-ye-that-daft look. "She was trying to kill *ye*. She blames *ye* for his death."

"But it's not my fault. If they hadn't tried killing me…"

Wolf snorted. "A demon cannot see reason."

"We must kill Morrigan. First, we have to get through Na'Rycha's army. You are the key." Silver flashed as Pepin worked.

"You keep saying that. The key. How am I the key?" I tried not to witness the rabbit's dissection, but my gaze kept gravitating toward the knife.

Wolf narrowed his eyes. "Have ye forgotten what you did when you were here?"

"You mean what my blood did." Not *me*.

"Ian drank your blood and died. But Evan drank your blood and lived…no longer a fasgadair. Same with Aodan before Morrigan killed him. And Wolf." Pepin aimed the bloody blade toward Wolf, then laid the cleaned rabbits aside. He groaned as he rumbled to his feet.

"What does that have to do with—"

"I don't know." Pepin shoved a stick through a carcass and balanced it on the spit. "But you were given your abilities for such a time as this."

"So, what's the plan? Let every fasgadair try to kill me to see if they live or die? Remember what happened when three fed on me in the same day?" I touched my neck as if expecting to find the wounds. "I was barely conscious. And they'll want me dead. What's to keep them from chopping off *my* head? I'm not immortal."

Concern darkened Wolf's hazel eyes.

"Na'Rycha must be stopped," Pepin said. "Since the gachen population has thinned, he's killing the pech."

"How? Aren't they underground?" The Tower of Galore wasn't. And it was visible for miles. I covered my mouth. "The Tower—"

"It's destroyed." Wolf peeked at Pepin then lowered his gaze.

A tear settled into Pepin's beard.

An underground world full of people, children. All I knew is what Pepin told me. If only they hadn't made me forget by forcing me to eat a glemmestein. I blinked back tears. My heart ached for them…for Pepin.

"We must trust and obey God in this. You *are* part of His plan. And He is with us." Pepin wiped a tear.

"Does Sully see what will happen?"

"Sully sees what God reveals." Pepin spun the rabbit on the spit. "He's not providing many answers. He tells us to do things that lead to more questions, such as waiting for you rather than going straight into battle."

"What about you? Before I left Ariboslia, you turned prophet on us. You told us what we should do and when. Do you still have any of that prophet thing going on?"

Pepin's braid bounced as he shook his head. "Like Sully, and everyone else, God uses us for His purposes at His appointed times."

"And Drochaid?" I pulled the amulet from my neckline. "It hasn't lit up once. Am I even supposed to be here?"

"I created Drochaid, and I don't understand it," Pepin said. "I've never heard of an amulet that acted as a guide. No pech has. If God made it so, and I believe He did, it probably wasn't intended to guide you throughout your life. It may have outlived its usefulness in that manner. For the moment, it still serves its intended purpose: as a key through the megalith and as a language translator. It was never more than a tool."

I groaned. My head hurt. Why couldn't anything be simple?

Wolf placed a hand on my shoulder. "None of this is yer fault. Yer the key to making it better."

I moved out of his reach. "That's what I thought. I was willing to die for it."

Wolf scratched his chin. "From my perspective, we've found a cure for fasgadair who wish to be saved."

"But that cure is *me*. *My* blood." All they have to do is kill me and take over Ariboslia. Doubts I thought I'd settled assaulted me. "There are so many of them and only one of me."

Wolf laid a hand on my shoulder, warm comfort issuing from his palm. "Yer loved, lass. Be at peace. God is with us. And we only need one of Him."

Pepin handed me a rabbit leg. I was hungry but had to force myself to eat. Each bite sank like a rock, weighing heavily in my stomach. Why had I been so eager to return? How could I help anyone? I put a target on their back.

I caught movement in my periphery. A blur pounced on me. Claws pierced my upper chest, pushing me back. My shoulder hit a rock. The coyote stood over me. Protruding fangs lunged at my face.

CHAPTER SIX

WOLF LIFTED THE COYOTE by its scruff. The thing snarled, snapping its jaw. Its body twisted midair. Wolf sliced its neck. Blood splattered my arm. I recoiled, and the coyote went limp. Wolf dropped it and rushed to my side.

"Are ye all right, lass?" Reaching out a hand, he helped me stand.

My body shook. My stomach threatened to bring back what little I'd just eaten. The thing's claw's ripped my T-shirt in several places. Scratches burned underneath. An ache radiated from my shoulder. "Is my shoulder bleeding?"

Wolf peeled back my shirt enough to inspect my shoulder. Good thing he was like a father, albeit a very young father. "'Tis red. 'Twill bruise. What about those scratches?"

"I'll be okay." I peeked beneath my neckline to inspect them all. "They're not deep." I stood and wiped at the coyote's blood, making it smudge my shirt. The rain had stopped. But there were fresh puddles. Good thing I packed plenty of shirts.

Wolf glanced in every direction. "What possessed that crazed beast to attack? 'Twas no coyote, that's for certain. Plenty of rodents roam these woods. It wouldn't have been desperate enough to go after something your size. But if it was a fasgadair, 'twas off its head. The beast had no chance against three."

I stared at the lifeless form. His nose had a fresh scratch. "This one attacked me earlier. Maybe it wasn't part of Morrigan's army. Maybe it wanted to die." I blinked back a tear. "What if I could've saved it?"

"What if it…" Wolf grabbed fistfuls of his hair as if he was about to pull it out, his face twisted in frustration. Then he let go and relaxed. "I don't even want to consider what it might've done to you. I won't let that happen."

I swiped at the blood on my shirt again. "Don't you have to remove its head, so it won't regenerate?"

"Aye. I will. No need for ye to see that. I'll take care of it when yer in the air."

The sky didn't look the same to me. It posed new threats. "I can't risk getting separated again. What if I ended up here alone, without Drochaid or clothes? I don't know where Kylemore is."

"Ye must." Wolf put a hand on my shoulder. "We need yer eyes. And we're close. Kylemore is southeast. If ye lose us, let yer bird senses guide you. If ye reach the ocean, you've gone too far."

I sighed. No point arguing. I changed back into a bird and retreated to the sky. My shoulder didn't hurt as much, and it was safer up here. I was the predator. The one to fear. Unless the bird following us was stronger. Given the lengths it went through to remain unseen, I doubted it was anything to fear. I hoped.

Still, I wanted to catch it.

The wind had shifted, making my flight easier. I flew faster, soaring ahead of my friends to turn around, hoping to catch whatever tailed us. Nothing but blue sky. If nothing else, I made it difficult to follow us without getting caught. My friends kept disappearing under the heavy brush. And the sun was lowering.

I wanted to call out. But after the coyote attack, I didn't want to bring on unwanted attention. Where were they? Had I gone too far ahead? Had I circled back in the wrong direction? I tried to tune in to my bird senses. Duh. Everyone who'd ever been to elementary school knew the sun rises in the east. The sun was behind me, and I need to go southeast. I angled myself toward the sun, keeping it to my left.

Wolf appeared in a clearing. He and Pepin were advancing at a good clip. I took a deep breath and soared after them, determined not to lose them again. The dense growth ended ahead, replaced by strange trees standing like bristled toothpicks in the earth.

No, not strange. Burnt. The smell of ash assaulted my bird-nose. Thick charred trees appeared to be upside down, their black roots jutting up from the ground. Plants looked like frozen, black snakes standing on their tails. A chill swept through my feathers. From this distance and height, the fire's path was clear. Nothing within it moved. Everything was dead.

But I'd be able to keep better track of Wolf and Pepin. And it would be difficult for any living thing to hide. I pressed on ahead.

Further up, life reemerged. The trees fattened. Birds flitted, crying out and scattering at my approach. Tree-dwelling critters chittered. Elephants trumpeted. Elephants?

Large gray bodies stood in a pond, which barely contained them. I angled back and perched on a tree. One elephant shot water at two others who trumpeted in return. The smallest one dipped its trunk, which swelled with water. Just before the blast hit the offending elephant's face, it lowered onto its front legs. Water sailed overhead.

"Analu, Keoni, Palani." A young woman called out in a hushed voice, sounding stern yet playful, matching her expression. Head tilted, hands on hips, she angled her piercing dark eyes at them and smiled. She spoke in a foreign tongue. I didn't understand a word without Drochaid. She spun her athletic frame, her long hair following in a wave, and sauntered down a wide path. The elephants ambled out of the water. On their way, the little one loaded its trunk and blasted the ammunition at the elephant it missed before, hitting its butt. The struck elephant swung its head, trumpeted, and followed the girl.

After they passed, I returned to the sky.

A strange sound, similar to someone running in corduroys, came from the trees. "Vvvvvt." Something shot past me.

An arrow.

Chapter Seven

"Vvvvvt." A sharp tip ruffled my feathers. No pain. It hadn't hit flesh. I tucked, dove a couple feet before banking to the left, descended another couple of feet, and veered back to the right, evading further attack. The dead area lay up ahead. I flapped with all my might.

I spotted Wolf and Pepin in the burned section. They were close. Too close.

I flew at Pepin, knocking him off Wolf. He pulled himself up and wiped the ash on his arm, turning his arm black. He threw me a stern look and shouted something I couldn't understand. I hopped around shaking my wings, kicking up soot.

Pepin abandoned my pack behind a thick, charred stub.

"Arrows." I didn't dare raise my voice too much, but I had to warn them. I changed in record speed and bolted out from behind the tree. "Shooting…" I pointed in the direction I'd come, gasping for breath.

Wolf sniffed at the air.

"Elephants…girl…"

"Ah." Pepin relaxed, returning his knife to its sheath. "Maili of Kylemore."

Doubled over, clutching my side, I turned to Pepin. "Huh?" Maili? Please, no. "Declan's betrothed?"

"She's why we're here."

"Well…she or someone with her tried to kill me."

****

The wide path where Maili had disappeared seemed like another world from the ground. Thick trees with trunks broad enough to house a small airplane lined the hard-packed dirt. Their branches formed a canopy about thirty feet over my head. The tunnel split off onto smaller passageways, but we kept to the main path.

I scanned everywhere for my attacker. How could they approach this place so boldly?

"Who are you?"

I jumped, turning to the sound. The voice, the same girl I'd heard earlier, came from overhead. I searched the trees. She stood with an arrow trained on us.

"It is I, Pepin." He pounded his chest twice and bowed—the traditional pech greeting. He motioned to Wolf. "This is Faolan of Notirr in wolf form. And…" Pepin tipped his head and gestured toward me, palm up, like a game-show host presenting a prize. "…this is Fallon of the human realm."

Oh brother. Had Pepin taken lessons from Ryann? Shouting our identities for any lurking creatures to overhear? Stealth. We needed stealth.

"We've been expecting you, Fallon." Maili lowered her weapon and returned the arrow to its quiver on her back.

"On a platter?" I asked.

"Pardon?"

Pepin stepped in front of me. "Please excuse Fallon. She believes someone here attacked her."

"The falcon was you?" Her arched eyebrows rose.

"Yeah." I crossed my arms.

"I feared the possibility. 'Tis why Zakur didn't shoot to kill. My most sincere apologies, Fallon. Zakur wouldn't have shot had he known it was you. We can't be too careful with Morrigan's spies lurking about."

"You can if it means impaling an innocent victim." I spoke under my breath.

Pepin threw me a warning glance.

"Please, come." She twisted a knot in the tree and slats emerged from the trunk, one at a time, starting from the top and winding their way down, forming a staircase.

I reached out to test a plank, yanking it up and down. It didn't budge. "Cool."

Maili tilted her head, her eyebrows pinched together. She knelt to touch the top step. "It doesn't feel cold."

"No, I mean—"

"Fallon has many interesting sayings." Pepin waved me off and started up the steps. I followed, hugging the tree, fighting the morbid urge to look down. Wolf came up close behind.

"Not him." Maili pointed to Wolf. "If you wish to enter our village, enter in human form."

Pepin threw the pack at Wolf then continued up the stairs through branches and leaves until nothing but greenery surrounded us. The world disappeared. The stairs seemed endless. We came to a platform leading to a wooden walkway with railings on either side. Wolf, in human form and dressed, caught up to us as I gawked at the treehouse village. Surrounded by leaves, it was easy to pretend we weren't so high.

When Wolf stepped on the platform, Maili twisted another knot. The steps disappeared into the tree as if they never existed.

"This way." She waved us on along the walkway.

"How did the stairway do that? Is it magic?" I asked.

She whirled around, her face darkening. "We don't use magic."

"Then how...?"

"We're tree-folk. Just as pech have abilities with stone, we have abilities with trees."

"I thought you were gachen?"

"We are. But not all gachen are the same, you understand."

No. I didn't. Other than the Treasach. But they're unnaturally big because they bred themselves that way. Then again, were the selkie, who transfigured into seals, considered gachen?

"Your mother's clan, the Cael, have abilities with dirt, which is why their homes are in mounds in the earth. Just as the selkie have abilities with water." She viewed me over her shoulder. "You didn't know this?"

I shook my head. There was a lot I didn't know.

We came to a broad platform. Wooden structures protruded from the trees, hidden among the branches. Decking and suspended walkways connected them. I spun, taking in the surrounding view as though seeing snow for the first time. "Amazing…"

Maili's face shone like the sun after a rainstorm. "You like it?" The light dimmed. Gray clouds overcast her face once more. "You should have seen it before." She glided along a walkway through more thick branches with a surefootedness I didn't possess at this altitude.

I struggled to keep up. "Before what?"

"I'll explain when we meet the others." Maili picked up her speed through the trees. She led us up a winding staircase to a building nestled between enormous branches seemingly growing flat and spread out just to provide support.

My foot slipped on the staircase. I caught myself on the railing. I couldn't see the ground, just a sea of branches and leaves. My surroundings wavered. "Oh."

Wolf came up behind me and grabbed my shoulders. "Are you all right?"

I gave him a weak smile and focused on the next step, blocking out everything else. I could change into a falcon and soar high in the sky, but I still had issues with heights in human form? It made no sense. If I fell, I could transform. Unless I got tangled in my clothes and…I shuddered, blocking out the horrid image I'd nearly conjured.

We reached a landing in the middle of a spacious room. The

railing continued beyond the opening in the floor. I clung to it until I reached the top. Rounded windows took up the far end on both sides. Birds twittered, flitting from branch to branch outside. Inside, wood covered the entire surface area, floor to ceiling—a hollow tree made so smooth the grain glistened. A green and tan carpet overlaid much of the floor. At one end, cushions and furs formed a circle. At the other, two men, both dark skinned like Native Americans, one bald, the other with shaggy, black hair, sat cross-legged on the floor at a round table.

When Maili approached the strangers, they stood. She waved first toward the older, bald man. "This is Shimri"—her arm moved to Shaggy Hair—"and Zakur, the one who shot at you."

Both men placed a hand on their heart and dipped their heads in respect.

"My apologies, Fallon." Zakur spread his dark hands, callused fingers held up and open. "My shots merely warned. We typically shoot to kill. But we've been expecting your arrival. These days, we can't even trust the animals. But I'm confused." He glanced at each of us. "If you're a pech and you're a wolf…who was the other bird?"

"Other bird?" Pepin, Wolf, and I asked in unison.

"Aye. There were two birds. Both big. I fired warning shots at both."

"See?" Hands on my hips, I spun to Pepin and Wolf. "I told you I saw another bird. I kept watching the skies to make sure it wasn't following us. It must've been flying low, out of sight."

"This is why we always keep watch. Now that you're here, they won't be warning shots." Concern masked Maili's face. "Shimri, please warn the watchmen about the other bird."

Shimri descended the staircase, disappearing in the hole in the floor. Wood filled the gap. Only the railing suggested a staircase existed.

"Have a seat." Maili motioned toward the table. "We've much to discuss."

"Is anyone else here?" Like Declan? I pushed the rising hope down, already sure of the answer.

"Just us and the men posted outside, keeping watch." She touched the wall by the window and leafy vines concealed the opening. Then she nodded to Zakur. "Will you light the room?"

I'd never seen the Cael do anything so impressive with dirt. I'd only seen the hill homes already built. I'd never seen one being built. But then, they're known for their pottery. Is that because they have abilities with clay? Did I have such abilities?

"We can't risk the fasgadair seeing our light." Maili crossed to the other window. "They think they've burned this entire village."

Faolan and Pepin sat on either side of me at the table. After Maili concealed the other window, she sat across from us while Zakur lit candles in a chandelier with a tiny torch on the end of a long stick.

"You want me to get those?" Before anyone could ask what I meant, I lit the candles in the other chandeliers.

Pepin scowled, crossing his stubby arms, while the two strangers stared, slack-jawed.

Maili whispered, "You have Cataleen and Aodan's gift." Her eyes glazed. Then she shook her head and rose. "Forgive me. You must be hungry. Let me get you something to eat."

The hole in the floor opened, and Shimri's bald head poked through like a whack-a-mole. "All is clear."

"Thank you, Shimri. Please share our plans whilst I prepare food for our guests."

As she strode away, he settled at the table. "As I'm sure you're aware, we're to provide safe passage through the Sea of Firinne to the Ain-Dìleas in Bandia. It won't be easy with the fasgadair watching the coastline."

"Why are they watching the coast?" I asked.

"They know gachen are seeking refuge in Bandia." Shimri stroked his short beard. "The mountains are only passable for a couple months. That window is nearly open. Regardless, the best way to Bandia is by ocean. Morrigan hopes to intercept anyone who tries to flee."

Zakur leaned in, his black eyes boring into mine. "You are the ultimate trophy."

I shrank back.

Shimri smacked Zakur's shoulder. "Pepin, what have you learned from your last visit with the pech?"

Pepin cleared his throat. "They're rallying forces, forging weapons for themselves and our people, and training while they wait for our arrival."

"Wait." I jolted. "The pech will help us?"

Pepin's eyes glistened. "After the Tower fell, they wanted to strike at once. We've been holding them back, convincing them to wait for us…for the right timing."

Maili set a plate before each of us. "We don't need the pech to get themselves killed. We need every able body."

"Aye," Zakur said. "This will be a war like Ariboslia has never seen. The clan wars won't compare."

War. What had I been thinking? I could come back, change a few people, and put things right? This was much bigger than that. Bigger than me.

My gut churned. "So, we're going to cross a sea just to pick everyone else up and return to war? Why not wait here for them?"

"Hear! Hear!" Zakur slammed his mug on the table, splashing liquid over the edge.

"Because…" Maili shot Zakur a look that made him focus on his food. "Sully made it clear. We are to bring Fallon to Bandia first."

"It doesn't make sense," I said.

"How often does Sully make sense?" Zakur chewed with his mouth open.

"How often has Sully been wrong?" Maili took a dainty bite.

"I don't know," he muttered under his breath, daring a quick glance at her. "I haven't heard everything Sully ever said."

"He speaks for God." Sweeping her glorious braid over her shoulder, she notched her slender chin up.

"Where are the others? My mother? Cahal and Evan?" I swallowed a lump in my throat, risked catching Maili's eyes, and whispered, "Where's Declan?"

She settled into her seat, exchanging a glance with Zakur that compounded the weight in my stomach.

"Most everyone is safe in Bandia." Zakur swallowed his food. "Last I heard, Sully sent your mother, Cahal, and Declan, among others, on a mission to travel Ariboslia, warning villages to flee to Bandia."

"You don't know where they are now?"

Chapter Eight

STILL GROGGY, I SMOOTHED my wrinkled T-shirt, then descended the spiral staircase, wishing it had a railing. How high up were we? Willing myself not to look down, I held on to Wolf's shoulder. My whole body groaned. Every inch ached. Had I gotten soft since my last visit to Ariboslia? Why did the Arlen sleep on the ground? They had cushions. Couldn't they make a mattress?

We arrived at ground level. I rubbed my shoulder, avoiding the bruise, and peeked at the still-dark sky. Weak rays of light poked through the trees from the east.

Something quacked behind me. I'd heard that sound before. I spun around. A furry lizard crouched in the crook of a tree.

"Aw. A fur dragon." I crept toward the creature and extended my hand to pet its mohawk.

"Fallon, no!" Maili lunged closer.

My hand stopped midair as the furry lizard opened its mouth. A stream of fire blasted toward me. Before the fire assaulted my face, it split in two. Separate streams shot past me on either side.

The lizard closed its mouth, and Wolf pulled me away.

"What's in yer head, lass?" He eyed the fur dragon as it scurried into the tree and disappeared beneath the foliage.

"I thought fur dragons were friendly."

"Aye. Fur dragons are friendly. But that"—he pointed to the tree—"was not a fur dragon. That was a fire dragon. Don't ye know the difference?"

How could I?

"First, fur dragons don't climb trees. If you ever see one in a tree, it's not a fur dragon. Second, a fur dragon has black fur surrounding its eyes. Fire dragons don't."

Seriously? Like that little detail was supposed to help? "Okaaay."

Maili edged closer, her delicate dark brows pinching a bit at the center. "Can you control fires too?"

"I don't think so. I can only start them."

"How did the spray split in two?"

I scratched my head. "Maybe it had something in its throat." I hadn't split the flame. Had I? It didn't feel like I had. Then again, I hadn't realized I'd started the fire the first time. Hadn't that emerged out of desperation? Perhaps I could control fire and I protected myself. "If it was me, I'm not sure how I did it. I never have before."

With a deep breath, Maili tipped her head skyward. "We need to get moving if we're to reach the ship on time."

"Should I fly ahead and scout the ground?"

Shimri shook his head. "We're better off fighting in human form."

I'd heard that one before, and I believed it after Ryann's death. I scanned the trees, suspicious of the critters and birds. "I'm a better fighter as a falcon." A picture of the fasgadair's eye skewered on my talon came to mind. I shook it off—the vision, that is. The eye had been harder to remove.

"You may be able to fight as a bird, but you can't kill a fasgadair if needed. We go together. On foot." Maili threw me a dagger in a leather sheath. "It's not far."

I fumbled the catch, stooped, and retrieved the weapon. "It's daylight. The fasgadair will be in animal form. Nothing will touch me in the sky. I'm the predator up there."

Shimri raised his eyebrows as though giving it serious

thought…or questioning God's choice in using me. "An arrow could kill you. Our allies on the ship won't know not to shoot you."

Right. Point taken.

Maili buckled a sheath around her tunic, emphasizing a figure to rival Kpop idols, and swept a stray lock of shiny, black hair from her eyes.

I buckled my sheath, puckering my T-shirt, as the men donned their swords. If only I could fly and escape the possible need to use a dagger.

The path thinned, and the forest thickened. We spent hours plowing through shrubs, avoiding roots, rocks, and debris. I was grateful for my jeans and sneakers for protection. So far, no one had commented on my strange attire. It was much better than a dress and flimsy, leather shoes.

Though the sun shone brighter, our way was dark, dappled in blinding light. A growl came from my right. "What's the matter, Wolf?"

"Huh?" Wolf, still in human form, responded from my left.

My head jerked in his direction. "Wha—? I heard a—" I pointed.

The others stopped and peered in that direction. Quiet.

Maili nocked her bow.

A low growl repeated from the thicket. Shimri and Zakur crept toward the sound with Wolf, Maili, and Pepin close behind. They armed themselves as they advanced. My fingers curled around my dagger hilt as I trailed a few paces behind. The growl deepened, gaining strength with each impending step.

The creature leapt from the bushes, snarling. Shimri struck it with the butt of his sword, and it fell limp.

"A raccoon?" I stepped toward the small animal with little ears and a masked face. It looked…cute. Now that it wasn't growling.

"A fasgadair," Wolf replied.

"How can you tell?" I didn't notice the electric scent. Do they only smell like that in fasgadair form? Right. Wolf hadn't smelled back when… I should've thought of that.

"A real raccoon wouldn't have threatened us, particularly during the day."

"Unless it's sick," Zakur said.

I hooked my thumbs in my sheath. "What are we going to do with it?"

"Kill it," Shimri and Zakur said in unison.

"Bring it with us," Maili ordered.

"Right." Zakur nodded. "Raccoons are good eating, fasgadair or not."

"Not to eat." She threw Zakur the look she reserved for him. "We have her." She pointed at me. "If we don't have to kill it, why would we? Let's get it to the ship and lock it up. If it's not a fasgadair, we'll have extra food. But if it is"—she eyed me askance—"we find out if it's redeemable when night falls."

Let the testing begin. My stomach twisted. I had expected this.

Wolf took a leather sack from his bag, shoved the raccoon inside, and flung it over his shoulder. "Let's go."

"Ummm." I tugged on my lip. "What if that thing changes into a fasgadair while it's in that pouch?"

"The demons aren't daft enough to turn during daylight. 'Tis much too painful." Wolf pushed a branch out of his way.

I surveyed the area. Nothing but shrubbery and dirt. Just like the woods behind my house. But everything was suspect. "What if there are more?"

"All the more reason to leave," Wolf called over his shoulder.

Shimri took the lead. "Be on the lookout for animal tracks, particularly as we near the shore. Our ship will meet us when the sun reaches its apex."

We must be close then. The sun had almost come to its highest point. Judging from the cool, salty breeze, we were nearly there.

The trees cleared, and the ocean spread before us. Maili and Zakur scanned the beach, dashed to an overgrown patch of rose-hip plants, and rooted through them. "We need to pull the dinghy from these shrubs. Be swift and stay low."

Wolf, Pepin, and Shimri worked to pull the rowboat free. I picked a rose hip. Bumpah showed me how to eat them, avoiding the fuzzy seeds. We munched on these tart little fruits whenever we passed them by at the beach. Bumpah swore those were the reason we rarely got sick. I plucked one, then remembered the blueberries. Or not blueberries. Whatever they were that nearly killed me. "Are these…?"

"Yes, you can eat them." Maili picked a few and shoved them in her pouch. "Grab some extras. These will be nice to have on the ship."

I took a bite of the fruit, careful to avoid the seeds. It tasted similar to the rose hips at home but, like everything else here, much better. I picked a bunch and crammed them in my pack's side pocket. I grabbed for another, and something bit my finger.

"Ow!" I jerked my hand back.

"Shhh!" Wolf came running, leaving Shimri and Pepin to carry the boat to shore.

I inspected my finger. Blood gushed from the wound. I wrapped it in my T-shirt hem as a high-pitched squealing rang from the rustling bushes. A weasel writhed on the ground. By the time he reached the thing, it stopped.

I backed away. He parted the branches to inspect it. "It's dead. It must've been an unredeemable fasgadair. Even in animal form, it can't ingest your blood and live." He let go of the branches and walked back to the dinghy, brushing his hands. "Good to know."

Yeah. Great. I couldn't wait to sustain more injuries to test fasgadair in human and animal form. Maili and I plucked a few more rose hips.

Zakur grabbed Maili's wrist. "I must get back to the elephants."

She stopped, her eyes glistening. "Keep them safe."

"I'll watch them well." His strong blunt hands patted her shoulders. Then, seemingly on impulse, he pulled her into his arms and hugged her. He kissed her forehead, then released his grip.

"Go." She squeezed his upper arms. "God willing, I'll return."

He hesitated a moment, his face pained. Then he took off in the direction we'd come while Maili headed to shore.

A roar thundered from the south. The ground shook. The cacophony of noises grew deafening. Each sound indistinguishable from another until a hyena's manic cackle, a large cat's snarl, or an elephant's trumpet rose above the din. Every hair on my body stood to full alert while I rooted to the spot.

"Get to the boat." Maili jarred me back to my senses.

So much for removing my shoes or rolling up my jeans. My feet sank into the sand, kicking it up against my calves, slowing my pace. The cold hit me like a walk-in freezer on a 100-plus-degree day. I inhaled sharply, sucking in my gut, and pressed on as fast as the water allowed. Maili grasped my hand to pull me into the boat while Wolf and Shimri pushed it through the surf. The dinghy collided with a crashing wave and rocked. Maili tumbled backward. My hand slipped from her grip, and my elbow smacked into the boat's edge. The shock from my not-so-funny bone traveled up my arm. I clung to the swaying boat and heaved myself up. Another wave pushed the bow up as I dangled on the side. The boat crashed back down. My bruised shoulder slammed against the seat. Searing pain pulsed from the spot. I righted myself and dragged myself to the seat across from Pepin. He sat in the stern, arms bracing himself on either side with eyes wide, frozen.

Shimri and Wolf scrambled into the rowboat. They'd need my seat to row.

"Pepin, you gotta move." I nudged his shoulder. His grip remained tight. I pried his fingers. He slid over and gripped the seat bench instead.

Shimri and Wolf sat in the center and took up the oars. Maili faced us in the bow.

We'd made it beyond the breaking waves. A mighty ship with a strange symbol on its masts steered our way.

"They're here." Relief smoothed the tension from Maili's face.

Horrific sounds vibrated from the shore. Mismatched animals appeared on the beach, howling, bleating, and screaming rage. A tiger, hyena, and elephant led the pack charging into the water.

I sat on the edge of my seat, gripping the boat. *Come on, boat. Move faster. Faster.* I rocked as if it helped increase its speed.

Maili shot the tiger. It roared, sending an icy shock through my body. The arrow slowed the animal but failed to stop its advance. The hyena burst ahead. An arrow struck its chest. It squealed and dropped into the water. The elephant caught up to the tiger. It stomped through the waves as if they were nothing. Each step sent up a spray and a wake.

"'Tis not one of your elephants, Maili. 'Tis a fasgadair. Shoot!" Shimri yelled.

Maili screamed. An arrow struck the elephant. It reared and trumpeted, then landed with a huge splash, sending a wave our way. Another arrow hit the elephant. And another. The elephant trumpeted again.

The tiger lost its footing but continued to swim. The elephant's wake crashed over its head. The tiger snorted, blasting water from its nose. One by one, the animals retreated.

The elephant's wake continued toward us, struck our dinghy, and sent it rocking. I tightened my grip. Pepin moaned.

The sound I'd heard when I was shot at in falcon form came from the ship. "Vvvvt. Vvvt. Vvvt." Arrows flew into the sky. Struck birds squawked and fell, splashing into the ocean. Their skewered bodies resurfaced and bobbed on the waves. How many of them were just birds? A full-body shudder shook me. *Thank you, Shimri.* Good thing I hadn't been in falcon form.

"Shark!" Maili hollered.

A fin cut a straight line through the water. Everyone braced themselves. Wolf, being the closest to the projected impact site, secured his left knee on the seat and right foot on the floor. He raised his sword above his head. Thrust the blade down seconds before the shark struck the dinghy, slowing the impact. I clung to the sides and planted my feet as the boat wavered. Murky redness spread from the shark as Wolf removed his blade.

I laid a hand over my racing heart and took deep breaths. The angry mob of animals shrunk, and their threatening cries dimmed as the distance increased. The mismatched group lining the coast looked bizarre, like something from a bad sci-fi movie.

Blood dripped from my finger over the rowboat. Salt water would help heal it. I peered into the water for danger, then dipped my finger under the surface. My pack sat on the other side of Wolf. Not wanting to interrupt his rowing, I wrapped my finger back up in my shirt.

Maili rooted around in her satchel, then handed me a cloth. "Here."

"Thanks." I bandaged my finger as waves lapped the boat.

Water sprinkled from the oars between dips beneath the surface. The sun warmed my skin, making the water shimmer. The tension in my body eased, and I zoned out, staring at the ship. Like something Columbus sailed, it dominated the water. But the flag was similar to a Celtic symbol. A tree. Its roots and branches fanned out and connected, forming a circle.

"There was nothing you could do, Maili." Shimri's voice strained as he paddled. "It wasn't an elephant. And you needn't worry about Zakur. He's in God's hands."

Turning her gaze from shore, she wiped her eyes. "I know."

We reached the ship and climbed a rope ladder. Wolf tried holding it steady. But each step jiggled. I lost my footing and dangled, wishing I could change shape and fly aboard but remembering the felled birds.

I neared the top to find a familiar face. I needed a second to place him.

"Evan?"

"Fallon. It's good to see you." He grabbed my arm to pull me onto the deck. "I wanted to greet you, but I was asked to remain with the ship."

"Well, you're here now."

He hugged me, filling me with warmth. This was what it was about. My purpose. To save more lives like his…and Wolf's.

Evan was the reminder I needed. Stepping back, I studied his face.

The friendly smile. The healthy glow. He still looked exotic with his dark hair and skin and bright blue eyes. Hard to believe he'd ever been a fasgadair, never mind my captor. But I'd seen it. I'd caused his transformation.

No. God had. But He used me.

It was worth it.

Thank You, God. Thank You for reminding me why I'm here. Give me strength to do my part....

Wolf dropped the bag with the raccoon at my feet.

...I'll need it.

CHAPTER NINE

I STARED OUT THE captain's cabin window, trying not to breathe in the stench of bad seafood mixed with ale and body odor. Tin mug in one hand, stale roll in the other, I sat on the window seat in the corner. The sun touched the horizon, illuminating both sky and sea in brilliant red and orange. The shore was long gone. I took another bite of bread, hoping to settle my stomach and keep down what the constant rocking threatened to bring up. Watching the horizon helped. But I needed to get back on deck for fresh air soon.

Pepin gripped the table edge. He hadn't touched his food. His ruddy complexion had taken on a green hue.

Maili and Shimri didn't look great either. Both were pale. But Evan and Wolf seemed fine. Comfortable even.

Evan took a swig from his mug. He sat on a bench at the table, facing me. "What are your plans for the raccoon?"

The water sloshed as I sipped, spilling onto Drochaid. I'd never get used to this rocking. "Find out if it can be saved, I guess."

"You're going to let it bite you?" He bit his roll.

My stomach lurched at both the swaying and the thought of facing the fasgadair. "Isn't that why I'm here? To rescue them if they can be rescued?"

Was I crazy to consider allowing these creatures to drink my blood? Was I playing a twisted version of Russian roulette?

Evan leaned back against the table, mug in hand, and finished chewing. "I suppose so. But you know nothing about this one."

"I didn't know anything about you…or your brother…or Wolf."

"Aye. But we'd been fasgadair for a long time. There's no telling how long this one has."

My stomach tangled like a drawer full of necklaces. "What difference does that make?"

After a long drink, he bent in toward me. His denim-blue eyes somber. "When you first become a fasgadair, all reason is gone. All that remains is a bloodthirsty monster."

"Isn't that how fasgadair are all the time?"

"Not always. It's difficult to explain. When you first change, you don't think at all. You feed. The longer you're a fasgadair, the more your mind clears. All are guilty of murder. Some fasgadair come to hate themselves for what they've done. Those, I believe, are the ones who can be saved. Others revel in their newfound powers and murderous nature, seeking any opportunity to kill. I think those die when they bite you. Others fall in the middle of the extremes. You never know which way it will turn out."

"So…" I crumbled an edge of the bread in my hand, bits falling on my lap before sifting to the floor. "Your theory explains how you were saved…and Wolf. But what about your brother? Why did he die and Aodan didn't? Look at all the evil Aodan did, threatening to kill his twin sister. And me. Why was he redeemed?"

"Perhaps there was something more to Aodan. Despite everything else, he protected the Cael from Morrigan. My brother?" Evan's lips pinched white as he gazed out the window. "I'm not surprised he didn't make it."

****

The dark waters swallowed the sun, and Evan brought me to the raccoon's hold on the main deck. The electric fasgadair scent strengthened. Shimri and Wolf sat on deck playing cards while supposedly keeping watch. I thought the cards would be a great way to pass the time. Perhaps bringing them was a mistake. These guys caught on quick and hadn't stopped.

"Oi! You there." A thick man with a cloth wrapped around his head pointed at Shimri and Wolf. "Are ye playing or watching for fasgadair?"

Wolf stood. "I assure ye, Captain, we are keeping an eye out."

Shimri moved to stand beside Wolf.

"Hmph." The captain crossed his arms and stood taller. "Night has fallen. Surely you understand what that means."

Wolf bowed slightly. "We do."

"Then yer aware those birds we dropped into the sea regenerated hours ago. They could fly on deck at any moment. Do you know how difficult they are to spot at night?" The captain paced before Wolf and Shimri. "Like charcoal in black mud."

"I—"

"And what of the sea creatures?" the captain cut Wolf off. "They're able to shift into their fasgadair form and climb on board. Those shifty beasts are skilled enough to climb without a rope. And they're quick."

"Aye, I—"

"Take starboard. And you"—the captain pointed at Shimri—"take port. Be vigilant." After pivoting on his heels, he marched away.

"Well…" Wolf smirked at Shimri. "I'd say our game is over for the night."

Grimacing, Shimri rubbed his bald head. "He has valid points."

"Aye, this is my first time aboard ship. Somehow, I thought a ship would be easy to defend," Wolf said. "Will ye be all right without me, Fallon?"

I shrugged. It's not like the fasgadair could bite him for me.

Maili and Pepin arrived. Pepin walked with his stubby legs and arms splayed.

"Pepin, why don't you lay in a hammock below decks?" Evan

placed a hand on Pepin's shoulder. "You'd feel better there."

"Fallon might need me."

Aww. Pepin's willingness to put aside his illness and hatred of all things associated with water was touching.

A grated hatch enclosed the hold. The moon shone bright, enhancing my already excellent Ariboslian night vision. Nothing stirred in the dark hole.

"Hello?" I called. "Are you in there?"

"Leave me be." A weak voice rose from below. Female. Somehow, that made me breathe easier.

Pepin, Evan, and Maili responded with shrugs and raised eyebrows. *Lord, help me.* I returned my attention to the thing in the hole. "Can I get you anything?"

"No. Please, leave."

"Aren't you hungry?" Why did I ask that? What would I do? Push in a few people for her to feed on? "Don't you want to go home? Anything?"

"No."

Full of inexplicable courage, I drew in a deep breath and nodded to Evan. "Lower me down."

Evan crossed his arms. "No way. She might kill you."

"Like you did?" When he didn't respond, I pressed further. "Like your brother tried to?"

"Fine." He dropped his arms. "Let her in."

They tied a rope and threw it over a wooden beam. I stepped into it and pulled it up to sit. Pepin held the other end.

Evan grasped the rope. "If she hurts you, burn her."

"You want me to set her on fire?"

"If you have to." He handed me a lantern.

The image of Aodan howling when I'd set his hair on fire resurfaced. Guilt washed over me. I shuddered as my stomach rolled. I wouldn't be able to set my worst enemy on fire…again. But Evan didn't need to know that.

The fasgadair scent increased to high voltage as I descended, mixing with rancid sea, mold, and decay. I gagged and tried to breathe through my mouth. Goosebumps broke out as I dangled, spinning midair, defenseless. Had I just delivered myself into the lion's den?

CHAPTER TEN

I TOUCHED GROUND AND stepped out of the rope. Moonlight shone spotlighted me. The ship rocked, and I nearly lost my balance. Dangling objects clanged. I planted my feet and splayed my arms.

"You plan to kill me?" A whisper came from behind.

I twisted around, expecting to find her right behind me. Nothing. I crept forward until dirty feet came into view. A young woman covered in muck huddled in a corner. She clutched her legs, head down, naked.

"Hey!" I yelled to the others. "Throw me down a coat or a blanket."

Within moments, a blanket floated down, and I threw it at her.

She pulled it over herself. Stringy hair fell in thin clumps down her face. She trained eerie eyes on me. "I'm ready to die."

"I'm not going to kill you."

"But that's why I'm here." Her voice rasped, coming from somewhere so deep inside her, somewhere she still had human thought, as though each word pained her to speak. "An angel. Promised redemption. I have to die."

Shivers coursed through my body. "An angel sent you here? To us?" God planned this?

"Aye." A bitter chuckle crackled from her chest. "He told me where to wait. When you'd arrive. He promised…" Tears coursed down her cheeks, trailing through the dirt. "I should have known better."

"What if you could be healed?"

"'Tis not possible. I'm damned. Forever." She lowered her head, resting it on her knees.

"Bite me."

She jerked her head up. "What sick game are you playing?"

"No games. Just bite me."

"Why would you ask me to?" Frigid anger chilled her voice, lashing out and shivering through the room.

"Because it will either give you your life back or kill you. Either way, you will no longer be a fasgadair."

She remained frozen, unblinking. "You're off your head."

"Well, that's debatable." I laughed.

She continued to stare.

"Well?"

"This is how the angel intended me to die?" Clutching the blanket, she stood and neared me. "I won't harm you?"

"You won't." Then I remembered the last times I'd done this. "Well…not much."

She shuffled into the moonlight. Creepy eyes focused on me. Cast against the moonbeams, she looked like something that crawled out of a crypt. Her eyes caught the light and flashed yellow.

I fought a shudder and the natural urge to run. Every hair on my body rose and quivered like antennae on high alert. Ignoring the warning, I averted my gaze from the eerie, searching eyes, gathered my hair away from my neck, and forced my body to stay in place.

Inch by inch, she crept forward, bringing the charged scent of death with her. She paused. My cells jerked, urging me to bolt, but I stood rigid, refusing to budge…or look at her. She bent over. Her breath moist, reeking of decay, her teeth broke my skin like an expert nurse at a blood drive, so gentle. I barely felt the simultaneous pinpricks or the slow draining of blood.

My head swam. She released me and backed away. Her freakish eyes widened as if she'd witnessed something gruesome. With her mouth frozen in a silent scream, she collapsed to the floor.

The boat swayed. I fell on my butt...hard. "Ow!"

"Fallon?" Evan, Maili, and Pepin's voices merged. All sounded prepared to jump to my rescue.

"I'm okay. You can come down." I didn't have the strength to yell. Hopefully, they heard me. Blood trickled from my wound. I pulled my shirt collar up and held my hand there to stop the blood flow.

Crypt Girl writhed on the ground, eyes rolled up in her head. A continual groan escaped her parted lips, like something from the *Exorcist*. Which was probably accurate. It was an exorcism. If she survived.

I pushed away from her flailing appendages. *Father, please let her live.*

The others lowered a rope ladder and climbed down. Evan rushed to my side. Maili and Pepin crowded the girl. Her thrashing finally ceased.

"Are you all right?" Evan nudged my hand away and inspected the wound. "Thank God. It's not bad. It's almost stopped bleeding." He pressed a cloth to my neck.

"I'm fine." I took the cloth to hold myself. "How is she?"

"She's coming around." Excitement heightened Maili's voice.

"Wha—? What happened?" Crypt Girl asked.

Praises erupted around her.

"You made it." I struggled to throw my voice the short distance to her over the cheering.

"What's your name?" Maili knelt before her.

Crypt Girl thrust an arm out and inspected her hand, then touched her face with both hands as if she didn't recognize her own body. "Rowan."

****

Shouts rang out above us. Feet pounded on the floorboards. Electric stench wafted down through the porthole.

"Fasgadair," I said, staring at the others.

Evan ran to the rope ladder, his feet slipping on the wooden rungs in his haste. Maili followed close behind.

Pepin held the ladder steady as Evan, then Maili disappeared through the hole. "Be ready to grab your weapon when you reach the top."

I fumbled my way up the ladder. At the top, I peeked into the ghostly silence. A headless corpse lay a few feet away. It shriveled up and disintegrated to dust. A breeze swept through, disfiguring the pile.

I climbed onto the deck and armed myself.

"Fallon. Watch out!" Wolf shouted.

I wheeled around, face-to-face with a bloodsucker.

Chapter Eleven

THE FASGADAIR'S EYES CAUGHT the moonlight. They gave off an eerie glow. "Fallon?"

What was this? The monster wanted conversation? Should I use my blade? Should I let it bite me? My hand gripping the blade refused to budge.

The thing jerked and fell toward me. When I jumped out of the way, it landed facedown, a blade protruding from its back.

"Where was yer head, Fallon?" Wolf came running. He pulled the dagger from the monster's back. Then turned in every direction, gaze darting.

I sniffed the air. It didn't smell like there were any more fasgadair on board. No live ones.

Wolf cleaned the blood from his dagger, then sheathed it. "Why'd ye stand there waiting for the monster to attack?"

"I was—I—It knew my name."

"They all know your name." He freed his sword and raised it above the fasgadair's neck.

"No." I held my hand up. "Don't kill it."

"Are ye daft? The thing attacked us. It killed a crewman."

"What if I can save it?"

"Not this time." He swung his sword, and the head rolled away from the body.

People began emerging from the shadows. Their low conversations growing louder.

A rough man with a row of hoop earrings lining his ear approached. "That's the lot." He brushed his hands on his trousers. "Best keep an eye out, though. Eh?"

"Why'd you do that?" I didn't care that a crowd was forming. My hands clenched, rage shaking my whole body. "It could have attacked me. It didn't."

Wolf wiped his blade on the fasgadair's tunic and returned it to its sheath.

"Don't you see?" I asked. "It stopped. It recognized my name. What if it wanted help?"

"And what if it wanted to kill ye?"

"If it had, wouldn't it have attacked?" I fought back tears. "Isn't this what I'm here for? He was down. We had the upper hand."

"What could we have done, Fallon? Ropes won't restrain a fasgadair. Should I have thrown him in the hold with Rowan?"

"Of course not."

"Perhaps we should drain some of your blood ourselves so next time we can force feed it to them before they regenerate and kill more of our people. Does that sound like a good plan?"

My fists shook at my sides.

"I will always look out for ye and our people before saving fasgadair. I won't apologize."

The captain approached adjusting his cap. "How many did we lose?"

"Two crewmen, sir," Earring Man said.

The captain sighed. "Back your stations. The night's not over."

****

Objects dangling from hooks and rafters clanged in the ship's sway, waking me. I rocked in my hammock while the scents of bad seafood and body odor sank into my consciousness, but it wasn't as offensive. I must be getting desensitized.

The ship groaned and creaked with each roll over the waves. Its rhythmic movement and sounds both comforted and disturbed me. The disquiet that kept me awake must've lulled me to sleep.

Sunlight streamed through the small portholes. Dust particles danced in the rays.

Most of the cots were empty. Shimri slept in one, his arms crossed behind his head. Wolf's arm dangled from another.

Wolf. At memories from the night before, I fought the rising anger as his chest rose and fell. He was still alive. Perhaps I shouldn't be so hard on him. It's not like we had a procedure manual outlining what to do. And we lost two men. This was war. We couldn't possibly rescue every fasgadair. At least we saved Rowan. For my sanity's sake, I'd have to follow the advice Evan gave last year and be thankful for the lives saved and leave the lives lost in God's hands. Who lived or died wasn't up to me.

I stood. Waves of nausea washed over me. I dressed and headed to the captain's cabin for food.

Evan was alone at the table, cutting an apple in half. "Good day, Fallon. Are you hungry?" He held out half his apple and thrust it into my hand.

"Uh. Thanks." I sat across the table from him, and he placed a roll and a hunk of cheese in front of me. I bit a chunk of apple, then the cheese. They tasted so good together. Like the snacks Stacy's mom used to serve. Sometimes I missed home. "When will we arrive in Bandia?"

"We've been blessed with the wind in our sails. At this pace, we should arrive in a few days. A week at most." He bit nearly half his piece of apple. It bulged his dark cheek as he chewed.

I groaned. A whole week? "Where's Rowan?"

"In the hold, sleeping."

"Still?"

He shrugged. "She didn't want to come up. So, we brought her food. She seems comfortable on the bedding we provided. Give her time. She has much to contend with."

"I want to talk to her." I popped the last bit of apple and cheese into my mouth, grabbed the roll, and rose to leave.

He grasped my wrist. "Remember what I told you? We don't know her story."

I returned to my seat, forcing my mouthful down as he released me. "I remember what you said, but so far four people have reverted from fasgadair to gachen. Morrigan killed Aodan too quickly, but both you and Wolf turned out fine. What makes you think this could be difficult for her?"

Evan's countenance sagged as if a great weight had settled upon him. He leaned back in his chair and crossed his arms. "Wolf and I didn't have time to dwell on it. We needed to escape Ceas Croi, return you to your realm, and flee to Bandia." His gaze moved to the floor. "I was just so grateful."

"As I recall, so was Wolf. Why wouldn't Rowan be the same?"

He twiddled his thumbs. "You don't know her story."

"You keep saying that. What difference does it make?"

He drummed his fingers. "I always looked up to my brother…though I shouldn't have. He drank, got involved with the wrong people…gambled." Evan chugged his cider, then set the mug back down and mopped his mouth. He watched his hands as he rubbed them together. "I found him, nearly beaten to death. Men circled him, taking turns kicking him." His voice cracked. "I wielded my dagger and killed them all. I don't even remember doing it. But I remember standing there, bloody knife in hand with felled men around me." He peeked my way, then dropped his gaze and swigged another drink.

Absorbing what he was saying took a minute. I couldn't imagine him doing something so heinous. Then again, he'd been a fasgadair when I met him. My captor. Whatever he was like as a fasgadair or before, he was different now. I touched his shaking hand to reassure him I didn't judge him for what he'd done.

He jerked away. "I carried my brother for miles. I had no idea where I was going. We couldn't go home. I couldn't help him. A fasgadair found us. Our blood attracted her.

"You can imagine what happened next. I was desperate for my brother to live. But she refused to help him unless I allowed her to change me too." He buried his face in his hands. "It was my fault."

My hand hovered over his shoulder. Was it a good idea to comfort him? Good idea or not, I rested my hand on his shoulder.

"You did what you thought was best to save your brother."

He swiped his eyes with the back of his fist.

I retracted my hand. "But you're okay now. I still don't see why you think it will be different, or worse, for Rowan."

He emptied his mug and placed it on the table. "The fasgadair blood didn't make me a murderer. I did."

"Wouldn't that be worse? Wouldn't that make you feel less redeemable, not more so?"

He rubbed his face. "I honestly don't know what's worse. But everyone has a story. We don't know what kind of guilt she's experiencing or how she'll handle it. She has time to think. That may not be a good thing. One thing I'm sure of...she became a murderer as a fasgadair, and that's not something easily overcome."

****

Evan opened the hatch, and I climbed into the hold. Though sunlight streamed through the slats overhead, the dank space was no less creepy than it had been the prior night. Impenetrable shadows lined the exterior. Hanging metal objects clanked, and wooden slats creaked as waves rocked the boat. The fasgadair smell was gone. Now it reeked of low tide and mold.

I stood in the spotlight. Blinded, I retreated into the shadows and waited for my eyes to adjust. Rowan lay curled up in the blanket, in a fetal position. She looked peaceful. I shouldn't wake her. I edged back toward the ladder.

"Fallon?" Her hoarse whisper sent a thrill through me. Another one lives.

I sat beside her. "How are you feeling?"

"I don't understand. I'm alive?" She picked herself up with the care of someone who'd been hit by a bus.

"Yes." My heart danced. "You're alive."

"Did I hurt you?" She pointed to my neck.

I touched the tiny bumps. They itched, like mosquito bites. Someone should invent a fasgadair-bite cream. But I'd be the only customer. "I'm fine. Don't worry about me."

"How are you okay? How am I alive?"

"I'm not sure. Last year, when I first arrived in Ariboslia, I thought I was here to kill my uncle. But it seems God had even bigger plans. My blood either kills or saves fasgadair." I spied the empty plate beside her. "Oh good. You ate something."

Rowan shook her head. "A bird took it."

"What?" No way had I heard her right.

"This morning. A bird took the food off my plate."

"A bird?" There were many gachen on this ship. Someone must've wanted more than their ration. I shook my head, disgusted.

"'Tis all right. I wasn't hungry."

I ripped my stale roll in half and held out the uneaten portion. "Want some?"

She reached for the bread. "So, you have the power to save us? Fasgadair rather? You speak as if it's nothing." She nibbled some and swallowed. "Who's your uncle?"

I studied her. She seemed sincere. Hadn't everyone around here heard of me? Or was that presumptuous? "Aodan."

She studied me as a baby does, never taking her eyes off me. It grew uncomfortable. Maybe that's why people babble at them, to break the uncomfortable silence. "You're the prophesied child."

"Apparently."

"Aodan is deceased?" Her eyes widened, full of hope.

"Morrigan killed him."

"I wouldn't have expected such a twist of fate."

"It was an accident. She was trying to kill me. How'd you become a fasgadair?"

She cast her gaze downward. "'Twasn't by choice." Bitterness and sorrow laced her voice. She tore off a morsel of bread. "I hated myself...what I'd become. I remained in solitude...in animal form. 'Twas a just punishment."

"Well, not anymore. You've been given a second chance." I patted her shoulder.

She raised her head, tears streaking her cheeks. "How can this be? Why me?"

"Why any of us? None of us deserves what God gives us." And only God knew who He'd choose to save through me next...if I survived.

Chapter Twelve

I HOPED THIS TRIP wouldn't taint my love of the sea. There was a good chance I'd go ballistic if I remained trapped on this ship much longer. An entire week had gone by, leaving me desperate to stand on solid ground.

"Land, ho!" The man in the crow's nest held his hands to his mouth to amplify those wonderful words.

The captain shouted orders. Some crewmen bustled about on deck while others climbed the masts.

I fought my way through the organized mayhem to the bow.

Someone rushed past me, pushing me into the rail. "Make yourself useful or get below decks," a surly crewman jeered over his shoulder.

Having no idea how to help and desperately wanting to see land, I kept moving. At the bow, I strained to see anything along the horizon. The man in the crow's nest had a bird's-eye view and a spyglass. Still, I prayed he wasn't seeing things.

I kept my gaze on the horizon, praying, hoping for something. A sliver of green between the ocean and sky revealed itself. *Thank God!* I gripped the railing.

The hilly landscape took shape, growing in size and definition, revealing a beautiful city protected by a wall. Buildings filled the hills and dotted the highlands. A castle stood in the center, partway up the massive hill. Pastures flanked the highlands. A fortress rested at the highest peak. Mountains framed the city. Protruding land formed an inlet lined with pillars, obscuring the kingdom's lower portion.

Evan appeared beside me.

"What are those for?" I pointed to the pillars.

He leaned on the rail. "'Tis the warning system. They're guarded day and night. If something goes wrong, the guard lights the fire. When the guard across the way sees the fire burning, they light theirs. They do this all the way around the city, so everyone can ready their weapons and barricade the passageway."

Pepin dragged ropes past us.

"Pepin, check this out," I called to him.

"Hmph. I'm getting off this unstable hunk of timber and onto dry land where God intended us to be." He continued past without glancing or pausing. "Pech weren't meant to teeter about..." His unintelligible mumbling faded away.

Evan and I laughed.

Wolf joined us. "Looks like yer having quite the blether. Does Rowan still refuse to come up?"

Evan scoffed. "Not even to see land. She doesn't seem to want to come out of the dark."

"Well, the lass can't stay on board when we reach port. 'Tis not our ship." Wolf headed toward the hold.

Rushing past, I reached out to slow him. "Let me talk to her."

I descended the ladder and searched the darkness. "Rowan?"

"I'm here." Just a hoarse whisper, her voice floated toward me.

"It's time to come up. We're almost there."

She pulled her knees up and hugged them tight. "Where?"

"Bandia."

"No!" Shaking her head, she buried her face in her knees.

"What's the matter?" I knelt before her. She refused to look at me. "Is there something wrong with Bandia?"

"No." She lifted her head. "There's something wrong with *me*."

"What do you mean?" I moved next to her, and the odor hit me. The musky stink of someone who'd gone far too long without a shower. I breathed through my mouth.

"Nothing." She gave me a pleading look. "I can't go there. Please don't make me."

"I can't make you do anything. But you need real food and a bath. And you can't stay on this ship."

Judging from her expression, she either didn't believe me or didn't care.

"If you're running from something, you're sure to get caught if you stay behind."

She closed her eyes and inhaled a deep breath. "Will you carry me in a satchel as a raccoon to your room?"

I studied her face. "So, you *are* hiding from something?"

"'Tis the only way I'll go." She crossed her arms.

She was about as likely to walk out of this hold with me or provide a solid explanation as Morrigan was about to hand herself over to my blood for testing. I groaned. "Fine. I'll carry you."

Rowan disappeared under the blanket, and a masked bandit peeked out.

****

We sailed into the inlet wide enough for one ship to pass through. Twin towers stood on both sides. A wall snaked away from each tower along the coast, lining the backs of the buildings within its perimeter. Guards armed with bows stood at the tops and base of each. The guard on the right walked in our direction, holding up his hand.

The man in the mast gestured to the guards and shouted.

Evan pointed to the harbor entrance. "See that chain?"

A chain—the width of my torso, covered in green slime, and strung between the two towers—hovered over the water's surface.

"Once they clear us, they'll drop the chain so we can pass."

We were approaching the chain at a decent clip. "The ship isn't slowing down. What happens if we run into it?"

"The ship will sink." Evan laughed. "Steady yourself. Your eyes are as wide as saucers. Not to worry. They'll lower the chain in time." He leaned over the rail.

The guards turned the cranks, lowering the chain. Expecting to collide, I braced myself as we sailed through, but we cleared it. The inlet was longer than it had seemed from afar. A guard stood by each of the pillars. We passed three before the inlet widened into a harbor where a fleet of similar ships and various smaller watercraft rocked on the water. The stone buildings lining the rocky coast grew more impressive. As did the elaborate archway lined with pillars and the enormous castle.

The crew continued bustling about letting down sails and tying them, heaving lines to men waiting ashore. The men on shore pulled the ship in while crewmen prepared to lower the gangplank.

Eager for land, I hoisted my pack over my shoulders and picked up Rowan in the sack.

Rowan hissed.

"Sorry," I whispered and repositioned her, hoping to make her more comfortable. Raccoons are bulky, awkward creatures.

She settled down without further complaint.

My arms grew tired as I waited for the crew to allow us to disembark. Pepin stood next to me, his body quivering. "Are you okay, Pepin?"

"I will be. Just anxious for land." His body continued to quake like the lid of a pot about to boil over.

The crewman with the hooped earrings waved us through, and I raced down the gangplank behind Pepin. The pier met a stone roadway leading up to a massive arch with a uniquely carved pillar on either side. Their enormousness made me feel like an ant. They rivaled the wall surrounding Gnuatthara. And their beauty was unmatched by any architecture I'd ever seen.

It smelled like the seafood section of a grocery store. Chatter and shouts mingled with lapping water, rocking boats banging against docks, ringing bells, clicking shoes, and other random thumps and clangs.

Pepin waited with me, on his knees. He raised his arms to the heavens, then kissed the ground. After Evan, Wolf, Maili, and Shimri filed down the gangplank, we set off down the road.

A little girl blocked our way. "Would you like an Aine?" She shoved a misshapen statue of an overly endowed woman in my face.

"Uh. No thank you." I strode past her, glancing into the bag full of similar statues on her back.

"What was that?" I asked Evan once we were no longer in earshot.

"A pagan god. The goddess of fertility."

"You don't believe in that stuff, do you?"

"Of course not."

I gawked, craning to peek down every side street as we wound our way up the hillside. The road leveled and ended before a large iron gate. When Evan shouted to those atop the wall, the gate lifted before us.

We entered the courtyard. Stone pavers covered the ground. Pristine gardens lined the interior wall and the building in the courtyard's center. A massive castle stood beyond, rooms and towers protruding in different directions.

I wished I could whistle. "This is unreal." Elaborate carvings and giant stained-glass windows adorned the building holding court in the center of the courtyard. I couldn't read the foreign writings. Too bad Drochaid didn't work on the written word. "What is that place?"

"Their place of worship," Evan grumbled.

"I thought they no longer worshiped God."

"They don't."

"Oh."

"Fallon!" a familiar voice called.

My mother rushed toward me, her blonde hair shining and pink-tinged cheeks fuller than when I saw her almost a year ago. When she hugged me, she no longer felt bony. She smoothed my hair. "You made it. How was your journey?"

"Fine." Aside from being attacked by a mismatched pack of animals. And stuck on a ship. This queasiness and feeling as if I were still rocking would pass. Right?

"Faolan." The tenderness in my mother's voice and the way she regarded Wolf before embracing him made me wonder, again, as to the nature of their relationship. It seemed more than friendship. But how awkward would that be? They were the same age, but he looked young enough to be her son.

Pepin cleared his throat, and the two parted. "Cataleen, it's good to see you again." He thumped his chest twice in a pech greeting.

I waited for Maili, Shimri, and Evan to exchange greetings with Cataleen. "Didn't you, Cahal, and Declan go on a mission together? Are you all back?" My hopes rose.

Cataleen dropped her gaze. "We got separated."

Uh-oh. That look. That tone. Bad news. My rising hopes dashed upon the jagged edge of reality.

Cataleen brushed something off my shoulder. "I haven't seen them yet. But they could arrive any moment. More arrive continually." She addressed the crowd. "The clans have been called together. Most are here. The Dosne and the Olwen arrived about a fortnight ago. We've been awaiting your arrival to discuss our course of action."

"Can I come?"

"Of course. You're our guest of honor."

****

I knocked on the bathroom door again. The thick wood hurt my hand. "Almost ready, Rowan?"

The door opened. Rowan emerged, brushing her hair. Though dark while damp, it looked considerably lighter now. "My apologies, Fallon. 'Tis been a while since I've cleaned up properly. So many..." She held onto a clump of hair, yanked her brush through, and grimaced. "...knots."

In the bright room, her face free from grime, she looked beautiful.

Her pale, smooth skin probably hadn't seen the sun in years. And she smelled better than she had as Crypt Girl or as a ratty raccoon.

I sat on the bed and bounced slightly. "It's fine. Are you almost ready?"

"Ready?" She stared at me as she placed the brush on the nightstand. "For what?"

"For the meeting with the elders."

Her ice-blue eyes glared at me as if I'd asked her to hand herself over to Morrigan. Her barely visible golden eyebrows rose, then lowered, pinching together. "I've no intention of attending."

"I just thought—"

"Fallon, whilst I appreciate the lengths you've gone through on my behalf, I must insist."

I leaned back as if she might bite me. Where'd this forcefulness come from?

A knock at the door made me jump. I hopped up and gave myself a quick once-over in the mirror.

The bathroom door closed.

I smoothed a stray strand of hair, opened the door, and deflated somewhat at the sight of my mother. "Oh, hi."

Cataleen raised an eyebrow and tilted her head. "You were expecting someone else?"

"No. Come in." I pulled the door open wide.

"Where's Rowan?"

I plopped onto the bed and waved to the closed bathroom door. "Back in the bathroom. She's not planning to join us, anyway."

"No worries. We can bring something up for her to eat when we return." As awkward silence quieted us, she turned to me. Her eyes roamed the length of my body like an MRI scan. She cleared her throat. "Do you have something more…Ariboslian?"

I checked out my jeans and T-shirt. "What should I wear?" I hadn't anticipated any formal events.

"Do you have a dress?"

"I have the dress the Selkie gave me. Will that work?"

"Much better."

I grabbed the dress and glanced at the closed bathroom door. "I'll just be a minute. Meet you outside?"

My mother nodded. "Be quick."

After she stepped into the hall, I changed and glanced at myself in the enormous mirror, light aqua shimmering over me in liquid ripples. Good thing I packed sandals. Hopefully, this would do. What if Declan was there?

What if he wasn't?

CHAPTER THIRTEEN

CATALEEN LED ME DOWN ornate halls and staircases. Her heels echoed on the freshly polished floor. Portraits of unsmiling men and women bedecked in jewels peered down at us. Their seeming endlessness and similarity reminded me of a Scooby Doo cartoon loop. I swear I passed the same picture more than once. Nervous energy made my fingers tingle as I half-expected to catch a portrait's eyes following me.

We came to the end of a long hall to tall, arched doors. Guards with swords at their hips pulled the thick doors open, allowing laughter and chatter to escape. The guards remained stiff as we entered a grand room. Intricately carved archways adorned with decorative lanterns and exposed beams lined the high ceiling. Arched windows twice my height with gold curtains covered the walls to my right and my left. People clumped together in cliques. The fancy chatted with those bedecked in elegant clothes and jewels; the not so fancy gathered among those similarly dressed in simple tunics or dresses.

Thank you, Cataleen, for making me change. As much as I loved them, it would have been embarrassing to show up in jeans and sneakers, even among the plainly dressed.

I searched for one thing. The Treasach stood a couple of heads and shoulders above the rest. I'd forgotten how short Cahal was in comparison. Cahal!

An attempt at a smile crossed his perpetually stern features. I started toward him, joy filling my heart. As I neared, his face morphed into something I'd never seen…not in *his* eyes. A cross between fear and hurt. His shoulders sagged, and I slowed. Cahal's feelings, if he had any, were usually impossible to detect. Something had to be terribly wrong to read his face…to sense it before reaching him. My feet continued forward despite my hesitation. Each agonizing step leading me to news I had to know but didn't want to hear.

Cahal crossed the gap and smothered me in a hug. He grasped my arms and leaned down, his gaze penetrating. "Are you well?"

"I'm okay. How are you?" Past the slight smile, his eyes held the truth.

He let me go and returned to his full height. Another shadow darkened his face. "Much has happened since you left."

"So, I've heard." Why did I feel like I was choking? I touched my neck. It wasn't my dress. My neckline didn't come up far. I swallowed hard. "How's Declan?"

His stoic expression cracked. Only raw pain there now. "I lost him in Diabalta."

Whatever held me in place began to falter. The room swayed. "Diabalta? Morrigan's empire? Why?"

Cahal wrapped an arm around me and led me to a chair at a nearby table. "We had to go."

I blinked to clear my vision. Tears stung my cheeks. "Is he… Is he…?" I couldn't ask.

Cahal's shoulders drooped. He shook his head slowly, eyes closed. When he opened his eyes, he kept his gaze downcast. "I don't know."

How could he say he didn't know? I rubbed my neck to soothe whatever choked me. "You were with him." Words clogged my throat. "What happened? Where is he?"

"We got separated. I went back for him, but…"

The way he spoke. His inability to meet my gaze. Something was off. The air felt heavy. Its weight made breathing difficult. "What aren't you telling me?"

"There is nothing more. We got separated."

"That can't be all. You would've gotten him back—no matter what."

His countenance drooped like a dog with his tail between his legs. "I'm sorry I've disappointed you."

"No. You're keeping something from me. What is it? Why won't you tell me?" Someone touched my arm. I didn't bother turning to see who. The weight of Cahal's words crushed me. Dead. Declan must be dead. He just couldn't bring himself to tell me. But that wasn't like Cahal, was it? He spoke his mind. In as few words as possible, but still. He didn't sidestep. He didn't hold anything back. Did he?

"My apologies, Cahal. I should have told her sooner." My mother pulled me to stand. "Come. Let's return to your room."

I shook free. "No." I needed to be here. To help Declan, I had to learn more. I had to find him. He couldn't be dead. He couldn't be. I sank back in my seat.

My mother sat on one side of me, Cahal on the other. Evan, Pepin, Wolf, Shimri, and Maili filled the surrounding chairs with Maili directly across the table. Sensing her there, I jerked my head up. Searched her face. Did she know what had happened to her betrothed? Did she care?

Bodies shuffled past, chairs scraped across the floor, and glasses clinked as I attempted to stop my cyclical thoughts. Speculating and worrying wouldn't help. I needed to know the plans to destroy the fasgadair and my part in them.

Guards with swords swaying at their hips escorted a man wearing a jeweled crown. Everyone stood. Including me.

"That's the high priest and the king's regent, Kagan." My mother whispered from my right.

The guards delivered Kagan to the head of the table. He remained standing while guards took position along the wall and in twos at each exit. Another guard remained behind Kagan. He sipped from Kagan's goblet, then handed it to him. Kagan lifted his glass. Shuffling cut the silence as everyone hurried to lift theirs. I raised mine last.

"Peace to all," he said and drank.

A chorus of "peace" rang throughout. Then Kagan sat, and everyone returned to their seats.

Clinking resumed as people reached for and passed around plates with sliced bread. A wonderful aroma wafted toward me. Servants in plain black attire lingered behind us with tureens. A serving girl waited behind me with a ladle.

"Oh. Sorry." I righted the upside-down bowl atop my dinner plate. She poured the steaming soup and moved to my mother. Garlic and other herbs teased me as I chased a dumpling in the broth.

Kagan's dark eyes roamed the crowd. Tufts of coarse gray hair seemed to hold up his jeweled crown. Matching gray dusted his darker, trim beard. Dark fabric covered his skull under the crown, probably to hide a bald spot.

A Merlin lookalike on Kagan's left stood. "Please allow me to thank our hosts, King Aleksander, Regent Kagan, and the king's successor, Prince Valter"—he motioned to the ruggedly cute guy on Kagan's other side—"and the generous people of Bandia, for giving us refuge." He raised his glass. Once all glasses hovered in the air, he said, "Enjoy the feast!"

"That's Abracham." Cataleen swallowed her mouthful of wine. "His father was king of Diabalta before Aodan captured him."

"Who? The one that looks like Merlin?"

"Who's Merlin?" She shook her head. "No, the man who was talking."

Yeah. The guy who looks like Merlin. Just once, it would be nice if people caught my references. I resisted rolling my eyes. "Is the king of Diabalta still alive?" *Dumb question, Fallon.* If he was, he'd have to be over a hundred, unless Abracham/Merlin was prematurely gray.

My mother grimaced. "'Tis possible. Rumor is Morrigan keeps a king collection."

Dare I ask what a king collection was? No. It sounded self-explanatory. And I wasn't sure I wanted the details.

Cheers and the clinking of glass filled the hall. Conversations hummed around me. I slurped some broth, the spices unfamiliar, but wonderful. Servants removed my bowl and spooned veggies, potatoes, meat, and gravy onto my plate. Sure beat rabbit, the stale shipboard food, and even the ramen I'd lived on back home. And I had no idea when I'd get another meal.

Declan. Heart twisting, I scooped another bite of potato. He must still be alive. Cahal didn't sugarcoat. If he knew something certain, as hard as it might be, he would've told me. So, there must be a chance. And I'd need to be in decent shape if I had any hope of helping him.

The servants began clearing our plates, and I shoveled the last forkfuls into my mouth.

Regent Kagan stood. "As unfortunate as it is to break this merry feast, we have urgent matters to discuss. If you are not a clan leader, kindly adjourn to the ballroom for dessert. For those of you who remain, not to worry. You will be served dessert as well."

The crowd politely laughed. Chairs scraped along the floor as people rose to leave. I moved to follow. My mother grasped my hand, rooting me. "Regent Kagan requested your presence. You are to stay."

I guess I expected as much. After all, they were waiting for my arrival to decide how to proceed, right? This should be interesting....

Chapter Fourteen

A CROWD GATHERED AT the door with Wolf, Pepin, Evan, and Shimri among them. A low murmur increased in volume as they exited. Guards shut the door with a clang, and silence reigned. Less than a quarter of the people remained, including Cahal, my mother, and Maili.

My mother and Cahal weren't clan leaders. Perhaps they were allowed to stay for my sake? And Maili? What had happened to her parents? Was she now the leader of her clan? Would I always be so self-consumed? I'd never made any attempt to get to know her. I needed to do better…to *be* better.

The servants placed a small pie before each of us. Off-white filling sprinkled with a brownish powder. I poked it with my fork.

"Custard tarts." My mother tasted hers and smiled. "Try it."

Smooth and creamy. Sweet and spicy. Delicious. I savored each morsel and scraped my plate for every minuscule crumb. Guilt sweeping over me, I frowned at the gleaming white plate. How could I sit here enjoying this food with Declan missing? Someone had to do something. *I* had to do something. But what?

The regent cleared his throat and stood once more. "I don't deny the enmity that has existed between us over the centuries. But the fasgadair banded us together for a common cause. As you're all too aware, they will overtake us completely if we don't act. We are the final remnant of our race. It's time we put aside our differences and join forces. We are stronger together."

Everyone applauded.

"And there's someone here to help us." He gestured a bejeweled hand to me. "Fallon, would you please rise?"

My mother nudged me.

"Huh?"

She jerked her head upward, urging me to rise.

"Oh!" My face burned, and my arms trembled as I stood.

Regent Kagan extended his arm toward me. "Fallon heals demonic fasgadair blood and returns them to gachen, isn't that right?"

He spoke as if I were powerful. But it wasn't me. And my blood sometimes killed. Another thing I had no control over. But I didn't want to get into a big discussion. I just wanted to shrink away from the eyes sizing me up. So, I gave a small nod.

"Thank you, Fallon."

I dropped back into my chair, wishing I could melt into it.

A slender man with a pointy beard rose. "I heard she could kill them too."

As he returned to his seat, murmurs intensified.

A young guy in brown leather stood. "How will that help us? Can she kill a number of them at a time?" He glanced my way before returning to his seat, his eyes apologetic.

Valid point. I can't.

"We need an army. The fasgadair destroyed our village," a man in a tattered tunic said. "There are a handful of us left. We're tradesman, not warriors."

"Aye!" A man with long sideburns tied into braids burst from his chair. "You must give us something stronger to go on than a little girl. 'Tis that all ye have?"

Who was he calling a little girl?

Kagan stood. "We are here today at Sully's insistence to await Fallon's arrival. We've complied, and I've no doubt her unique abilities will prove useful. But the plan hasn't changed. We will send three separate groups: one through the mountains and two by sea. Both ships will navigate southwest. One will disembark on Notirr's shores. The other will continue further south toward Kylemore. The three groups will reconvene at the Somalta caverns to join forces with the pech. Fallon will join my troop toward Notirr."

Pandemonium ensued as leaders argued amongst themselves.

The commotion died down as if by force as a strange substance filled the air. The room grew warm and tingly. Gooseflesh broke out over my arms as a chill coursed through me. Sully stood. I hadn't realized he was here. He remained rigid, his gray eyes wide, staring straight ahead. "In a land with no natural enemies, you war amongst yourselves. Your murderous hearts are intent only on evil. Repent! Destroy your idols! Return to your first love so God may bless you. Or face judgment." Sully relaxed, scanning the room as if he could see, then gripped the table as he lowered himself with the care of a man befitting his advanced age.

Whatever had filled the air was gone, replaced by a suffocating silence. Had God spoken through Sully? Some remained still, scarcely breathing, their eyes riveted on Sully, while others shifted uncomfortably.

"Was that a prophecy?" someone asked.

"God has spoken," Sully said. "We must destroy the idols and return to Him."

Kagan, still standing, clapped in a slow, mocking way. "Well done, Sully. That was a wonderful performance. Very convincing. I wonder…are you merely attempting to delay our attack? You convinced us to await Fallon's arrival. Now this? Will your demands never cease?" He scanned the crowd. "As the king's regent and high priest, I cannot allow our gods to be defiled. If any zealots among you continue to insist that the only way to unite ourselves is to forsake our gods, put away our idols and sorcerers, and bend the knee to your God, we must decline. Do not expect us to respect your values if you cannot respect ours. If you respect our ways, our traditions, you may continue to take refuge here. But those who are incapable, I grant your leave."

Abracham cleared his throat. "I know not all of us follow the One True God…"

Groans and murmurs erupted along the ranks.

Abracham held up his hand. "…but I trust Sully's prophecy. Going against God's will by ignoring His instructions and proceeding with these plans will result in disaster. We need Him. If we want Him to go before us, we must do as He asks before attacking the fasgadair."

A man with a cloth wrapped around his head smacked the table. "Don't let Sully rattle you. He's off his head. And, as Regent Kagan pointed out, he's an excellent performer. We must stick to the plan. We need every able body to fulfill this quest. Please don't tell me the believers in the God of our ancestors won't join us if we disregard this request."

Abracham stared the man down. "Why do you think our ancestors believed in one God? They knew. One God pulled us from the human realm to dwell here. Our ancestors were witnesses. It's written in our annals. And evidence surrounds us. Gateways between this world and the world from which God removed us still function. And you dare to mock them? Their beliefs? You mock us for remaining faithful to one God? He *is* the only God. I pray none of His believers will fail to trust Him, ignore His command, and go with you."

The audience broke out in firm nods and grunts of approval or shaking heads and offensive remarks.

"What is this?" Braidburn nearly toppled his chair. "Your father was ruler of Diabalta, a free city. He was not a believer in one god. Do you dare disgrace his memory by attempting to convince us one little god will save us?"

"My father could not save himself or his people. Not by his own will. Had he served God, things might've been different."

Various snorts, expletives, and guffaws broke out around the table while others threw those people contemptuous looks.

Braidburn remained standing, nodding toward a group of

complainers. "We believed you could lead us because you held the loyalty of all the clans." He grew louder as if fueled by the naysayers. "We believed you could unite us. You mean to tell us you're a zealot?" He spat the word. "Was this your plan all along? To trust in a god that doesn't exist? He can't help us. He would have done so already. Tearing down our idols will only anger our gods and guarantee our failure."

The noise level increased as people spoke over one another. Abracham leaned across the table. He spoke so quietly everyone hushed to listen. "Have you forgotten?" He scanned the crowd, searching each face. He repeated the words until conversations ceased and all eyes were on him.

Braidburn lowered himself to his seat.

Abracham tugged his Merlin beard. "How long has it been since your fathers stopped reading and teaching from the annals? How long that you've forgotten our God and what He's done for us? Do you even know our history?" He pushed himself back to full height. "We were once the mightiest race in Ariboslia. We worshiped God, and He blessed us abundantly." He pushed his hands together as if praying and pressed them to his lips. "Do you not know?"

Some sat rigid while others squirmed.

Abracham paused, catching each eye in turn. "How is it you can come to trust in gods you've never seen? Gods with no history? Gods your forefathers invented? We're not awaiting God's judgment. His judgment is here. The fasgadair are God's judgment upon us. In His infinite mercy, He's giving us a chance to turn this losing fight around. Does it make sense to keep disobeying and dishonoring Him and expect things to change? This is our chance. He's told us exactly what to do. If we obey, He will bless us. He will be with us. He will free us from the fasgadair." Abracham took a deep breath. "Is it so impossible to believe we can unite once more? We are at death's door. Our clans are devastated. Many of our loved ones are enslaved. Will you not destroy statues that can't help us and turn to the God who can?"

Regent Kagan smoothed his green surcoat with gold

embellishments, his rings sparkling. "We're all too familiar with the twisted views of intolerant zealots. I never took you for one, Abracham. You defame your father's legacy. We will not destroy our gods. Look around." He motioned to the room. "Our gods protected us. That's why you're all here. Bandia is the only refuge. What has your God done for you? You're the ones who lost loved ones and lands. You are the ones displaced. Our gods protected us and will continue to protect us. Think carefully. Do you really want to risk the futures of your few remaining clansmen? Do you really want to put it all in the hands of one god and a few zealots when we're offering you a battalion and the return of your father's lands?"

Abracham lowered his head. Was he considering Kagan's offer? At length, he raised his gaze just enough to meet Kagan's. "I follow your logic. I want to unite and attack as you planned. But God's ways are not our ways. And I cannot move forward without following Sully's advice. I can't convince you of God's greatness. He will reveal Himself in due time, I've no doubt. But you're right. Our numbers are dwindling. There's little left to lose, but so much to gain if we stand united."

"Not for Bandia." Regent Kagan smoothed an eyebrow. "We've lost nothing. We've merely come to your aid."

"Sir Kagan is right. The gods protected his people here. I must protect the few remaining among my clan," Braidburn said. "I won't risk angering our gods."

Nods and murmurs swept up the air as I sat stunned. I could see both points. And I could understand why these people couldn't trust God. They weren't believers. But to place their trust in their false idols, to the extent that they weren't willing to follow the God Who'd actually spoken to them… That, I couldn't understand.

Cahal's chair fell to the floor with a crash in his haste to stand. "I've returned from Diabalta." His voice thundered over the din. The crowd silenced. "Na'Rycha has built an army greater than Aodan could conceive. They're coming. They won't stop until all of Ariboslia is theirs. The ocean and mountains won't hold them back much longer." He righted his chair and sat.

"We should flee to the land in the east," the young guy in leather said.

"The land in the east?" multiple voices questioned.

Another man, darker skinned with a shaved head, stood. "We know nothing of that land other than it is rumored to be selkie territory. We've no idea how long it would take to cross it nor what we might find when we arrive. Other vessels attempted the voyage and failed to return."

"'Tis our best chance to protect our race. Our chances of survival are slim if we stay." The guy held his ground. "The mountains are passable. Na'Rycha and his army will come…particularly now that the snow has nearly melted, and she's arrived." He pointed at me. "Morrigan must already be aware of her presence. We must act quickly."

"Do you suggest we hand Bandia over to the fasgadair?" someone asked.

"Of course not." The vein in the guy's neck protruded. His face reddened.

Kagan smacked the table. "Fleeing to an unknown land which may or may not exist, from which no one has ever returned, is not an option. We have plans to meet the pech. They are a formidable army with no zealots among their ranks. The question is—do we move forward with the plan as it was previously agreed to, convene with the pech, and face this evil together? Or do we allow ourselves to be coerced into turning our backs on the gods who protected us by destroying our relics to unite and fight this battle together? Since destroying our relics is not an option, the question is this: who is going to ignore Sully's performance and join us in battle?"

The arguments continued well into the night. It became a debate, each side attempting to convince each person individually to switch sides. What began as a welcome distraction had become tedious. I melted into my chair, wishing to escape to my room, desperate for sleep. No one needed me here. I was nothing but a mascot for the away team. A mascot the home team wanted to steal. These people would never agree. Sadly, the number who supported Sully seemed considerably smaller and grew smaller still as the arguments continued.

"Enough." Kagan didn't bother to rise. His crown was askew, and his face drooped. "Prepare to move forward with our original plan. We will finalize the preparations for our ships and depart in three days. Those who refuse to join us are welcome to go wherever they wish, but they will no longer be welcome in these lands. You have three days to choose—fight with us or seek another place to take refuge. Either way, our idols will stand. Anyone who dares raise a hand against them will face severe consequences."

No way would my friends go against Sully. But where *would* we go?

CHAPTER FIFTEEN

REPLAYS OF THE ARGUMENTS resounded in my mind like a bad song. I tossed on the hard mattress, coverings twisting around my legs. How long had I lain here? Sleep. I just wanted to sleep.

A beam of bright light blinded me. I squinted and wiped away the tears, then held my hand like a visor, shielding my eyes. My surroundings came into focus. The beach. The beach in my dreams where I'd always seen my mother. Someone stood in her place. No billowy dress or blowing hair. A man.

I stepped forward. But, like my mother had in the dreams before, he remained the same distance away. What was this? Who stood there in my mother's place?

The man pivoted. He looked like… No, he couldn't be Declan.

A popping sound rang out on my right. The circle of swirling lights. But how? Aodan was dead. No one else had ever penetrated my mind. Was it part of the dream? Could someone else breach my mind as Aodan had with his sister? As he almost breached mine?

One way to find out. I inched toward the swirling lights as they formed a hazy image.

"No!"

I jumped.

"Stay away from him, Fallon."

"Declan!" I ran toward him but failed to get any closer. Then, as in the dreams past, darkness swept over the landscape, swallowing the light. I blinked, and Declan stood before me. His face morphed into a fasgadair as he lunged.

Someone shook me. "Fallon. Wake up."

Flickering light swept past me, traveling next to the bed. Who woke me? Where was I? A wave of memories crashed over me. I was in Bandia sharing a room with Rowan. But that wasn't Rowan. Groggy, I wiped my eyes.

"From the looks of it, you were having a nightmare." My mother lit the oil lamp, and light flooded the room.

I groaned. What was she doing in here? What time was it? Early. Too early. My body ached. I just wanted to sleep. I'd struggled to sleep despite my exhaustion. My mind ran like the Energizer bunny.

The hard mattress didn't budge under Cataleen's weight as she sat, but the covers tightened around me. I fought the urge to push her off as I adjusted myself to relieve the pressure.

"Do you want to talk about it?" she asked.

No, I want you to go away and let me sleep. "It was nothing." I had no interest in talking about how the bizarro dream that used to haunt me had returned, except it was Declan haunting me. And, oh yeah, the swirling lights, a sign Aodan was attempting to take over my mind, had returned. Except Aodan's dead, so I had no idea who the culprit was this time. Unless Aodan was able to reach me beyond the grave. I shuddered.

Then again, she'd dealt with this with Aodan. She experienced a complete takeover. He succeeded in having her harm herself, which is how she ended up in my realm to begin with. If that hadn't happened, I never would have been born. But, if anyone would understand, she would. Should I tell her? Or would that just create another issue to contend with?

"Get up. I'll be back in a few minutes to bring you to the dining hall. And wake Rowan too. We need to discuss our plans since we're no longer welcome here."

"Right." Perhaps I'd talk with her another time. I yawned and closed my eyes.

"Fallon?"

"I'm up." I swung my feet out from the covers and sat.

Satisfied, my mother left the room.

Something bugged me. Aside from the fact that I was in a strange world rooming with a girl I'd transformed from a monster, Declan was missing, and we now had no plan or allies in the war against the fasgadair. Was it Cataleen? As much as I'd wanted to have a mother, as much as I'd envied Stacy even when Stacy was irritated with hers, I didn't like having someone mother me. I'd grown up without one. I didn't need one now.

Blankets covered Rowan's head. "Psst. You awake?"

She freed her face. "They're making you leave Bandia?" She slipped out of bed and moved to the door. She secured the latch and returned to bed.

Good idea. "You mean we? Yeah." I sat cross-legged on my bed, facing her.

"I can't believe they'd do that. Of Bandia's problems, lack of hospitality has never been one." She propped herself on one arm. Blonde waves tumbled down.

"Sorry. I would've told you last night, but you'd already fallen asleep. We brought you food." I pointed at the table by the door where the food still sat. Untouched. "I'm sure it's bad now."

Rowan waved her hand. "I'm not hungry." She laid her head back on the pillow.

When was the last time she ate? How was she not starving?

"When are we leaving?" she asked. "Where will we go?"

"Good question. Kagan—I mean, Regent Kagan gave us three days to prepare. In the meantime, I'm headed to breakfast. Want to join us?"

She shook her head and rolled over.

****

After breakfast, I walked outside to get fresh air. Something about the castle stifled me, despite its enormous rooms and windows. I had no desire to hang out with Rowan, and she refused to leave. And I had even less interest in subjecting myself to the agony of listening to the leaders deliberate. So far, they were getting nowhere. We had two options: meet with the pech despite Kagan or to flee to the unknown lands to the east. Both were bad ideas, and I had nothing valuable to add. I'd settle for the CliffsNotes from my mother later.

The sky darkened in the distance. It wasn't raining yet. All the more reason to get out now. I passed the place of worship, keeping a suspicious eye on it. What did they do in there? What gods did they worship? For what purpose? Did they make blood sacrifices? I shuddered, skirting it as if the place might shoot out mind-altering waves to suck me into their way of thinking.

"Ah, Fallon. I've been looking for you."

Darn. I'd almost made it to the gate. I swiveled to see who spoke.

Valter stood a few feet from me, his gold-embellished doublet a fantastic fit that showed off his shoulders and the *V* of his chest tapering into his waist. A sword hung from his hip. I didn't care for his air of importance, but his smile softened me. "I wonder…might you join me in a tour of the kingdom?"

My heart skipped a beat. What made me so nervous? "Uh. I guess. Sure."

Valter motioned to the temple. "Shall we?"

"Ummm…" I took a couple steps back.

Laughing, he grabbed my hand and led me inside. Color blasted my eyes as if a rainbow had thrown up and splashed every surface from the stained-glass windows and painted walls to the red cushions and spackled gold floors. White statues and carved pillars with images and lettering I couldn't read somehow missed the spray and offered relief from the visual assault.

People kneeled on the cushions hunched over in prayer, facing several statues before a massive window.

Something beyond the Skittles decor bothered me. Something intangible. I sensed it like a fasgadair's presence minus the smell. "Is it your time of worship?" I whispered.

"The temple is always open for worship. But attendance has grown as more refugees arrive and fear spreads."

A woman brushed past us, down the aisle in the center of the rows of cushions, to an enormous statue. She bowed and dropped a package at its feet.

"What's that?" I nudged his elbow.

"She's leaving a grain offering to Camalus, the god of war."

Many packages lined the feet of the so-called gods, but Camalus had the most by far.

"Are those packages food?"

"Aye."

"I guess they're not hungry." I stifled a snicker.

Valter threw me a disapproving glance.

Did they expect the gods to consume the food? What would happen to it? Perhaps that's how the priests earned a living. Maybe they shared it with those who might not be able to afford food. I shook my head. Didn't matter. The whole thing was wrong. A stone remains a stone no matter how you carve it.

The woman retreated to a cushion. She rocked back and forth, wailing, with her arms in the air.

Okay, time to go. I launched myself out the door. Once I felt a comfortable distance and the hairs on my arms relaxed, I slowed.

Valter caught up to me. "I apologize if she scared you." As we approached the gate, he signaled the guards to raise it. They bowed and rotated the cranks. The iron gate rose with a painful squeal, like a stuck pig with a megaphone. "She's afraid for her family and rightfully so."

Passing underneath, I eyed the gate's sharp points. What if the rope holding it broke at the wrong moment? I quickened my pace.

"You've seen the wharf on your arrival, I gather," Valter said.

"We passed through."

"Perhaps we can visit another time. Follow me." He veered in the direction opposite where we'd arrived, uphill, keeping the castle wall on our right.

People walked along the streets carrying heavy loads on their backs while children zigzagged around them. All stopped to bow as Valter neared.

Should I have bowed? I eyed him askance, and he threw me a reassuring smile.

The side streets and stone buildings thinned. The incline steepened. Lush grass replaced stone. The clouds hadn't yet caught up to the sun. Thick, humid air weighed down my lungs, making breathing difficult, particularly uphill. A soft breeze swept through, cooling my skin. I put my arms out and splayed my fingers to allow the breeze to swarm and refresh me.

A fortress stood at the crest. "Is that where we're going?"

"Aye. Whatever you do, don't look back." He winked. "Not yet."

The stone fortress was chilly. Openings along each side allowed the breeze to sweep through. We ascended a staircase to a tower protruding from the roof. Four posted guards remained rooted, keeping at each compass point. Tweets echoed as birds flittered about the rafters.

"Step aside." Valter motioned to a guard.

The guard slid over but remained rigid, still facing out his window.

Valter beckoned me. "Close your eyes."

I hesitated. I didn't know this guy, and he was leading me to an open window many stories high. He was next in command. Who would stop him from...

He tilted his head and raised his eyebrows. "Please?"

I closed my eyes.

He grasped my shoulders and guided me to the wall. "Okay," he whispered, his breath hot at my neck. "Open."

"Wow." I hadn't realized how far we'd walked or how high we'd come. Castle towers partially impeded the view. The ocean shimmered. The bustling city and wharf seemed so peaceful. I've never flown over a populated area before or the ocean. "It's beautiful."

Folding his arms over his gilded chest, he stepped to the side and beamed.

"Have you always lived here?"

"Aye. This is my home."

"If you leave to fight in this battle, how do you plan to protect it?"

Sunlight rippled over the golden doublet as a heavy breath filled his lungs. "Regent Kagan plans to leave a few men behind. He believes our gods and our natural defenses will protect our people."

I recalled the fasgadair's swiftness, the control they'd had over me before I came to believe in God, the cavern full of monsters where I awaited my death. And Na'Rycha had built an even larger army? "He's wrong."

"I'm concerned too. But the king is ill. Bandia law dictates the high priest act as regent as long as King Aleksander lives and is incapable of ruling."

"Who will rule if the king dies?"

"I pray King Aleksander will not hear Aoibhell's harp. But, should he pass from this life into the next, the crown will become mine." Gazing out at the sea, he narrowed his eyes. His Adam's apple bobbed as he swallowed. "The king had only one heir, Princess Arabella, my betrothed."

"What happened to the queen and princess?"

"The queen died in childbirth. Arabella disappeared seven years ago. We awaited a ransom demand. None came."

He leaned against the post and inspected his fingers. "But Druantia used the tragedy to protect us. Arabella's disappearance motivated King Aleksander to put these security measures in place. Now we're prepared for the fasgadair." He stretched his arm out in front of me, pointing to a clearing in the trees, outside the city walls. "See that tower there?"

"Ay—Yes." I giggled. I'd almost said aye.

"Guards are posted there." He moved his hand further up. "And there." He pointed to the left. "And the rest up the row. Should a threat arise, the guard stationed at the post will light a fire. The other guards, as they see the signal fire, will also light their fires. We have posts surrounding this point along the bay and abutting the mountains behind us."

I resisted the urge to grasp his arms and shake sense into him. "But what good is that? Once you're alerted to an attack, what will you do?"

"If they arrive by water, the chain across the canal will keep them at bay. The guards will set the closest ships on fire. Archers will handle anyone who tries to climb ashore."

"What if they pass through the mountains?"

"If they dared venture the terrain, we'd defend ourselves. Our archers would attack. The enemies fallen would take many more down with them. We have other hidden dangers in place to eliminate threats." He chuckled. "Regent Kagan has quite the imagination. I, too, trust we are well protected."

"How?" One foot tapped an impatient rhythm. "They have a large army. Many fasgadair can transfigure into a bird or something capable of mounting the wall, attacking from the inside, and letting others in. How will you protect yourself? There won't be many here to defend the land. And fasgadair...*don't*...die." At an image of Aodan's hair set on fire, blackening before returning to its fasgadair pale, I shuddered. Even his hair regrew to its original length. "From what I understand, decapitation is the only way." Besides my blood. "You can't decapitate them from a distance."

Valter shoved away from the pillar and elbowed in beside me. He braced himself against the lookout wall, his arms propped up on the edge. "That is why we need to stage our attack. We've already wasted so much time waiting for your arrival." He spoke under his breath. It sounded like he said, "Sully." His sudden puppy-dog look melted my heart. "That's why we need you."

"I'm sorry, Valter." I tipped my face to the sun, letting light and warmth soothe the aches from my temples. "I wish I could help. Really, I do. But unless we follow Sully's instructions—"

"You saw those people in the temple, Fallon. We can't destroy it. The gods are our only hope…aside from you."

"They're wasting their time and energy on man-made statues who can't eat their food. Their hope should be in God. He's the only One Who can help them."

"Even if that were true, we can't go against Regent Kagan." Straightening, Valter swept something off the windowsill—did he sweep my warning away just as casually? "And isn't this why you're here? Why we waited for you? To rescue us from the fasgadair? That is the prophecy."

"I thought the prophecy was about me and Aodan."

Valter shook his head. Blond curls brushed his forehead. "It's much deeper."

He moved to touch my shoulder.

I stepped out of reach. "What do you care about a prophecy given by God, spoken through Sully?"

Valter shrugged. "There's much truth to what Sully says."

"Then destroy your idols and return to God."

Something flashed in his ice-blue eyes. Anger? "It's not so simple."

"Actually, it is. If you believe God speaks through Sully…if you believe the prophecies about me, then you must do as he says. You can't pick and choose. If you accept part, you must accept all."

"Kagan is high priest and regent. He will believe in your God among his gods. But he will never destroy the idols or submit to one God."

"Then we go our separate ways. You with your people and me with mine."

Chapter Sixteen

I SAT ON MY bed and stared at Rowan absorbed in her book. My legs itched, antsy to do something. I sprang the mattress and pulled the heavy curtain aside. Clouds blocked out the sun, allowing diffused light to turn the landscape gray. Rain pelted the glass. Going outside wasn't an option unless I wanted a shower. But sitting in this room wasn't a choice either. "Let's explore the castle. Prince Valter gave me a tour of the kingdom earlier. You should see it."

Rowan's book fell to the floor. "Valter?"

"Yes. He was the princess's betrothed."

"Is he meeting you here?" Her wide-eyed glance darted to the door.

"No. He went to the throne room."

Relaxing, she stooped and scooped her book off the stone tile.

"Come check out the castle with me."

"Check out?"

"Not like a library book…" Not that she'd know what that meant either. "I mean—"

"No thanks."

I let out an obnoxious huff. "Fine."

As I left, Rowan shoved the book in front of her face.

I lingered in the hallway like a kid waiting for someone to come out and play. I didn't want to spend the day with Cataleen. And she probably had more important things to do. Wolf hadn't left her side since arriving in Bandia, other than to sleep. Pepin or Cahal wouldn't be interested. I barely knew Shimri or Maili, but I doubted they'd be interested either. Evan was my only chance. But I felt funny knocking on his door.

Knock, knock, knocking on Evan's door. I laughed as the tune with altered lyrics rang through my head.

I made my way down the hall toward the stairwell, checking over my shoulder in case someone should open their door, and crashed into someone as I rounded the corner.

"Oh!"

"Sorry, Fallon." Evan backed away, blushing, hands up.

"My fault. I wasn't looking where I was going."

"No, I was going too fast. I needed to get away from the politics and scoffers."

"I hear that. But I can't stand sitting here for another moment. Why Rowan is content to stay there, cooped up in the room, I'll never understand. It makes me feel like a caged animal."

He offered his elbow. "Then let's take a tour of the castle, shall we?"

"You read my mind." I accepted his offer by grabbing his elbow and laughed.

The castle was an endless maze. So many rooms. So many halls. Arched windows, lining some halls from floor to ceiling, helped us get our bearings. With the storm, even those halls were dimly lit. We relied on lanterns and wall sconces. A cool draft and the eerie Scooby Doo portraits sent shivers coursing through my body. If only I had a sweatshirt. And a Scooby snack.

I chuckled. Evan gave me the look. The one that silently questioned if I'm right in the head. I brushed it off.

Evan and I explored the castle as if it were a video game and clues might lurk in any corner. We poked our heads in every unlocked room, skipping those with guards. Some were barren with white sheets covering furniture. But, with the extra guests, many bedchambers were in use. Their occupants were likely meeting to discuss the plans to depart the following day. In other bedchambers, maids were changing bedding or tidying up. They watched us suspiciously, and we quickly shut the door. Each room had an elaborate fireplace, which would be nice despite the warm summer days. The castle felt perpetually chilly.

Evan and I ascended to one of the upper levels. The rain had stopped, but the sun had set. No sconces were lit, and our lanterns only offered a few feet of light. Cobwebs dangled from the ceiling. Something scampered through the halls, scratching the floor.

"Oh!" I jumped and grasped Evan's arm.

He laughed. "I'm sure it's just a rat."

Just a rat? What planet was he from? "Yeah. That's what I'm afraid of." I raised my lantern, suspicious of every dark space.

Wherever we were, it appeared abandoned. Rodents and spiders the only residents these days. That and whatever they ate. Ick.

"What's that?" I pulled a sheet off an odd-shaped object, sending up a cloud of dust. Coughing, I waved the dust away. "A rocking horse."

Evan peeked under a sheet. "There's a crib over here."

"I guess we found the nursery."

I caressed the rocking horse's intricately carved and painted face. His eyes sad from long abandonment. "Is this part of the royal quarters?"

"It may have been at one point. It certainly isn't now."

"Where's the king?"

"Wherever he is, I'm sure he's well protected."

"Too bad he's sick. He might've been willing to work with us. I wonder what's wrong with him?"

Evan shrugged. "I've heard rumors of poison, but nothing based on any evidence."

I pushed open a little door toward the back of the nursery, kicking up more dust. I sneezed.

"Bless you." He lifted his lantern over my head. "Looks like the nurse's room."

The modest room held a small bed, a dresser, and a bedside table. We passed the meager items to another nondescript door on the opposite wall to a massive room. Another cloud of dust elicited more sneezes. A chaise lounge lingered by a window, draped in thick curtains. We passed a table and chairs to an imposing canopy bed. A dominating portrait hung above the fireplace. I lifted my lamp, illuminating the full picture, and drew in a sharp breath.

"What is it?" Evan asked.

"The princess isn't dead."

Chapter Seventeen

I BURST THROUGH THE bedroom door. Rowan jumped, her book smacked her in the face.

"You're Princess Arabella."

"Shhh!" Her bulging eyes dominated her pale face. Her neck spun in every direction as though there were someone else in the room…or the walls had ears. "Shut the door."

I scanned the hall before pulling it closed. All clear.

"What gives you such a preposterous idea?"

"I saw your portrait."

Rowan fumbled with the book, trying to lift it from her chest, but her hands shook. "I must look like her."

"I'm not a fool, Arabella." I stressed the name, not allowing her to derail me. "You refuse to leave or see anyone. You're jumpy. You hide when people are near. You lock the door. And you totally freaked when I mentioned Valter."

"Freaked?" She waved her hand. "You say strange things."

"Don't change the subject. You understand what I'm saying. You're afraid of getting caught. Admit it."

"I'll admit no such thing." She placed the book beside her, sat up, and crossed her arms.

Drawing in a deep breath, I plopped next to her. "What are you afraid of?"

She hung her head. Blonde waves shielded her face.

"I won't tell anyone, but you need to give me a good reason why I shouldn't."

Hands shaking, she brushed those waves aside and, slowly, so slowly, lifted her head. She searched my face, then closed her eyes. "Because I'm a disgrace. I wasn't abducted as I led everyone to believe. I ran away." She lowered her head, protected once more by the curtain of blonde. "I'm a traitor to my people…to my crown."

"Why did you run away?"

"I was betrothed to Valter, but in love with another."

Sounded familiar. "What happened to the other guy?"

"H–he—" Her voice cracked. "He wasn't worthy of my love."

"Oh." Didn't sound like it ended well. I hoped something similar wouldn't happen with Declan. If he was still…

No. I had to stop thinking like that. This was about Rowan. Did I dare ask what happened? "How did you become a fasgadair?"

"I realized my error and was on my way home when a storm hit. We sought refuge in a nearby village. The fasgadair attacked that night. Jacobus, the boy I ran away with, knew he had no chance of stopping me from returning home. But if I was a fasgadair…I'd never return. He begged them to turn him…and me. I'd have rather died. But a fasgadair turned us both against my will. I can't…" She buried her face in her hands.

If Evan's description of the bloodthirst was accurate for all new fasgadair, I didn't want to imagine what atrocities she'd committed. Or how to help her overcome them. Right now, she had too much time on her hands to relive the past. That couldn't be good.

She wiped her tears. "I escaped and made my way on my own in the woods, as a raccoon."

So, as Wolf had, she'd chosen to remain in animal form to avoid the monster she'd become. But she was back, changed. And she seemed to believe in God. She'd be a much better leader than Kagan or Valter. Perhaps Arabella could convince these stiff-necked people to destroy their worthless idols. "Don't you think your people would want to know you're alive?" I touched her shoulder. "Don't you think it would give them hope?"

She jerked away. "No, I ran away. I'm a disgrace. The throne no longer belongs to me."

I placed my rejected hand in my lap. "Your father is ill. What if this is your last chance to see him…to make peace with him?"

"I can't." Misty eyes peered into mine. "Don't you understand? I'm not worthy of my father or my people."

"I get why you've been holed up in here. But do you have any idea what's happening? God spoke through Sully. He warned us we need to destroy the idols and return to Him. I fear what will happen if we don't, but Kagan refuses. He's forcing us to leave, and we have no plan…no place to go." I stared at her as if my eyes had the power to convince her. "We need you to claim your right and help us."

"No. As long as my father's alive and unwell, Regent Kagan will remain in control. My reappearance would make no difference."

"But you could talk to him, convince him to change his mind."

"Nothing would change. I'd only create chaos when we can little afford turmoil. Nothing will ever convince Regent Kagan to tear down the idols. And I'd be forced to marry Valter."

"Would that be so bad? The guy is hot." I chuckled. Despite the tenseness between us, I could imagine worse fates than being stuck with Valter.

Arabella's eyes narrowed at me. "Hot? Is he ill too? Does he have a fever?"

I burst out laughing. She gave me the usual look—like I might infect her with whatever possessed me—and backed away slightly.

"No. I just mean he's…" What word would I never use that she might understand? "Handsome."

"Truly? He was such a scrawny boy. Perhaps he's grown into himself. It has been a number of years. I suppose he's older than me now since I haven't aged." She seemed to contemplate the idea, then shook her head. Blonde curls bounced around her shoulders. "It makes no difference. Valter isn't worthy of the crown. I could never convince my father of that without evidence. But I'm sure Valter hasn't changed enough to be worthy now."

I had a hard time seeing anything in Valter unworthy of kingship. He seemed far better suited for the position than Kagan with his multiple gods and intolerance to our God. But what did I know of the burden of a crown? "I don't know about ruling a country, but if he shouldn't be king, wouldn't it be best if you were there to watch over him? To keep him in check?" What was I suggesting? That she should marry for her country rather than love? That she sacrifice her happiness for others? Was that what Declan attempted to do? Was that better? "I still think you should reveal yourself."

Her curls resumed their emphatic bounce. "Valter will have full control as king whether I'm by his side or not. My awareness of his poor decisions will only succeed in hastening my death. And there's no way out of this alliance without Valter revealing himself as a traitor to Bandia or dying." She grasped my sleeve. "Please don't tell anyone, Fallon. I beg you."

"Fine." I let out a dramatic sigh and rolled my eyes. "I'll keep calling you Rowan so I don't slip up. Evan already knows my suspicions, but I'll ask him to stay quiet. And I won't tell anyone else." For now.

Chapter Eighteen

IN THE DINING HALL the following morning, my stomach growled for the eggs, ham, and potatoes we'd had the previous day. But the aroma wafting from the tureens the servants brought in smelled nothing like breakfast. It smelled like soup.

A servant scooped a pale, lumpy, semiliquid substance into our bowls. I gave it a sniff. "Soup for breakfast?"

"It's porridge. Try it." Cataleen ate a spoonful.

I took a nibble from the tip of the spoon, expecting the consistency to make me gag. But it wasn't unpleasant. A little gingery. I ate the remaining spoonful. Not bad.

Abracham stood. "Thank you for joining me this morning and for your prayers. I ask, has anyone received clear direction from God?"

A diminutive bald man rose. "I have."

"And what is the answer you've received?" Abracham prompted.

"We are to travel the Bàthadh Sea to the east and the land beyond." He returned to his seat.

"We've discussed this," said someone with a deep, guttural voice.

"Aye, no one has ever survived the trip," rang out another.

The voices grew to white noise. Only a few words stood out. Abracham pounded the table with his fist until the shouts and murmurs died. "We're aware of the arguments. There is no time nor reason to rehash them. It is time for action. There is one claim to have received a revelation from God. Can any confirm?"

A handful of men and women stood, Sully among them.

"He has given you all the same message?"

Ayes and nodding heads came from those standing.

Abracham lifted his hands and gaze toward the heavens. "Thank You, Lord, for revealing Your will to us. We shall travel to the land beyond the Bàthadh Sea. Go with us." He returned his gaze to the crowd. "I shall meet with Regent Kagan to arrange travel."

****

In the king's massive throne room, I didn't have to fight the crowd to see Kagan. An ornate throne dominated the dais while a glass dome above angled the sunlight to spotlight him.

Abracham had finally gotten through the line. He knelt on the steps to the throne between two guards holding spears.

"Silence!" Kagan pounded his scepter on the floor. He glared at the buzzing crowd before giving his attention to Abracham. "What is your request, Abracham?"

"With your permission, Sir Kagan, as we are no longer welcome in Bandia, we request a ship to sail to the east."

The regent tugged on his immaculate beard. "As none who have traveled east have returned, I expect my ship will not be returned. What have you to trade?"

"As you are aware, Sir Kagan, we are refugees from our lands. We have few resources and are in need of what little we possess to see us through this journey."

"You are asking me to *give* you a ship?" He stressed the word *give* and laughed. Valter stepped up behind him and whispered in his ear.

"Allow us a moment to deliberate." Kagan followed Valter and a guard to a room behind the throne. The door closed behind them.

An incomprehensible hum filled the hall as conversations resumed then hushed when Kagan reappeared and reclaimed his throne. "I shall grant your request, Abracham. Consider it aid in a time of war. In addition, we will provide supplies. I will not expect you to repay the debt. Remember the favor Bandia bestowed upon your people."

Abracham bowed. "We are grateful for your generosity, Sir Kagan."

"A crew will ready your ship to set sail tomorrow morning." Kagan waved Abracham off.

Why was Kagan being so generous? He had laughed at the idea of giving us a ship. And now he was offering us supplies too? What did Valter say to him? Arabella was wrong. She had to be. He must've changed.

"So, you're leaving then?" Valter startled me. How long had he been at my side? I hadn't even seen him leave the room with Kagan.

"Yeah. Thanks for whatever you said to Regent Kagan to change his mind."

"Ah." He waved it off. "Why have you decided to go east?"

"Sully received a revelation from God."

"Did that revelation specifically include you?"

"I'm among those who won't disobey God, so yes. Besides, I can't abandon them."

"Why would God want you to travel east? For what purpose?"

Good question. One I'd asked many times. I squelched rising doubts. "Sully speaks for God. I trust him. I want to do God's will. Even if it doesn't make sense." In my limited experience, it usually didn't.

"You'd rather die on a fruitless mission than join us in our quest to destroy the fasgadair? We have an army, weapons. For the first time in history, the pech have agreed to fight on our side. They have staggering numbers and weapons. And they're strong. With us, you have a fighting chance." He laid a hand on my shoulder and gazed into my eyes. "Think of the good you could do restoring fasgadair back to who they once were." With his other hand, he motioned outside. "But out there… You have no idea what's there. You have no plan. Why flee when you can take a stand?"

All good points. Going with him made far more sense. But what could I do? "Destroy your idols."

"Hmph." A scowl crossed Valter's face, and his grip on my shoulder tightened. "You still have the night to think it over." He released me, flashed a winning smile, then walked through the parting crowd like Moses walked through the sea.

What was that? I rubbed my shoulder. Had I met one of his other personalities? Or was it my imagination? It had to have been. Unless he had split-second personality changes.

Why didn't Valter use his position to change Kagan's mind? He clearly had influence.

****

I lay in bed. Wind drifted through the open window, ruffling the curtains. Shadow monsters shifted, creeping back and forth from their hiding places. Sleep refused to release me from my overwrought mind. Valter's request to join him resounded over and over and over. How could I even consider it? I couldn't leave my friends. But he had a plan.

We had a plan too. But it was weak. It wasn't a plan at all. What kind of plan was it to sail to an unknown land from which no one had ever returned? For what purpose? What would we do when, and if, we arrived?

This was based on Sully's words. Were they truly from God? Was he always right?

But others confirmed it before Sully spoke. They weren't all mistaken. Was it possible they might think they received this revelation because of what Sully said at dinner with Kagan?

Why would God tell us to tear down the idols, then course correct and tell us to go east? God knew everything. He didn't have a Plan B. He had to know we'd fail. He didn't expect us to go against Kagan, did He? Or should I sneak out and smash them myself?

I shuddered, thinking what would happen when I got caught. What would Kagan do to me?

Would Valter take my side? Something in the way he grabbed my

114

shoulder… His eyes. His voice. And his expression when I told him to destroy the idols. Was he following Kagan's orders, or did he also believe in the false gods? He must. He grew up here.

These thoughts and images tormented me. Despite my desperation, sleep lingered just beyond my fingertips.

Bright light blinded me. I wiped the tears away and held my hand up, shielding my eyes from the beam. My surroundings came into focus. The beach. The figure…Declan.

I moved forward. As always, he remained the same distance away.

Why was I having these dreams again? Why was I aware I was dreaming? Why was Declan here, in Cataleen's place?

The popping sound rang out on my right. The circle of swirling lights emerged. Who was trying to take over my mind? Who had the ability to try?

I had to know.

The swirling lights combined, forming a solid circle. I stepped toward it.

"No!" Declan called to me. "Stay away from him."

The Declan on the beach was like my mother had been. Unreal. Part of the dream. But the person on the other side of the swirling lights was real. I had to find out who…

I took another step.

"No!"

As I turned back to the voice, the fasgadair version of Declan pushed me away from the lights.

I bolted upright in bed, chest heaving. Declan…. He pushed me? But how? I rubbed my arm. I still felt the pressure of his touch.

"What was that?" Rowan lit the lamp, and light flooded the room. She stood and closed the window.

"What was what?"

"Something flew in here." Hugging herself, she stroked her arms.

"What?" Is that what I felt? No. I felt hands. Cold hands. I searched the room.

"It's gone," Rowan said.

Someone rapped on the door. Rowan bolted to the bathroom.

When I cracked the door, a guard grabbed me. "Come with me. We're under attack."

Chapter Nineteen

I TUGGED MY ARM to pull away, but he held fast. "Please, I need to grab a few things." I wasn't leaving without Rowan.

The guard hesitated.

"I'll come with you. But let me dress and gather a few things."

The guard glanced up and down the hall, then released my arm. "Be quick."

He didn't seem to have any intention of leaving my room, so I carried my things into the bathroom.

"Quick," I whispered to Rowan. "Get into the sack."

"Something's not right. I was just at the window. The signal fires weren't lit. If we're under attack, why aren't the signal fires lit?"

"I don't know, but if you want to come with me, you better change now."

She stood there. Jawline set. Hands on her hips.

"Or you can chance them finding you."

"Very well." Rowan disappeared under her nightgown. The neckline caught around her middle as she tried escaping in her raccoon form. I snagged the gown. She wriggled free and crawled into the sack.

"Are you talking to someone?" The thick wood softened the guard's voice.

"Just thinking out loud." I dressed, threw my things into my backpack, and heaved it over my shoulders.

A sharp rap rattled the door. "I said be quick."

"Coming." Cradling Rowan, I opened the door. The guard fell inside, so I stepped out of his path.

"Come with me." He hustled me along.

I eyed the two mussed beds. They must employ this guard for muscle, not powers of observation. Either he was oblivious to the fact that I shared my room with someone or he didn't care.

My eyes darted toward the others' rooms. "Where are my friends?"

"There's no time. We must hurry." He pulled my arm.

"No." I yanked my arm away, nearly dropping Rowan, and planted my feet. "Where are my friends? I won't go without them."

A couple more guards appeared in the hall. As they approached, I backed away, then turned and ran. They caught up to me and grasped me bodily, lifting me. I kicked as Rowan plunked to the ground. The first guard picked her up and flung her over his shoulder while the other two carried me down the hall. "No! Let go of me. Cahal! Wolf!"

The two guards swept me away. The first guard trailed, carrying Rowan. Thank God, he was unobservant.

God, please don't let him discover the princess. Please let her stay with me.

Maybe her discovery was exactly what I needed to get out of this mess. Was I praying for the wrong thing?

As we traversed many halls and descended many stairways, a sense of déjà vu overcame me. This had happened before by Aodan's guards in Ceas Croi. But these weren't fasgadair. What did they want with me?

We arrived at the throne room. Clones of the guards opened the doors in time for us to pass through. Kagan occupied the throne, despite the hour. He leaned to one side, his scepter angled in the opposite direction. He straightened as I approached.

After the commotion earlier in the day, the room felt oddly

empty. Why was I getting private time with Kagan?

Wrong question. Why was I being *forced* to have private time with Kagan?

The guard who pulled me from my room pushed me forward to the steps before the throne. I caught myself, but my backpack threw me off balance. I steadied, keeping a distrustful eye on Kagan.

"Welcome, Fallon." He aimed his scepter at me. It hovered there. Then he took a deep, impatient breath and waved the scepter. "You are supposed to touch it."

I creeped up the steps and poked the scepter with my finger.

Kagan rolled his eyes and drew it back to his side. "I've requested your presence to implore you to stay."

"You're asking me?" I scoffed. "Your guards kidnaped me. They told me we were under attack."

Kagan stared at his guards. They lowered their heads. Crinkles appeared in the corner of Kagan's eyes. He found this amusing? "My most sincere apologies for my guards. They can be a bit"—he tugged on his beard—"enthusiastic?"

Sincere? Yeah, right. "Call it whatever you want."

"I didn't call you here to debate my guard's methods. They were effective. That is all I ask. But what of my offer?"

"Stay? Here? What about my friends?"

"The invitation is extended to you alone. I'm intrigued by your…abilities. You'll prove to be quite useful, I imagine."

"I need to go with my friends."

"Give it a day to think it over."

"I don't have a day. You banished them. They're leaving this morning. I'm going with them."

"Guards, bring Fallon to a suite in the west wing where she'll be comfortable."

"But I told you, I can't stay." I fought against the guards. "Let me go. I can't stay!"

They carried me to a room and shoved me inside. The one carrying Rowan dropped her on the floor. I tried to push my way out behind them, but they shoved me back in and shut the door in my face. A lock clicked in place. I wiggled the handle, then banged on the door. "Let me out!"

"Don't waste your energy," Rowan called behind me. "They're not going to release you...us."

I spun around. Rowan must've changed in record time.

She rubbed her back. "I must say, getting dropped and tossed around in a bag is not a pleasant experience."

"What am I supposed to do? I can't stay here. The ship is leaving today. This morning." Spotting the window on the opposite wall, I ran to it. Bars. Closely spaced. Even as a falcon, I'd never squeeze through. I squeezed my hands over two and tugged. They didn't wiggle in the slightest.

Ships in the harbor were barely visible in the dim morning light. "How can I tell which one is ours?" I turned around to an empty room. "Rowan?"

"I'm looking for a way into the tunnels." A tapestry bulged as she moved along the wall behind it. She came out, hair ruffled, and blew a blonde tuft from her forehead. "If there was one, they sealed it. Where's a pech when you need one?"

"Rowan, can you tell which ship is ours?"

She crossed the room and stood beside me. "Isn't Kagan giving you a ship? There's no way to tell which he'll offer. Unless they've stripped the flag. They won't allow your people to wave our flag."

"So, it won't be any of those." I pointed to a fleet flying the same white flag with what appeared to be four spirals or a mirror image of a short tree with two long curly branches.

"Right. The symbol for strength. They're likely readying those for battle."

"The flag on the ship we arrived in was white with a circular symbol of a tree with roots."

"Kylemore's symbol."

"Would they use that flag?" Panic welled up within me as I scanned the flags. "I don't see it."

****

"You're going to wear a hole in the rug."

I stopped pacing and glared at Rowan lounging on the massive bed.

"What else am I supposed to do? I'm trapped like an animal!" I shouted at the door as if someone listening might realize their error and let me go.

"I take offense to that." She yawned.

"It's getting dark out." I motioned toward the window. "My friends might've left without me, and I've been *kidnaped*!" I shouted the last word toward the door again. "And you're sitting there like nothing is wrong. How can you be so calm? What if you get caught? What if they come back for me and I can't bring you with me because you're not in the bag?"

"Perhaps it's my royal training." Sitting up straighter, she spoke the words with genuine curiosity as if she too hadn't a clue how she was so calm. "Or maybe not. Somehow, I know this is in God's hands. All will be well."

"How is that? Didn't you grow up here?" I twirled around, arms up, putting our cage on display. "Don't your people believe in multiple gods and things?"

"I did. But something happened when I drank your blood."

Just the distraction I needed. "What?" I plunked down beside her. The transformation completely intrigued me. Her experience might unlock some of its mystery.

"I remember being in pain. But it was strange. It wasn't a physical pain."

"Really? You were writhing on the ground. You looked like you were in agony."

"Aye. I remember. And I was. But it wasn't physical. It was as if God was showing me all I'd ever done wrong." Her face twisted at the memory. "It was the worst thing I've ever experienced."

"How'd you know it was God? Did you see Him?"

"No. But I sensed His displeasure…and His love. He wanted me to change. And as I relived every horrible thing I'd ever done, I cried out for help."

"I didn't hear you."

"Not out loud." She placed her hand on her chest. "In my heart." She moved her hand to her temple. "And in my mind." She gazed at the ceiling, a smile replacing the sorrowful twists. "He answered." She refocused on me. "He said He made a way for me to live with Him forever if I chose to turn to Him. If I believed. I did. I did believe. I do."

"And you didn't think to mention it? Man! Has this happened to everyone who changed back or just you?"

She shrugged. "I can only speak from my experience."

"But why did you choose to stay in the dark?"

"God has forgiven me. But I'm still working on forgiving myself. He loves me. But I'm struggling to love myself."

Her words struck me as if this was something I should see in myself. How did she see these things so clearly? Was that the reason for her calm in this storm?

I walked toward the window. Distraction over. "We still have to get out of here…somehow." A light flickered in the distance. "Uh…what's that?"

Cloth rustled as she moved beside me. "The signal fires."

"Would they light the signal fires because of my friends?"

"No. We must truly be under attack. The fasgadair must be…"

A shrill whistle pierced the darkness.

"…here."

Chapter Twenty

Shouts accompanied clanging shoes outside the room.

"We have to get out of here," Rowan said. "Now."

"How? We're trapped?"

"Think, Fallon." She laid her hands on my shoulders, fingers clenching into my flesh, and peered into my eyes. "Why is Kagan desperate to keep you?"

"Because I can turn fasgadair back to gachen, like you."

"Is that all? That's not useful on a battlefield. Knowing Kagan, he has bigger plans."

She was right. My ability was useless on a battlefield. So, what would he want from me? A light sparked. Fire. "I can start fires."

"What?" She released me and stepped back. "How?"

"I don't know. By thinking about it."

"Why didn't you tell me before? Burn the door down. Get us out of here!"

Why hadn't I thought of that?

My heart raced as I ignited the wood surrounding the lock, careful not to overdo it and trap us inside until it cooled or fell away. Rowan morphed into a raccoon. I gathered her clothes and shoved them in the bag. I pushed her fuzzy butt in after them. She chittered in protest. Probably not typical royal treatment, but I needed her with me wherever I ended up. And to get her out of here alive.

"What in Druantia's name? The door's on fire!" someone yelled from the other side.

"Kick it in. We have to get to her," came another shout.

A loud thump accompanied splintered wood, and the door burst open.

"Quickly. Come with us." Two guards waved for me.

"Where are my friends?" I stood my ground.

"Their ship sailed hours ago."

My legs nearly gave out. They left? They actually left? Without me? No way. They couldn't have.

One guard clenched my arm. "If you value your life, you'll come with us now."

I yanked my elbow out of his grasp. "How do I know we're really under attack?" I'd heard that once before. But then, what purpose would it serve to lie to me now? I was already their prisoner.

A shrill scream sounded like a horror movie blaring on a television in the next room. Close. Too close. I gathered my bag with Rowan into my arms and caught a faint whiff of a fasgadair.

They were here.

One of the guards held a finger to his lips, peeked out the door, then signaled for us to follow. So far, they didn't seem to be falling under the fasgadair spell. The bloodsuckers must be too far away. Or otherwise detained.

Either everyone had dispersed or whatever caused that scream was still feeding on its victim. I had no desire to find out. I kept stepping on the lead guard's shoes while the guard in back gripped my arm. Was he being protective or fearful, hoping *I'd* protect *him*?

I followed the guards to the throne room, empty but for the electric fasgadair scent. It wafted from the halls along with screams and animalistic snarls that sent shivers coursing through my body, urging me to flee.

What was I doing? Wasn't I here to help? But what could I do? They'd kill me too. But lighting them on fire might slow them down and save people. I stopped.

The guard behind me passed and tripped, nearly losing his grip on my sleeve. "What are ye doing? Let's go!"

"I can't. I can save them. I can set the fasgadair on fire."

The guard released his grip. He looked at me with new respect. Or fear. "If that's true, it's too late. This place is overrun. We have to go. Now!"

"I have to try."

"Don't be a fool."

I'd be on my own. My friends were gone. Only unbelievers remained. They'd be like flies in a spiderweb awaiting their demise once the fasgadair were close enough to enact their mind control. Remembering what it felt like to be paralyzed in their mind-grip, I shuddered.

Save Arabella.

What was that? Was that God? Was this somehow His plan? I hugged the bag tighter and gazed down the hall. It sounded like someone watching *The Walking Dead* had turned up the volume. The electric odor strengthened, mingling with a metallic blood scent. Did God really want me to leave them?

I had to follow His plan.

The guards ran into the small meeting room behind the throne. I hurried after them. The first guard had disappeared. The other held a tapestry away from the wall and motioned for me to come. Thank God, he waited.

A false wall closed behind us, immersing us in complete darkness. We waited as the guard who wasn't clinging to me fumbled with something, probably a torch.

We had to move. But I didn't want to light the wrong thing on fire, so I groped in the dark until I found the torch in the guard's hand. I felt my way to the tip, removed my hand, and set it on fire. He jumped and dropped the torch on the stone floor.

"So 'tis true." He retrieved the torch from the ground. "You can light fires. I hope the other rumors are true as well. C'mon."

The light illuminated a few feet of the dingy hall strung with cobwebs and laced with mold. We pushed through the tunnels, the torch singeing cobwebs along the way. The unpleasant aroma, like burnt hair, mingled with the mold or mildew…something dank. The air was oppressive. I imagined mold spores filling my lungs as we ventured deeper. My feet kept slipping on the slick stone. But we pressed forward.

"Where are we going?"

Both guards ignored me. As the distance between us and the fasgadair grew, so did my resistance to meeting the fate that awaited me, wherever it was. The guards gained distance.

Perhaps we were safer in these tunnels? But then, how long would the torch last? There was nothing else to ignite, other than spiders and rats.

I quickened my pace.

We descended several flights of winding stairs to a dungeon. The stench of human waste hit me like a wall. I staggered. Ammonia made my eyes water. Grimy gaunt faces peered through the bars we passed. Spindly hands reached toward us, mouths gaping like fish as if they'd been away from humanity for so long, they no longer knew how to speak. Some managed to squeak out "help" and "save us."

I stopped.

"What about them?"

The second guard looked back. "The prisoners? What of them?"

"Set them free."

"Bah! I've no authority to do such a thing."

"Isn't everyone fleeing Bandia? They don't stand a chance to survive if everyone leaves. If the fasgadair don't get them, starvation will. There will be no one to feed them."

Highlighted by the torch, indecision twisted the guard's face.

"At least give them a chance."

He groaned and threw me a key. "Be quick."

My heart raced as I unlocked the doors and the prisoners shuffled out. Rushing feet clanged on the stone close by.

"We must go now!" the guard yelled in a hushed voice.

I glanced back at the poor souls. "We have to help them."

"We did. We set them free. But if you want to catch the boat, follow us. Now."

The guards ran ahead. I tried not to think of those poor prisoners. At least they had a chance.

I ran to catch the guards. Stamping feet echoing in the hall followed—from the prisoners, other escapees, or the fasgadair?

It couldn't be the fasgadair. We'd never outrun them, and I couldn't smell them. Only mildew. Thicker and stronger than before, it felt as if it were taking up residence and accumulating in my nasal passages. I covered my mouth. Who knew what disease-inducing spores were down here.

The tunnel sloped in a never-ending downward curve to the left. I slipped on the mucky bottom multiple times trying to keep up with the guards. Rats squeaked and hissed as we dodged each other.

The ground leveled, and a breeze swept through carrying salty air. I inhaled as if smelling the sweetest perfume. But the breeze passed, and I choked on the musty air.

The guard stopped at the end and put his back against the wall before peering, FBI style, into a cavern. He beckoned us and hurried to a row of boats tied to a platform at an underground lake. No, not a lake. It smelled like salt water. It had to be an inlet.

The boat rocked, pulling the rope and clanging against the platform. I knelt and placed Rowan in the skiff. The guard held my hand to steady me as I stepped in, toppling into my seat. I grabbed the bag and placed it on my lap, hoping I hadn't hurt her royal furriness.

The lead guard placed the torch in a slot at the helm while the other untied the boat. Once the second guard boarded, they picked up the oars and pushed off. My heart continued to race despite the calming rhythmic motion. Water dripped from the oars and lapped against the chamber walls. Rowan remained tense on my lap. Her claws had pierced through the bag. I petted her, hoping I wasn't irritating her. She became slightly less stiff.

Where were these guys taking me? Where were my friends? Had they really left without me?

I had no idea how much time passed. What felt like an hour was probably only fifteen minutes. Cool air swept through my hair, and I took a deep breath. Dim light dawned before us as the tunnel opening grew. Moonlight sparkled on the rippling waves. The guard yanked the torch from its holder and extinguished it in the water. It let out a soft hiss as the sea swallowed the flame.

Fresh air swirled around me, but I held my breath, certain fasgadair would spot us. Highlands surrounded us at every angle. Where was the harbor?

"Where are we?"

"Shhh!" The lead guard raised his finger to his lips.

We continued on forever. My body felt heavy, and my eyes threatened to close. My mind kept wandering to the horrors I'd left behind. Would the prisoners survive? How could I just leave?

As we drew nearer to the land, the hills parted, revealing a canal. We passed through. On the other side, it opened once more. On the open sea, the waves strengthened. The tiny skiff rocked. Sea spray accumulated, flooding the floor, soaking my shoes.

Please don't let us sink.

When I'd get carsick, I'd open a window and close my eyes. That usually helped. I closed my eyes and clung to Rowan and the dinghy.

I jostled and woke, nearly falling off my seat, and caught Rowan mid-fall.

Hushed voices called out. "Someone's here!"

The guards hopped out and dragged us ashore. "We have Fallon."

The wide-eyed faces surrounding us relaxed. "Come inside."

I followed the guards across the pebbly beach through a gate lined with more armed guards to a fortress.

"What is this?" I asked. "Where are we?"

"The king's stronghold."

In all the talk about defenses, Valter failed to mention this.

"Ah, Fallon," a relieved voice greeted me as I crossed the entryway.

Facing Kagan, I tensed. I was still a prisoner. We may have escaped the fasgadair. But my friends were gone. He was responsible. "What do you want from me? Where are my friends?"

"We may need to test those abilities of yours sooner than expected. Please go rest. My guards will call on you when your services are required." He signaled the guards. "Bring her to the upper room, next to my chambers."

The guard who led me out of the castle nodded and tugged me. I nearly dropped Rowan.

"Need me for what?" I called behind me.

Kagan turned his back to me and walked away. I had been dismissed.

I glared at the guard.

He released his grip and held his hand up, showing he meant no harm. "My apologies, I'm merely following orders. But you're safe here. You and whomever you're smuggling in your sack."

He knew I carried someone. But he didn't know who.

"The name's Sandor." He bowed.

Was he afraid I might go on a rampage and set everything on fire? If that was the case, he clearly didn't know me. But then, perhaps it was best he didn't.

Was this all God's plan? He'd told me only to save Rowan. I glanced at the bag in my arms. Better play nice. For now.

Chapter Twenty-One

My door burst open, and light rushed toward my bed. I wiped my eyes and tried to make sense of what was happening.

"Wake up, Fallon. 'Tis time. Regent Kagan has requested your presence," Sandor said.

I threw the blanket aside. Still fully dressed, I followed Sandor and glanced under the bed at the empty bag. The fur-ridden clothes were the only evidence of Rowan. Was she still in raccoon form? Where was she?

Sandor led me outside—so dark.

I tripped over myself. "How long was I asleep?"

"About an hour. Come." He quickened his pace up the steps to the top of the wall.

"They're coming, Fallon." Kagan spoke without looking my way. "Can you see them?"

I peered in the direction of his gaze, squinting my left eye. "I see dark spots where the waves don't reflect the moonlight."

"Aye. Those dark spots are a fleet." He handed me a spyglass.

I closed my left eye and peered through the spyglass. "Are they coming to rescue us?"

He took a deep breath. "I'm afraid not. Those ships are full of fasgadair. They've overrun Bandia and are continuing their attack."

"What if they're more citizens of Bandia or refugees who escaped?"

"Only an enemy would pursue us here with an entire fleet. My men would stay a safe distance away and send a scout."

"What do you want from me?"

He stared into my eyes as if attempting to hypnotize me. "Set them on fire."

"What?" I jerked back. "How can you ask me to?"

"If you don't, we will die."

"What about your archers?" I nodded at the row of armed men alongside us, atop the wall, arrows ready. "Why don't you shoot them with flaming arrows?"

Kagan squinted as if giving my idea thought. "Flaming arrows?"

"Yeah." Had they never heard of that here? "Wrap the tips and ignite them."

He gave me the look. "You want me to unbalance the arrows by adding weight to the front? How accurate could such an arrow be? How far would it fly?"

"Well, I—"

He raised a hand to silence me. "Wouldn't the arrow's speed extinguish the flame midair?"

"I don't—"

"And should the arrow miraculously meet its mark from such a distance with the flame alight, wouldn't the fasgadair stomp out whatever minuscule flame remained?"

I didn't bother to respond. Why did the movies make it seem so easy?

"Enough nonsense. We can't defeat such an enemy with man-made weapons from this distance. But you!" He stepped forward, a sick smile overtaking his face, reminding me of the Joker. "You can look at those dark spots and set them ablaze. *You*, Fallon." He grasped my upper arms and gave me a little shake. "You have the power to save us." He smiled at me as if I was his favorite toy.

I edged back, but his grip remained. "Those are people!"

His smile twitched, and his eyes narrowed. "Those are murderous demons!"

How could I trust him? Any of them? His people were liars.

Then again, there's no way he wanted me to kill his people. Who would he rule? "Are you sure they're all fasgadair?"

"Do you care to wait until they arrive to find out?"

"Yes. I can save them."

"You can't." He shook his head emphatically, shaking me in the process. "Not before they storm this beach and annihilate us." He released his grip. "How many can safely feed on you at most? Three? Four? Any more than that would kill you. Fallon, can't you see? You can't save them. But you can save *us*." He sighed, took a kerchief from inside his jacket, and dabbed his brow. "I realize my methods of detaining you were a bit…forceful."

Understatement, buddy.

"I'm merely trying to protect our people and my king. If I thought there were any captives, I wouldn't ask this. But we have eyewitnesses. My men saw the fasgadair pilfer the ships and kingdom. Is that correct, Tyge?" He glanced at a guard holding a bow. "Tell Fallon what you told me."

Tyge kept his eye on the sea. "The bloodsuckers arrived with a fleet the likes of which I've never seen. The other guards froze. They just…let the monsters kill them. I didn't understand why until the bloodsuckers got too close to me. It was like… like…"

"You were paralyzed?" I asked.

"Aye." Tyge nodded, still facing the threat from sea. "Somehow, they missed me at my post. They passed by, and I could move again. I followed along the shore to the harbor. Thousands of the beasts rushed the piers killing everyone in their path. Others took over our fleet. Probably to pursue us, waving our flags, hoping we'll think just what yer thinking." He leaned his bow against the wall, wiped his palms, then armed himself again. "Once they're close enough to paralyze us, there'll be no stopping them."

"We can't let them reach our shores." Kagan's eyes implored me. "We rescued the king. My highest priority is to protect him. We need *you* to protect *us*."

Black dots bobbed on the waves, growing larger. Hadn't I just been willing to ignite fasgadair to save Bandia? Wolf would tell me to light them up too. I envisioned Aodan's head when I lit it on fire. It hurt. He'd howled in pain. But his scorched skull returned to normal. His hair even grew back perfectly. The worst I could do was maim them and sink their ships. Then what would happen? Would they swim? Or would they drown, regenerate, then drown again? Would they spend their lifetime drowning over and over in this sea? If any of them are air or sea creatures, they'll transition and attack. "What if all I manage to do is anger them?" I swiveled back to Kagan, beseeching any goodness I hoped lay within him. "If they're fasgadair, it won't kill them. And if they're not…" I gulped. My stomach lurched.

Tyge shot an arrow. It arched into the sky and skewered a bird. Both splashed into the sea. Tyge readied another arrow and scanned the sky.

"They *are* fasgadair. And you're right. You'll likely only delay them. We can only hope they'll continue to drown to buy us more time to find a way to get to the pech and win this war. We can pick off one or two at a time. But if even one ship reaches our shores"—he held up a finger to emphasize his point—"if just *one* shipload of bloodsuckers charges this castle, our fight is over." Kagan watched me with such intensity, I feared he might set *me* on fire. "It's our best chance. If you don't try, those monsters will kill us. They will kill *you*." He pointed at the dark spots taking shape. "Our race is on the verge of extinction. You're our only hope."

Tears slid down my face. How else could we get out of this?

I remembered God's words—*Save Arabella.* Was this the only way? Where was she?

The fleet closed in. I lifted the spyglass. The flags…Bandia's quadruple spiral. Yes, they'd attack us in Bandia's own ships.

But how could I set these people on fire? People who might have another chance at life? How could I torture them like this? I collapsed to my knees, my heart wrenching as if squeezed in a vice grip.

"Please." Kagan held a hand out to me. His face and his voice softened. "Ariboslia needs you."

I grabbed his hand. As if in a trance I stood, my limbs numb. How could I not?

"They're getting closer."

I studied the ships. Sobs choked me as I stared at my target. *It's like lighting candles in a chandelier, Fallon. They're just candles. This is nothing.* The lead ship erupted in flames. The others slowed. My legs gave out, and I fell on my butt, crying, while praises rang out around me.

"Well done, Fallon!"

Cheers erupted along the wall while I cried for the lives I tortured…possibly ended. I hoped they truly were fasgadair. No captives. But if that were true, what would become of them? Had I taken away their only chance for redemption?

"They're still advancing!" someone called out.

I stood. The ships circumvented the one in flames.

"Please, Fallon. You need to get them all."

How many people did I have to kill? Why didn't they turn around? "I can't!"

"You have to. We need you."

"They're gaining speed," a voice called from the darkness. "What are your orders?"

"Fallon?" Kagan pressed.

Two ships now took the lead. *Just candles. Nothing more.* In turn, they burst into flames. Apathy set in as the ships behind the three in flames changed course.

"They're retreating!" Cheers erupted from every direction as a part of me lay dying.

I dropped to the cold, unforgiving stone. What had I done?

Chapter Twenty-Two

I TOSSED IN BED, turned the pillow to the cool side, and flipped myself over. Like a fish on land, I kept flopping. The blanket twisted around my legs. I kicked them free. Worst-case-scenario images flipped through my brain like a sped-up slideshow.

Had the prisoners gotten out? What had I done to the people on the ships? They had to be fasgadair. They *had* to. Would they eventually have a chance at redemption? Or would they spend the rest of their lives dying under the sea?

I needed my friends. Had they really abandoned me? Like Cahal abandoned Declan? Where were they? Were they okay? Wherever they were, they were better off away from this place.

I deserved whatever fate awaited me.

My mind wouldn't stop. Like clothes in a dryer with a broken timer, they just kept tumbling and tumbling—the prisoners, the ships, my friends. The prisoners, the ships, my friends.

Had I done the right thing? Had I bought time to find a way out?

This whole time, I'd killed some poor little weasel and possibly a jail and three ships full of people. I'd redeemed one. Only one.

A match struck, and light illuminated the room. Rowan replaced the glass on the oil lamp. "You weren't sleeping. Might as well plan our escape."

I sat up. My puffy eyes hardly open. "I shouldn't be here. I'm making things worse."

"You did what you had to do." She pushed hair out of my face and frowned.

"Did I?" I couldn't get Aodan's reaction to having his head set on fire out of my mind. That's what I'd just done to three ships' worth of fasgadair.

God, I'll never survive this if they weren't fasgadair.

"Three ships," I said.

"I understand. There are seldom any decisions that don't result in casualties during war. We'd all likely be dead if you hadn't acted. Push these feelings aside. Let's plan our escape."

"How? We're on an island surrounded by guards. And I'm *not* lighting them on fire."

"I may know a way." Her lips slid into a mischievous grin.

"I'm not going to threaten to…"

"I wouldn't ask it of you." She waved her hand dismissing the thought. "Kagan will have potions with him. Tomorrow, when he and his guards are away from his chambers, I'm going to find a potion we can use to get past the guards. Something to knock them out long enough to get into the tunnels. There are boats on the other side of the island. Once we're on a boat, there's nothing they can do. They won't chance killing you. And now that they've seen what you're capable of"—she laughed—"they'll be too afraid to try."

Her words pierced my heart. People had reason to fear me now. What kind of monster had I become?

****

I pushed my porridge around the bowl. Disquiet loomed. Men wearing the same black garb were engaged in heated conversation. Their voices differed, but they looked the same. Guards. Keeping me here. Trapped. Occasionally, my name pulled me out of my trance. But they talked about me, not to me.

Women and children sat at other tables. Mothers scooped

porridge into their children's bowls from their own. Whenever a child's gaze drifted my way, they looked away or received a stern warning.

I was a pariah.

With my half-empty bowl still on the table, I returned to my room. Had Rowan been successful? I couldn't wait to escape. "Rowan?"

The room was empty.

"How could you!" a voice shouted.

Rowan? I peeked into the hallway, grateful for the lack of locks, not that they needed locks when the entire place was a jail. Two guards ran into the room beside mine. I followed.

"Calm yourself, Your Highness," Kagan said.

Facing Kagan, Rowan stood next to a withered man in the bed. She held a knife in the air, ready to strike. "You're killing him. You're killing him with your potions!"

"Princess Arabella?" one of the guards spoke quietly to another.

Kagan held his hand up to keep them at bay. The guards watched, like coils ready to spring should Kagan give the word.

"With all due respect, Your Highness, you're mistaken." Kagan moved his arm so he now defended himself against her. "I've been keeping him alive."

The knife dropped slightly, then sprung back into the air. "You expect me to believe that, you manipulative, power-hungry vulture?"

"Leave us." Kagan waved us away.

The guards hesitated.

"Go." He stepped toward us, waving his arms.

We retreated into the hall. I returned to my room and put my ear to the wall. Nothing. I searched along the wall and found a crack between bricks. Only Rowan was visible.

"When you left, your father became ill."

"Aye. You made him ill." Her voice was murderous.

"Arabella. You're a smart woman. Think about what you're suggesting. I know my potions. If I'd wanted the throne, I would have used the right potion, and he would be dead. I would be king. But that is not my desire. My allegiance is to my gods and to my king…to the royal family, chosen by the gods. And to the crown."

She waved the knife in the air. "Valter would've inherited the throne. You're keeping my father alive to maintain control."

"Had I wanted the throne, I'd have killed Valter as well. My loyalty has always been to the gods and to ensuring their blessing on those in power. The crown belongs to your father…to you. It's your birthright. It would be my honor to return the crown to its rightful owner."

The knife lowered. "Then what's happened to him? This isn't natural."

"This was a murder attempt by someone unskilled in potions. I made a buille cridhe to keep him alive while I sought a better solution. I've pored through my books. I've sought counsel from apothecaries, herbalists, sorcerers, diviners, and other priests. I've searched the lands for anyone who might revive him. But alas, there is none. The buille cridhe is keeping him alive. If he goes twenty-four hours without it, he will die."

"Who tried to kill him?" Low and lethal, the question seethed from her lips. Her hand shook.

"Jorge Durnin."

She covered her mouth with her free hand. "Jacobus's father?"

"Aye," Kagan said. "He faced judgment and was beheaded."

"Sir Durnin knew nothing of potions."

"I was surprised as well. But we found evidence in his home. The potion that put your father in this state. Rest assured. We caught the criminal. Justice was served."

"I just can't believe—what was his motive?"

"Jacobus went missing the night you were kidnaped. We took his father in for questioning. Sir Durnin insisted his son was not involved in a plot and had likely been kidnaped as well or harmed in an attempt to rescue you. He became bitter and angry toward the king for making accusations and tainting his son's name. He spent his nights in a tavern where he spoke out against the king to anyone who'd lend an ear. His assassination attempt came as no surprise. Though I'm dumbfounded as to how he got so close. If it had been the right poison…"

This had to be killing Rowan. She'd blame herself now.

She wiped a tear. "How long has he been like this?"

"Six years. And a few months."

"You've been giving him buille cridhe every twenty-four hours?" Dropping the knife, she sat beside her father. She brushed his cheek. "He must be so weak. Have you considered the side effects? Even if he wakes, he'll never be the same. He'll never rule again."

"If you're willing to claim your throne, I'll cease the treatments. If that is your wish."

"I could never wish my father dead. There's truly nothing more you can do?" A tear slid down her cheek.

"I wish there was."

"How can I leave him like this?" Rowan leaned down to kiss her father. Blonde waves fell onto his face. "Forgive me for abandoning you, Father." She dabbed her tears from his face.

"Princess." Kagan stepped into view. "These are the direst of circumstances under which to receive your crown. But it is rightfully yours." He cleared his throat. "Do you wish to fulfill your duty?"

"I didn't think I could after what I've done. But what other choice is there?"

"From my perspective, you are evidence that our gods have not abandoned us. I'll give you a moment alone with your father and speak with my men…*your* men." Kagan bowed and left the room.

I spun, slid down the wall, and sat. There was no hope of leaving with Rowan now.

CHAPTER TWENTY-THREE

I POKED MY HEAD outside my chamber for the hundredth time. Rowan still hadn't returned. Where was she? I slipped through the door and slinked down the staircase like a kid sneaking out of time-out.

Someone familiar walked past. "Valter!"

He swung his head. His hair disheveled, dark bags under his eyes, he flashed me a fake smile. "Fallon. Good to see you." His words didn't match his tone. He glanced around me as if searching for someone.

"Were you here the whole time?" I closed the gap between us.

"Aye. I haven't had much rest. I have no idea how many of the birds I shot out of the air were just birds. But we'll eat well tonight."

Did he know my totem was a falcon? I'd hate to end up on someone's platter. I'd probably skip the meat tonight.

"Thank you for that valiant rescue last night. I hate to imagine what might've befallen us had it not been for you."

"Please, don't mention it." Seriously.

"If you'll excuse me." He pivoted to leave, but a guard approached.

"We caught them trying to sneak up on the east end," the guard said.

"Evan! Cahal! Sully?" Heads down, they stood with hands tied behind their backs. Dirt smudged their faces and matted their hair. Why was Sully with them?

A couple more guards strode by with Wolf and Shimri.

They glanced my way as they were swept past. I followed them into the courtroom where Kagan and Rowan stood.

Valter stopped short, his mouth ajar.

One of the guards gasped. "Princess!"

"Princess Arabella?" another said.

"What is all the commotion?" Kagan asked.

"Sir Kagan." The guard bowed. "We found these men bringing a longboat ashore on the east end. What shall we do with them?"

Kagan bowed slightly toward Rowan and motioned for her to reply.

"Release them." How regal she sounded.

"Thank you, Your Highness." Evan bowed. "We have a ship. Please, come with us."

"To what end? To where shall we flee?"

"The land to the east," he said.

Kagan rubbed his chin. "Your Highness, if they have a ship, we should convene with the pech as planned."

"With these minuscule forces? And what of the women and children? Are we to bring them into battle as well?" She inclined her head to Evan. "Pray tell, what is the situation ashore." Her voice, her stance—so authoritative. Shoulders back. Head high. She must've been trained for this and, like riding a bike, had never forgotten.

Evan's shoulders drooped. Pain twisted his face. "It's a bloodbath, Your Highness. We're uncertain of the death count. Many were taken captive and are being held in the castle. The fasgadair were boarding the ships."

"And how did you escape?"

"Regent Kagan banished us. Our ship was already out of port."

"Then why aren't you currently aboard your ship headed east?"

Straightening his stance, he met Rowan's gaze. "We couldn't abandon Fallon, Your Highness."

"I see." She threw me a quick look. Like we shared a secret. The friend I'd made was still there. Just putting on a show. "And the fasgadair. What are their numbers?"

"Countless." Evan stepped forward. "I understand your desire to reclaim your kingdom. But first, you need to find more support. The monsters decimated your army. Fallon was able to fend off the first attack to this fortress, but the ocean has merely slowed their progress. They will come."

He knew what I'd done to the ships? A pang twisted my gut. At least now I knew they were fasgadair. Or…mostly fasgadair.

"Let them come." Kagan motioned toward me and laughed. "Let them keep coming. Fallon will take them out, one by one. The princess will have her country back."

Evan bowed. "I'm sure Your Highness has considered every possible scenario. But the fasgadair will regenerate under water. What will you do when they swarm your shores? Will Fallon have to set them on fire repeatedly until guards can come remove all their heads? Those guards will likely become paralyzed. And what if the fasgadair decide to wait you out? They have a kingdom. You have a stronghold. How long will your supplies last?"

Kagan scoffed. "We sha—"

Rowan put an arm out toward Kagan, stopping his retort. "Thank you, Evan. We shall take your warning under advisement. Please allow me to meet with my council to discuss the matter, then give my father a proper funeral. We shall join you later."

Gasps filled the room.

"The king is dead?"

"My father has been dead for nearly seven years. I won't dishonor his memory by allowing him to remain in such a state a moment longer."

Sully cleared his throat. "Your Highness, may I approach?"

When she beckoned him forward, he tripped, then righted

himself. "Might I see the king?"

"For what purpose?"

"To do what only God can do. What your potions, sorcerers, and priests could not."

****

Those Rowan allowed to enter the king's chambers crowded the room. Sully stood by King Aleksander's side and raised his hands skyward. "Almighty God, reveal Yourself to these people. Show Your power and compassion. No one else on this earth or in the heavens could raise this man from this state. Only You, O God Most High. Restore King Aleksander to the crown You bestowed upon him. Show the people of Bandia Your power and glory, so they might honor You and praise Your name alone."

I held my breath. The room silenced as if someone hit a mute button.

The king's sunken cheeks swelled. A rosy color swept over his face and neck. His body filled out, raising the blanket higher.

King Aleksander's finger twitched. I jumped. The king blinked and turned to the crowd. His alarmed gaze fell on his daughter and softened. He reached out to her.

"Praise God!" Sully said, and others followed.

With tears spilling from her wide eyes and her hand hiding her mouth, Rowan crept toward her father and eased onto the side of his bed.

"My daughter. You've returned." He touched her cheek.

"Aye." She grasped his hand and kissed it.

King Aleksander sat up. "What has happened? Why is everyone in here?" He glanced about. "Are we in the stronghold?"

"Aye, Father. Much has happened. Perhaps you should rest."

"Nonsense. I don't need rest. I feel fine." He let his gaze roam the crowd once more. "Kagan? Is that my crown?"

"I…" Kagan removed the crown he'd worn for almost seven years. The cloth covering remained. His cheeks reddened.

143

Seeing him falter for the first time, I smothered a laugh.

"Valter?" King Aleksander scratched his head as Valter stood rigid, mouth agape. "That can't be you. You're so…so…"

"Old?" Rowan asked. "Father, it's been… It's been nearly seven years."

He pulled back. "Seven years? But you—"

"I'll explain everything." She nodded to the crowd. "Please leave us."

Everyone filed out while Valter remained frozen. He snapped back to reality and caught me watching. We moved toward the exit. Valter rubbed his temple and motioned for me to go first.

****

I sat on the edge of the bed, pulling pills off the blanket. As much as it killed me, I refrained from peeking through the hole in the wall. I had to give them their privacy. But my eyes kept wandering to it.

I stood and began inching toward the hole. The door opened, and Rowan entered.

"I guess I won't be carrying you around in a sack anymore, huh?"

She threw me an apologetic smile. The old Rowan was still there. "Aye."

"Is your father okay?"

"After learning what's transpired over the past few days, never mind the past seven years, he decided he needed to rest after all." She giggled.

"What happened to you?"

She cocked an eyebrow at me. "Pardon?"

"You were like a different person."

"Oh." She waved a hand. "Years of training for such a time as this. I was mistaken to think I could turn my back on my duty. No matter what I've done in the past, I'm obligated to serve my country and my people."

"What's going to happen now?"

"'Tis my father's decision. But I will encourage him to allow you to continue your quest. They never should have taken you captive."

"What about you?"

"If he heeds my counsel, we will join in your quest. It may be too late to destroy the idols, but I will try to convince my father to follow whatever Sully advises. After you saved me, I knew your God was powerful. Since Sully revived my father, the others should know it too. And from what I've seen so far, your God—*our* God—has a way of getting what He wants."

CHAPTER TWENTY-FOUR

KING ALEKSANDER SEEMED TO shrink as Rowan filled her father in on their current circumstances. He'd started out sitting high in his chair with a world-conquering smile. Now, he drooped in his seat like he needed an antidepressant.

"This is much to take in." He rubbed his temples, then adjusted his crown.

Rowan had given him the highlights of the past seven years. Now she ripped the bandage off by telling him bloodsuckers had overthrown his kingdom.

"I understand, Your Highness," Sully said. "You wish to save the Ain-Dileas. You also want to do God's will. We missed the opportunity to destroy the idols. But God's message is clear. We are to travel east."

"So, you said. Yet I fail to comprehend the wisdom in that maneuver." King Aleksander leaned in to Sully as if Sully could see him. "Kagan's advice to travel southwest to the pech is more logical. How can I abandon my people? What do I tell them when they ask why I didn't return for them? How many am I sending to their deaths?"

Listening to the king's concerns, I felt connected to him. I understood the agony of making life-or-death decisions. No matter what choice he made, he'd live with regret. If he survived.

"Tell them you chose to obey a higher authority. It's a big step of faith—I understand. But many more will die if choose your own path." Sully clasped his hands. "I've been following God for a long time." He drew out the word *long*. "I'll never understand His ways. But I don't question Him as I did in my youth. He's never failed me. I can't tell you how traveling east will save the Ain-Dìleas. I can't even tell you that it will. All I can say is you have a choice to make. Who are you going to trust? Yourself and your own human inclination? Or God?" He pointed skyward.

"Whether or not I trust God isn't the issue here. But do I trust that *you* speak for Him?"

"Your Highness, if I may." Kagan had replaced the crown with a strange pointy hat more befitting a priest. "You can't be considering following Sully's so-called god. They have a ship. Our ship. We can still meet with the pech and fight for our land."

"I don't appreciate your condescension toward Sully's God. Were your gods able to revive me?"

"No, Your Majesty." Kagan bowed low.

"Please." King Aleksander waved his hand. "Leave me to ponder this dilemma."

"As you wish." Sully stood and bowed.

Shoes clicked on the stone floor as we vacated.

"Arabella, stay with me please."

"Very well, Father." Rowan bowed and returned to the throne beside him.

Someone needed to make a decision and get us off this rock. I rubbed a knot in my shoulder. My body was so tense. The ocean always calmed me. "Do you think they'll let me sit on the beach?" I asked Evan.

"Not a chance."

Guards tugged the heavy main entryway doors open as we approached. Night had fallen. Dang. No way would they let me out the gate. Nor would I want to. I'd keep imagining monsters crawling out of the sea. I even smelled them.

Wait.

"Fasgadair!" came a shout.

"Defend your post!" a guard shouted.

The corduroy sound blasted from archers in succession.

"Boann's well!" another guard cursed and darted past us.

Another round of arrows shot into the air. A vampire lunged atop the wall and bit a guard's throat. Crimson drops rained down, splattering on the stone before me.

Sandor and a few other guards shoved us inside the stronghold and dropped a wooden barricade in place.

"This way." Sandor ushered us into the dining hall.

They pushed the bulky table aside, rolled back an ornamental carpet, then lifted a trapdoor.

People rushed into the room—women and children, the king, and Rowan. Sully fumbled through the crowd.

I fought my way to him and grabbed his bony hand. "Follow me."

"Hurry!" a guard whispered, then addressed Sandor. "Get them to the east gate."

Sandor disappeared in the hole in the floor.

"Your Highness." The remaining guard motioned to King Aleksander and Rowan. "This way. Please hurry."

"Let the children and their mothers go first." King Aleksander rested a hand on Rowan's shoulder. "You lead them."

She gave him a quick hug and hurried down the ladder with the children.

Wolf pushed me to the ladder next, and Sully followed.

We scurried like quiet mice through the passageway. I clung to Sully's hand. Sandor held a torch high above our heads. Silhouettes pursued the light. Sully tripped, and I slowed my pace. An image of him falling in this darkness, trampled by the panicked mob, crossed my mind, and I grasped his arm tighter.

People continued to trickle in behind us. How many had made it? Had the guards closed the trapdoor before the beasts found the tunnel? Would anyone remember them for their sacrifice?

I sniffed what little air existed in the stuffy tunnel. No electric smell. Yet.

The path split four ways. We followed Sandor across the way, continuing in the same direction. Sully and I slowed considerably, falling behind the crowd. A dim speck of light emerged at the end of the tunnel.

Sandor stopped at an iron gate ahead and extinguished the light. The gate creaked. They must be letting people out. Bodies pushed us forward as I clung to Sully. Dim moonlight cast shadows on the heads around me. I was squeezed in, drowning in an ocean of warm bodies stealing my oxygen.

I sucked in as much air as possible. But I wasn't getting any. I took a few more deep breaths, then couldn't stop. The tunnel darkened, and my legs gave way.

"Fallon?" Sully held me up. "Oh dear."

I slumped against him, gasping for breath.

"Help! We need help," Sully called.

The group shifted, allowing Sully to guide me through to the gate. I grasped the bars, pushed my face through the opening, and filled my lungs. My breathing returned to normal. I peeked at the crowd behind me. Wide eyes stared as if my head might pop off.

A guard crept up the beach, waving. Sandor unlocked the gate and eased it open. Like an amusement park ride attendant, he ushered a group out. The children had already gone. A few mothers remained. I didn't see any of my friends, other than Sully. Rowan must've gone with the kids. But where were Evan and Cahal?

Evan had been with me when the fasgadair attacked. I left him to help Sully. I searched for his face, but those out of the moonlight's reach were just shadows. I'd have to go without him.

I pulled Sully out. Guards surrounded us as we pounded sand

across the beach to two approaching longboats. Wolf jumped out of one and lugged it ashore. I wanted to hug him, tell him how happy I was to see him. But we had to be quiet. And quick. He gave me a wink as he helped Sully and me into the boat. Once the remaining seats were occupied, Wolf and a guard pushed us off, then hopped in and took up oars. We floated to the ship in silence.

The commotion on the opposite side obscured any noise we made. Dancing light brightened the sky. The stronghold was on fire. Those poor people.

The longboat hit the vessel's side with a soft thud. Wolf held the rope. When it was my turn to climb, he tugged my sleeve. "I'm going back for more. I'll return," he whispered.

"You better." How many trips would it take?

Abracham helped me climb aboard. Gachen clogged the deck. My mother ran to greet me. Pepin hung back, away from the edge.

Wolf returned for more people.

Please, God, save them.

Maili slipped in next to me. "Where's Shimri?"

I stiffened—whether in concern for Shimri or just having a hard time warming up to her, I didn't want to analyze. Not wanting to analyze it apparently didn't stop me from trying. "He's not on board?"

She shook her head. Black strands too short to stay in her braid fell into her face. She pushed them behind her ear. "He went ashore with the others."

"I'm sorry. I haven't seen him."

Abracham approached. "Please follow me to the captain's quarters."

"No, I need to be here, watching for my friends."

"My apologies, Fallon. But I must insist."

I gripped the rail. "What? Am I now *your* prisoner?"

"Far be it, child." Abracham threw me an apologetic smile. "We can better protect you below decks from the fasgadair and others who might harm you."

By others, he must mean Kagan.

Maili touched my arm. "I'll watch for them, Fallon."

Wolf's boat had almost made it to land. This side of the island was still quiet with no vampires in sight. Or smelling distance. I'd prefer not to light any on fire if I didn't have to. And a fire might attract attention. They'd call me if they needed me. "Thanks, Maili." I followed Abracham.

I moved from darkness to more darkness. We weren't allowed to light a lantern. Only a blurry light from the stronghold's fire was visible through the window in the captain's galley. Thank God, we got out in time.

Someone sat next to me. "You made it." Rowan. She sounded relieved.

"Where are the children?"

"In the crew's quarters. There weren't enough hammocks. Most of them are sharing."

Every nerve in my body fired, ready for action. I was desperate to flee. But I needed my friends to make it to the ship. I almost *wanted* to be attacked, just to have something to take my pent-up energy out on while I waited. Anything would be better than sitting here…helpless.

****

My mother hung blankets over the windows, so we could light a lantern. Although still dim, it was better than sitting in the dark. Maili opened the door. "Two more boatloads arrived." She didn't sound happy.

King Aleksander appeared in the doorway. Rowan vaulted into his arms.

Kagan and Valter plodded past them and sat at the table. Kagan's pointy hat was askew, and Valter's hair stuck out in every direction.

"Did Ev—"

"I'm right here." Evan stood behind Maili with a huge grin. "That *is* what you were going to ask, right?"

I ran to hug him.

"Cahal is helping Wolf bring more gachen on board," Maili said. "What about Shim—"

With a quick headshake, Maili closed the door between us.

Chapter Twenty-Five

I STOOD IN THE field of my dreams, facing Declan on the shore. Someone was trying to enter my mind. This time, I'd find out who. I watched the lights popping in the air, waiting for them to swirl into a window to the perpetrator's mind.

The lights merged to blackness. Frustration filled the air as if attempting to prick my mind and frustrate me as well. A sliver of light appeared, then grew. A grid covered the light. No, a gate. The end of the tunnel to the beach. Whoever's mind I saw through ran to the gate, flung it aside at an inhuman speed, then stood staring at the sea. "Noooooo!" The image dropped as if the person had fallen to their knees.

Nothing moved on the shoreline. If I was looking at present time through the mind of someone standing on the sands we'd just left, it was sunrise, and our ship was gone.

The frustration magnified a hundredfold. Whoever this was, they were in pursuit. That meant… It was a fasgadair.

Avoiding the window, I searched for Declan to pull me out before the monster caught my presence. Declan wasn't there. I ran. Something smacked my forehead.

I woke with a start. I'd banged my head against the table. "Ow." I rubbed the sore spot and sat up, then stretched my aching back. All was quiet. Like me, everyone had fallen asleep where they sat. But blankets no longer shrouded the window. The early signs of dawn bathed the sky in gray. How much time had passed?

I got up to leave. When I pulled the door open, a guard faced me. "Where's Wolf?"

The guard stepped aside and motioned up the steps.

Wolf sat by the bow with a bandage around his arm.

I ran and hugged him. "You made it."

Wolf laughed, but it sounded sad.

I cuddled up next to him and pointed to his bandage. "Are you okay?"

"Aye. 'Tis a scratch."

"Did a fasgadair do that? Can you get reinfected?"

"Nah. Ye need to be bitten and drink their blood to become a fasgadair."

I shuddered, unable to imagine him doing that. But that was the past. "I'm glad you made it. I was so worried. What happened? Did everyone get out?"

"No." He wiped his eyes. "Shimri insisted on returning with Cahal and me. On our last trip, some bloodsuckers found us. Only a few. Probably scouts. We killed them, but not before…not before…"

I wrapped my arms around his good arm.

"He didn't make it."

"Shimri? Or Cahal?" I barely breathed.

"Shimri."

I took a deep breath. Was it wrong to be relieved? "Does Maili know?"

"Aye."

I didn't know how close they were, but they'd been among the last of their clan remaining in their village. She'd been so concerned last night. She must be devastated.

I wanted to ease his pain. But what could I say? Sorry? How was that helpful? A conversation with Declan last year came to mind, and I squeezed his shoulder. "You are loved."

****

I never thought I'd be so grateful to be on board a ship again. The land was gone, the vampires far away and growing further still. I breathed in the cool, salty air and watched the horizon. A half-sun rested on the sea before us, its reflection making it appear whole, casting brilliant red and orange light. For the moment, I felt good. I had my friends back.

As the day wore on, we breathed easier. We'd gotten far enough to sea that birds were no longer a threat. And no vessels pursued. Even if anyone told the bloodsuckers of our plans, they'd be insane to pursue us on a suicide mission. They'd taken over Bandia and driven out the rulers. For them, it was a win. Morrigan might be upset over missing the opportunity to add to her king collection, but she'd survive. For now.

But whoever's mind I'd spied on…that person was furious.

****

That evening, Rowan insisted we celebrate. "Our king was nearly dead. He's returned. If we can't celebrate that, we've already lost."

She had a point. "And their princess has returned."

We attempted to celebrate despite the tragic events. We needed it. King Aleksander and Rowan danced together. Other gachen danced around them. One man drummed on barrels while another beat a pan. Someone played a wooden flute. It was like a medieval party boat.

But the atmosphere was odd. A strange mixture of emotions darkened King Aleksander's countenance. Joy filled his eyes when they landed on his daughter. But he looked as if something had broken inside him when he surveyed the crowd.

Profound sadness laced the festivities. Everyone had lost their families, their homes, their country…friends. Maili remained below decks. I understood what she was going through. I'd experienced it last year with Ryann. My heart ached for her.

Try as we might to celebrate, monsters occupied Bandia. That overshadowed all else. But I was glad to have my friends with me.

"I was so afraid I'd lost you," I said.

"We'd never leave without ye." Cahal took a swig of ale from his mug.

That's what I would have thought. But he'd left Declan.

Evan clinked his mug with Cahal's. "Thank God, we had a ship full of supplies for a long voyage and Sully knew what to do." He watched Rowan and her father, smiling. "If events hadn't transpired as they had, how many more lives would be lost?"

Valter stood in the shadows, leaning against the rail, every bit of his posture exhausted.

The sun sank, and the deck grew dim. A giant moon filled the sky, casting a brilliant reflection on the sea. The party dispersed, and the crew rotated shifts. The king and Rowan had long since disappeared. But I wanted to bask in this feeling of victory.

Valter approached me. "Princess Arabella requests your presence."

"Okay." I followed him to the captain's quarters where Rowan stood with two guards.

"Leave us." Rowan flicked her hand, dismissing Valter in a way only trained royalty could. "Please have a seat." She motioned to a chair and sat behind a desk. "Fallon, I wonder if you'd assist me?"

"You don't have to speak so formally to me…or do you?"

"Perhaps not when we're alone." She relaxed her shoulders. "I'd like you to stay with me, as a protector of sorts."

"I'm not much of a protector."

"Well, you're female for one. I enjoy your company for another. And I know you'd keep me safe should any real danger arise."

Me? Keep anyone safe? Did she want me to set fire to anyone who threatened her? She knew where I stood with that. "I can't do what you're asking me to do."

Rowan waved as she had when dismissing Valter. "My request is merely that you stay by my side. I'd never expect you to use your fire-starting ability on any living creature." A mischievous smile curled her pink lips into oh-so-pale skin. "But, once your reputation spreads, anyone who wishes to cause me harm will think twice before attempting to harm me with you present."

Great. More reminders of a reputation that made me ill. I didn't want it. Any of it. But I she had a point. And this would help ensure we sided together. "I can't make any promises. I don't know what will happen, but while I'm able, I'll try to stay by your side. But, if you don't mind, I'm going to keep calling you Rowan."

"Interesting request." She laced her hands and rested them on the desk, her lips quirked. "Not that I mind. Keeps me humble. But what is your reason?"

"I just think I'd be more comfortable being myself around Rowan than Princess Arabella."

She loosed a throaty laugh that made me flinch. "By all means. Just further evidence as to why I like you. Here…" She sat on the bench and patted the seat beside her. "I agree to your terms. I'll be much happier with you by my side…as well as safer. My people aren't pleased that my father has decided to side with Abracham and Sully and sail to the east. Who knows to what lengths one might go to turn this ship around."

CHAPTER TWENTY-SIX

ROWAN AND I SAT at the table in the great cabin. My stomach growled, ready for my evening rations. I hoped for something more substantial than the meager breakfast and lunch. So far, I'd had oatmeal, a rock-hard biscuit, sardines, and a piece of lemon. Rowan made me eat the whole lemon, peel and all, insisting I'd need it to keep from getting ill.

Others filed in, filling the seats other than the head. Sully, one of the few of my friends invited to sit with us, sat on my opposite side. Probably because he'd saved the king's life.

Valter, Kagan, and Abracham settled across from us. Dining with nobles still felt strange.

The king entered, and everyone stood. I followed their example.

"Greetings." King Aleksander smiled at Rowan and me, giving us a wink, and took his place at the head of the table. There was something about the king. Something genuine. His presence was both intimidating and inviting. *How* was he both?

A crewman gave us plates of salt pork, peas, fermented cabbage, cheese, a biscuit, and three little green things. Another poured wine. Sully prayed over the food, and I picked up a piece of cheese. Food aboard a ship with no electricity or refrigeration left much to be desired. The biscuits didn't seem stale. Rather, they'd been created to withstand Armageddon. But the cheese wasn't bad. I tried to pace myself to make it last.

"What is this?" I held up one of the green things to Rowan.

"It's a sirist." Her lips matched when she said the name. It must not exist in my realm.

"What's a sirist?"

She laughed. My pronunciation must be horrible. "It's a fruit. Eat them whilst they're available. This journey could take months. You'll need them to keep you well. But don't eat the pit."

Other than the pit part, it was the same spiel she'd given to convince me to eat the lemon peel. My mouth puckered. I nibbled the fruit. Sour. But not like the lemon. More like a kiwi. And sweet too.

The door to the great cabin barged open. A greasy boy in a white apron appeared, sheer panic masking his face. "Stop!"

I dropped the sirist on my plate.

A guard latched onto the intruder, pinning his arms behind him.

"Don't drink the wine!" the boy yelled.

King Aleksander, Abracham, and Kagan jumped to their feet.

"What is the meaning of this?"

The boy fought to catch his breath. "The wine barrel… Someone tampered… Six crewmen… dead!"

Gasps rose. I eyed my goblet as though something evil lurked inside, waiting to attack. Thank God, I hadn't taken a sip. Or soaked my otherwise inedible biscuit in it. Had anyone taken a drink? I searched the faces for signs.

"What is this nonsense?" Kagan asked. "I took a drink, and I'm perfectly well." He surveyed us. "Anyone else?"

We shook our heads.

"Release him." King Aleksander commanded the guard holding the boy.

The guard let go, and the boy tugged his sleeves back in place, throwing the guard a venomous look.

The king looked at the boy. "Thank you for the warning. You may go."

The boy darted out the door.

"Start an inquiry and report back." King Aleksander turned to the crewman who served us. "Remove these goblets and serve us ale until this issue is resolved." He eyed Kagan. "And call the apothecary."

The man nodded and gathered the goblets. I gave him plenty of room to take mine away.

Kagan loosened his collar. "There's no need for the apothecary. I'm an expert in potions. Don't you think I'd know if I ingested poison?"

I stared at him, waiting for something to happen.

"Oh, screaming banshees. I don't know what game they're playing at, but I'm fine." He sat and took a bite of cheese.

Abracham and King Aleksander returned to their seats. The crewmember returned with new goblets. Pouring ale, clinking utensils, and chewing filled the space. I kept peeking at Kagan.

Did I dare touch the ale? Or the rest of the food? I watched the others. Their eyes kept roaming to Kagan, but they didn't stop eating or drinking. My stomach growled as if voicing its opinion. I'd die if I didn't eat. Better to die quick with food in my stomach. And if ships had taught me anything, it's to eat when food is presented, even if it's a rat from the hold.

I dipped my biscuit into the ale, so I could chew it. Not the tastiest thing I'd ever had, but tolerable.

I peeked at Kagan again. Sweat wetted his sideburns. Was he just nervous, or was the kid right and the poison was taking effect? Did anyone else notice?

I caught King Aleksander's eye and motioned my head toward Kagan. The king wiped his mouth and moved to Kagan. "Where's the apothecary?"

Kagan's eyes rolled up in his head. Foam oozed from his mouth. He fell backward into King Aleksander's arms.

A man carrying a carpetbag rushed to their side. "My apologies, Your Highness." He peeled back Kagan's eyelid, then felt his pulse. "I was attending the others."

"Is there anything you can do?" King Aleksander asked.

The apothecary reached into his bag, clinking small bottles, and pulled one free. He uncorked the top. "I'm not familiar with the potion used. Whatever it is, it spreads quickly. The others didn't survive." He opened Kagan's mouth and peeked inside, then inserted the bottle.

Kagan gurgled and spat most of the liquid out. It ran down his neck.

The apothecary made another attempt. "I don't know if this will help. But I'm at a loss for what else to do. I have limited supplies on board. 'Tis a miracle I escaped with what I have."

Kagan's back arched. He remained tensed as if an electric current coursed through his body, the veins in his neck bulging. Then his body fell limp.

The apothecary felt for Kagan's pulse again, then leaned his ear to his mouth. "He's dead." He picked up his bag. "I have a sample of the wine. I need to run tests, but I'm limited without my laboratory."

"Do what you can, Graer," King Aleksander said.

Sandor appeared in the doorway. "Your Majesty, we believe the entire cask was poisoned."

"Graer." The king half rose from his chair, hands grasping the armrests.

The apothecary stopped at the door. "Aye, Your Majesty?"

"Have a sample taken from every cask aboard. Ensure they're not contaminated."

"As you wish." Graer bowed and left the room.

"You"—Valter shook an accusatory finger at Sully—"failed to see this coming?"

Sully's eyes widened, revealing more of his eerie gray irises. "Am I God?"

"How did you know I was talking to you?" Valter asked. "I'm not convinced you're blind."

Sully sighed. "I see in my own way. But I can assure you, I was unaware."

"You're not at fault, Sully. You wouldn't have raised me from the dead to kill me now." King Aleksander shot Valter a hard stare. "You'll do well to hold your tongue, Valter. At the present, I trust Sully more than my prior successor."

Ouch. That had to hurt.

King Aleksander eyed us each in turn. "Either the murderer was too intent on killing one of us to concern himself with the remaining casualties…or he meant to kill us all."

****

The next few days were quiet. The air brimmed with suspicion as people kept a watchful eye on one another. Thank God, I could trust my friends. Rowan and King Aleksander kept me and Sully close.

But who wanted to kill us? And which of us was the target? The king? Was the person who'd attempted to assassinate him in the past aboard the ship? Kagan must've been telling the truth. He wouldn't have been so desperate to kill the king that he'd drink the same poison. It served no purpose.

Rowan rarely allowed me to leave her side, but I needed air. So, she accompanied me on the deck. The ship banked portside, and I planted my feet. Then stepped carefully toward Evan leaning over the bow.

"What are you doing?"

He pointed into the water. "Look."

He eased aside to give Rowan and me a better view.

Dolphins, a ton of them, leaped in the wave created by the bow.

"Wow." I wanted to jump in the water and swim with them. Watching them frolic in the wave filled me with peace and awe. Not like flying, but close.

"Aren't they amazing?" he asked.

"Mmmm." I could watch them all day. Too bad gachen can't change into any animal whenever they chose. Then again, that would make the fasgadair even more of a nightmare.

"How's the investigation going?" Rowan folded her arms on the railing, still leaning over the side.

"There are no suspects yet, Your Highness. The apothecary is doing his best to analyze the poison."

"Who'd want to kill so indiscriminately?" I asked. "I mean, what if he'd killed everyone. What if he'd been left without a crew?"

"It doesn't make sense."

I shuddered. A killer in our midst. That freaked me out more than the fasgadair.

Shouts behind us made us turn. A guard pushed Valter, arms behind him, starboard side. An angry mob followed. Shouts of "murderer" and "killer" stood out over the ruckus.

Valter looked like he'd taken a few serious blows to his face. Redness indicated bruises to come. A cut above his eyebrow dripped blood past his eye.

"What's happening?" I rushed over with the others.

A crewman following the crowd turned toward us. "Valter murdered my mates. He's going to be reunited with them." He caught up to the crowd.

"What are they going to do?" I asked Evan.

He shook his head.

The crowd stopped at the railing. King Aleksander approached. "What is this outcry?"

The captain stepped forward. "The apothecary confirmed the potion was uisge bàs."

"Well…" King Aleksander clasped his hands behind his back. "There's not much reason to possess a potion that accomplishes nothing but death." He eyed Valter until Valter lowered his gaze, then moved on to the captain. "And I assume by the rope around Valter's wrists that he stands accused."

"Aye, Your Highness. They found a flask with the poison amongst his things."

"I'm not aware how you run your ship, Captain. In my kingdom, we have processes for a man who stands accused. I expect that process to stand even on the high seas without my presence. I can't imagine you planned to throw this man overboard without a proper trial?"

"Of course not, Your Highness." His face reddened. "My men got a little…zealous."

"Of course." King Aleksander smiled at the men. "You want vengeance for your fallen men. I understand. But I daresay, once our blood has cooled, we'll agree justice is better than vengeance."

"I most emphatically agree, Your Highness." The captain glared at his men. "I assure you this is not how we handle such matters at sea."

"Then let us proceed." With his index finger, King Aleksander lifted Valter's chin and peered into his eyes. "Valter, you stand accused of killing seven men. How do you plead?"

"Not guilty, Your Majesty." He licked his lips as if he wanted to spit something out.

King Aleksander dropped Valter's chin and rubbed his fingers together as if removing Valter's filth. "Have you an explanation for the uisge bàs in your possession?"

"Someone planted it there, Your Majesty."

"Who, pray tell, has the motive to incriminate you?"

"I don't know, Your Majesty."

"Is it true that, during the night, you attacked the sailor at the helm to turn the ship around?"

Valter hung his head. "Aye."

"For what purpose?"

"This is a fool's mission." Valter's bulging eyes scanned the crowd. "We're running from our home, our country. Not to gather troops to return and rescue our people or reclaim our lands, but to follow a crazy man who thinks he hears from God. We need to gather forces with the pech and take back what is ours."

"Is that why you tried to kill me?" King Aleksander asked.

"We need leaders who will make the right decisions. Decisions to protect us…protect our lands. Kagan understood that. He made such decisions until you returned."

"So, you admit to the assassination attempt."

"What? I—"

"No need to confirm, nor deny. We heard your confession." King Aleksander straightened to his full height, his regal posture giving off an aura of greatness. "Thank you for simplifying the investigation. Valter Scholz, I, King Aleksander of Bandia, convict you of murder and treason." He faced the guard holding Valter's bound arms. "Shackle him and put him with the ballast."

"Your Highness, aren't we going to throw him overboard?" a crewman asked.

"'Tis the rightful punishment for treason, Your Majesty," another said.

"Indeed." King Aleksander threw Valter a sidelong glance and frowned. "There is much to consider. But I won't throw a man overboard without considering the facts. Rest assured, he will face punishment for his crimes, starting now. Lock him up."

Chapter Twenty-Seven

ROWAN AND I SAT in the captain's quarters. Everyone else was either working, keeping watch, or sleeping. Sometimes I wished I had more to do. Hanging out with royalty on a ship was mind-numbingly boring. They blathered on as if they had control and accomplished very little. Their issues ranged from navigation and rations, to plans for making peace with whatever natives we came upon, to dealing with Valter's continual complaints about someone stealing his food. He probably wanted more rations. But our rations were dwindling.

"So, I guess your betrothal to Valter is off, huh?" It was a dumb question driven by sheer boredom. Sitting next to her, watching her study supply charts and take notes was getting stale.

Rowan took a deep, satisfied breath as she studied parchments. "That's a safe assumption."

I glanced at the foreign scribbles. "I'm surprised your father didn't kill him."

"Indeed. The king I remember as a child wouldn't have hesitated." She swapped the parchment to another that looked identical, dipped her fountain pen into the ink, and jotted something down.

"Have you talked to him?"

She sighed and dropped the pen into its holder. "I tried. It's dangerous to keep Valter on board, even in shackles. But my father insists he stay alive…for now."

The boat lurched with a loud slap. Rowan and I braced ourselves. Shouts sounded above decks.

I jumped past Rowan to see what was happening.

She caught my sleeve. "Why is it you always run toward trouble?"

"I don't." Did I? "I have to know what's going on. Don't you?"

"I want you to remain here with me, safe."

"How am I supposed to stay safe if I'm not aware of the problem? Do you think we're safer sitting here? What if we sink when we'd had a chance to get to a longboat?"

"Very well." She rose. "But I'm going with you."

The deck was wet, but there was no rain. The crew scurried about, shouting. A giant tentacle lined with suckers slapped the deck. Cahal thrust his battle-axe down, slicing the end off. Purple slime spurted from the wound, and the creature shrieked. The arms slithered away, and the creature dropped back into the sea.

"What was that?" someone hollered.

"'Twas a sàl samhanach."

Wolf charged me, his dark hair tousled like a young mad scientist. "What were ye thinking? Are ye so daft as to run toward a giant sea creature? Ye put the princess in danger."

I slapped my hands onto my hips. "What if that thing tore the ship apart? We could die down there."

"For the love of all that is holy, Fallon, do yer job. Keep the princess safe." He spun on his heels and raced toward the men lifting the severed tentacle.

"Aye," the captain chimed in. "The chances of survival aren't good if you leave the ship. But, in the direst of circumstances, if we must abandon ship, someone will fetch you. Until then, stow away in my quarters when danger arises." He joined the other men and shouted more orders while Rowan and I retreated to the captain's cabin.

A crewman ran up to the captain. "Sir, the sàl samhanach took out our rudder."

The rudder? Isn't that the thing that steers the ship?

****

I was beyond sick of life at sea. We drifted for weeks with minimal winds and no rudder. But the crew was optimistic. The stars guided them. To me, it was just a sky full of glowing dots. But, if we continued in the same direction, we'd have to hit land…eventually.

After a meager breakfast, Rowan and I took our daily walk on deck. The temperature had dropped. A bitter wind blew my hair into my face. "It's so cold." I rubbed my arms, wishing I had a sweatshirt, but I'd lost my pack during the fasgadair attack. Choppy waves slapped against the ship, making it sway more than usual. Good thing I'd finally gotten my sea legs.

A weary crewman approached the captain. "There's a westerly gale."

"Aye. A storm's rolling in." The captain gazed at the sea.

"What are your orders, sir?"

He narrowed his eyes toward the darkening west and sniffed. "Stow the aft sails. We don't need this thing pushing us sideways. Raise the foresails and hope this wind pushes us ahead of the storm. We won't survive it without a rudder. But be on the ready to stow the sails at my command. We'll need them if we make it through this."

That didn't sound promising.

"Aye, Captain." The crewman turned on his heels and barked orders to others. The crew climbed and shimmied along the rigging.

"Take shelter below decks," the captain ordered us.

On our way to the captain's quarters, Evan rounded the corner and almost collided with Rowan. "Oh!" He bowed. "My apologies, Your Highness." Then he dashed up the stairs.

Was Rowan blushing? She'd been acting strangely around Evan for days. I had to confirm my suspicions. "Do you like Evan?"

Her eyes bulged. "Wha—I—How—" Her cheeks grew redder.

"You do." I chuckled. "It's okay. I won't tell. He's a great guy. Cute too."

Rowan laughed. "This is why I enjoy your company. You don't treat me like royalty."

"Sorry. My people aren't so civilized. I don't have the first clue as to how to treat royalty. Other than what I've seen on TV. But sorry, no. That's not me. That is why you will forever be Rowan to me."

"What is TV?"

"Uh." How to explain? "Moving pictures?"

Her eyes bulged. "You have portraits that move?"

I needed to remember to be careful about what I mentioned from my realm. "Sort of." The boat swayed. I grasped the bed's railing to keep from falling and gazed out the porthole. The sky had darkened fast. "That doesn't look good."

The door burst open. Evan poked his head in the room, his eyes wild. "Come with us to the great cabin. We need to tie ourselves to the ship."

The ship pitched forward as we followed Evan. We fell and slid toward the front of the ship into Pepin tied to a chair. I pulled myself up, fighting the ship's sway. Wolf rushed to me. He helped tie me up as Evan helped Rowan. Rowan and I stared at each other. The fear on her face likely a mirror image of my own.

Everything not nailed down rolled from one side of the room to the other. The ropes burned my skin. Winds howled, wood groaned, and waves crashed. The door broke free of its hinges and flew toward us with a rush of water. I fought against the ropes as everything went black.

CHAPTER TWENTY-EIGHT

BARKING WOKE ME. I groaned. Where was the barking coming from? There were no dogs on board.

Every bone, every muscle, every fiber in my body ached. My head pounded. I blinked. A cool breeze rustled leaves, and intermittent light blinded me. I held my hand up to protect my eyes. Waves lapped upon the shore. Another bark startled me, and I nearly fell. I grasped a branch and steadied myself. How did I get in a tree?

My legs dangled over one branch while another, thicker branch supported my back. A dog barked at the trunk, leaping up at me. He stood on his back feet, front paws against the tree, staring up at me, his tongue lolled out to the side as he panted. I sat up and stared out toward the shore. I didn't see any people or wreckage debris, just one set of footprints leading to the tree.

One set? Had I walked here and climbed myself? No way. I hadn't regained consciousness until now. Had someone carried me and put me here? On purpose?

"Quiet, Rác." A muscular guy in a sleeveless tunic approached the dog. "What have you trapped this time?" He peered through the branches. "A girl?" Running his hand through his black waves, he laughed.

I straightened and felt the lump on the back of my head. "It's not funny."

"Mm." He sucked his cheeks in, and his eyes, straining to be serious, sparkled.

The guy knelt and allowed the dog to kiss his chin. "You needn't have climbed the tree. I can assure you Rác is harmless."

"I didn't."

"You didn't what?"

"Climb the tree."

"How'd you get up there?"

"I don't know."

He waved toward the footprints. "There's only one set of prints."

"I noticed."

He cocked his head and squinted one eye. "Someone carried you across the beach and put you up there?" He paused as if expecting a confession. "Then where are they? There are no footprints leaving the tree."

I shrugged.

"Why would anyone put you in a tree?"

"Good question."

He scrunched his eyebrows together and scrutinized me as if wondering if he should help a compulsive liar...or a psycho. "Want me to help you down?" He held out his arms, planted his feet, and looked up at me. Deep dimples appeared as he smiled.

Guess he decided to help despite my mental state. But that wasn't going to happen. I didn't know him. I couldn't trust him. What guy happily helped a potential psycho? And he was big. At least six feet. With menacing, straight eyebrows. And all dark. Dark hair, dark clothes, dark eyes, darkish skin. He looked like he could make himself scary if he wanted.

Yet there was something playful about him.

Didn't matter. "I think I can jump."

He took a step back and waved his arms as if relinquishing the space to me.

I leaned over. It was high. Too high. "Maybe I should…" Should I tell this guy I could change into a falcon? I'd have to give him my clothes to put somewhere for me to change. That wasn't gonna happen. I should jump. It wasn't *that* high.

"Maybe you should what?" He squinted up at me.

"How high do you think this is?"

"Six cubits, give or take."

"Do you know how many feet that is?"

"Feet? You want me to walk up the tree and count the steps?"

"No."

He ran his fingers through the thick mass on his head again. His waves fell back into place partially across his forehead.

"Are you sure you don't want me to catch you?"

"No. I mean, yes." The ground was sand. There'd be some give. Right? I had to stop overthinking it and jump. One…two…three… I pushed off and landed…hard. My left foot twisted outward, and pain shot up the inside of my ankle. "Ow!" I fell backward onto my butt.

"Are you hurt anywhere?" Dark Guy asked.

"I think…I twisted my ankle."

"Here." He reached out a hand. "Let me help you."

I glanced at his hand, then his dark eyes, and my heart ached. Why'd he have to be so cute? I clasped his hand and tried to stand. "Ow!" A twinge sent my foot buckling underneath me, and I grabbed his arm for support. His eyes sparkled as he grinned. I pulled away and shifted my weight to my good foot.

"Lean on me. I have supplies at home."

Home? His home? No. I nearly stepped back, faltered, then righted myself. "My friends might be hurt. We were shipwrecked."

"I haven't seen anyone. And you can't search for them. Come with me. I can take care of your ankle and come back to check the beach while you rest."

Sure. No problem. I was in another realm, in the middle of who-knows-where, shipwrecked without my friends. And I'm supposed to go with this strange guy? To his house? Where he could do who-knows-what? "I don't think so."

He put his palms up. "I promise you'll be safe with me. I can't promise you'll be safe out here without me." He offered his hand again. "What other choice do you have?"

"Ah…" The beach was bare for miles. Dunes, rocks, and bushes ringed the side opposite the ocean.

I hobbled up a sandy path lined with beach grass, trying to bear the weight on my right foot.

Dark Guy scooped me up. "Are you crazy?"

"What are you doing? Put me down."

He dropped me, and I fell into him. My face grew hot as I peeled myself away and glared at him.

He smiled, and those dimples appeared. Rude. "You don't have a choice. You can't walk. Your friends aren't here. What are you going to do when night falls, and this beach is crawling with crabs?"

"Crabs?"

"Yes. Big ones. With large pincers." He pinched his thumb and pointer fingers together.

"I know what a pincer is." I knocked his hand away. "Is that why I was in the tree? Someone was protecting me from crabs?"

He narrowed his eyes at me as if to say, "You're still sticking to that sad story?" then crouched, wrapped my arm over his shoulder, and helped me hobble to a rock. "You sit here while Rác and I search the beach. If we don't find anyone, you're welcome in my home. I promise you, it's much safer."

I stared at him as if you could tell a person by their looks. Supposedly, Jeffrey Dahmer was charismatic. Well liked even.

I scanned the beach once more. I'd have to find shelter inland if I stayed. How would I do that with an injured foot? I had no tools. No pack. Did it get cold here at night?

I had no choice but to hope this guy wasn't a cannibal luring me home for dinner. With a weak nod, I eased myself onto the ground.

Dark Guy whistled. Loudly. Then clapped his hands. Rác tore

himself away from a shrub he'd been inspecting and bounded toward his master. Ears flying, tongue flapping to the side. The dog trusted him. Dark and Rác headed down the beach. They shrunk smaller and smaller until they were out of sight completely.

My stomach growled as I waited for their return. How far had they gone? Had they found anyone? Had they decided to leave me here? The sun hadn't set yet, but it was on its way. When did the crabs come out? The bushes rustled behind me. Birds squawked as they flew overhead.

My ankle had blown up to almost twice its original size. I rested my head on my arms.

The dog blasted past me, kicking up sand. Dark Guy came up the beach from the other end. He circled behind me?

He sat next to me. Close. I shuffled away. Did he have no sense of personal space? "I checked the beach on both sides and the paths off the beach. There are no traces of people or any shipwreck debris."

My stomach growled. How many rations had I missed?

Dark Guy laughed, stood, and held out his hand. "Now will you let me take care of your foot and get you food?"

I stood. He scooped me up before I had a chance to object. How humiliating. But, like he'd said, what choice did I have? My right arm dangled awkwardly. The only place for it was on his shoulder. So, I let it rest there.

He flashed me his dimply smile, melting my heart. His tan skin was smooth. No stubble. "I'm Kai."

"Fallon." I fought the urge to run my fingers through his hair. His earlobes peeked out beneath tufts. I'd never been so close to anyone before, especially a man. I could smell him. Pine and something else. Intoxicating.

The sand gave way to a steep rocky incline. He was right. I wouldn't have made it. Sweat beaded his forehead, but he breathed steadily.

We crested the hill, and a gorgeous lake with brilliant blue water came into view. He carried me along a steep path to a dinghy at the water's edge. I groaned.

"Do you hurt?"

"No. I just don't want to see another boat."

"We can walk around, but we won't get there before nightfall."

"It's fine." How far were we headed? My friends wouldn't able to find me.

Sitting in the rowboat with him on the opposite side, I looked him straight on. I couldn't guess his age. The sun at my back blinded him every time he cast his gaze my way. He looked cute when he squinted. Angry and tough, but cute. His muscles flexed as he rowed.

Rác stretched out on the floor between our feet and yawned.

"Why don't your lips match your words when you speak?" he asked.

Uh-oh. Just how close *had* he been watching me? Was it a bad idea to tell him about Drochaid? "Um… Well…"

"Your speech is off. Yet you speak perfect Cianese. And you have black hair. Otherwise, you don't look like you belong here."

Cianese? Where was I? "You don't speak Ariboslian?" I'd never come across anyone who didn't speak Ariboslian. Or had I? Wait. What was that language Evan and his brother spoke last year when they thought I couldn't understand? Was it Cianese?

"I do. But why should I when you speak Cianese so well?" He cocked his head at me, squinting. "You don't know what language you're speaking?"

"Um… About that…"

"Welcome to my home." He pointed to a house built on a cliff high above the water. A stone staircase descended below water level. He rowed us to a platform between two half-submerged balconies. Rác jumped onto the platform, shaking the boat. "Here. Let me help you. Do you think you can make it up these steps?"

A long, narrow stairway ridged the hill. "Uh."

"I didn't think so." He stooped, offering his back. "Climb on."

I didn't even know this guy, and he had touched me more than anyone else in my life. And now I needed to climb onto his back? I was eighteen. Legally an adult, even if it was otherwise debatable. How much more humiliation could I take?

But the steps were steep. And there were a lot of them.

I swallowed my pride and climbed his back. His hair tickled my nose. Why did he have to smell so good? We ascended the stairs to a covered porch. He delivered me to a wooden couch lined with cushions. "I'll return shortly."

I gaped at the turquoise water, reminding me of pictures I'd seen of the Caribbean. Hills surrounded the lake on every side. If there were other dwellings, they were hidden in the greenery.

Kai returned with a mug, a tiny bowl, a thin board, and a bandage.

"What kind of shoes are those?" He motioned toward my sneakers as he placed his armful on the table.

"They're sneakers." I pulled the strings loose and dropped them on the floor.

He raised an eyebrow. "Are they for thieves or something?"

"No." I laughed. "They're just a type of shoe."

"Your clothes are strange too."

Time to change the subject. "What's the board for?"

"To keep you from moving your ankle while it heals." He scraped a greenish, black grainy substance from the bowl and rubbed it on my ankle. "This will help with the swelling." He then placed the board along my ankle and bandaged it.

"My friends will never be able to find me here."

"Shhh." He handed me the mug. "Drink this."

I put the mug on the table. No way was I drinking that.

Kai grabbed my mug. "Do you think I'm trying to poison you?" He took a sip. "It's just water. You're the one in my home wearing sneakers." He put the mug back in my hand. Now he expected me to drink after him? "Where are you from that you are so untrusting?"

I set the mug back down. "America."

"America? Where is that?"

"Nowhere near here."

"Excuse me, Fallon. I'll get us something to eat."

How had I ended up here? Was it wrong that part of me was enjoying this?

CHAPTER TWENTY-NINE

SOMETHING LICKED ME. I opened my eyes. A black nose filled my view. A pink tongue appeared. I dodged and took it on the chin. "Rác!"

The dog whined, wetted my cheek, then sat in front of me, shuffling his feet into a more comfortable position. I wiped my face while he watched with eager anticipation as if I might say, "oh, go ahead," and allow him full access to my face. Yeah, right. He was adorable though. A white patch ran down the middle of his forehead and covered his muzzle. Black surrounded his eyes. Like someone painted his eyebrows and the sides of his mouth brown with clown makeup. He licked his lips, then opened his mouth, panting.

Kai laughed. "My apologies. He loves everyone and doesn't see many people around here. He's deprived. I'm afraid he plans to take it out on you."

Good thing he was cute. The dog too.

"Aren't there other people around here?"

"Mm." He handed me a plate and sat next to me. "There are villages. But I prefer to keep to myself."

I poked the food with my fork. Fish. Mussels. Some wet, leafy substance. The fork wouldn't pierce it, so I slid it between the tongs. It dangled over the plate, wiggling as if it were alive. "What's this?"

He picked his up with his fingers. "Feamainn." He took a bite. "It will help the swelling in your ankle." He kept chewing, motioning me to try it.

I picked it off my fork. He'd eaten some. What could he do to it? Lace it with poison? But why would he have poison in a secluded area, population of one? Unless there weren't any other people because of him.

I shrugged off the thought and tried some. The bitter sting of way-too-much salt assaulted my tongue. I fought the urge to spit it out. As I chewed, the saltiness dissipated. I gnawed the flavor right out of it, and it still wasn't swallowable. After several more chews, it was small enough it shouldn't choke me. I gulped it down. My first and last taste.

Kai opened a mussel and sucked the meat out of the shell. "I'll try traveling north tomorrow to find your friends or signs of a wreckage."

"Tomorrow?" Why did I act surprised? Coming here rendered me stuck. I faced the incredible lake and breathed in the sweet air. There were worse places to be stuck. But what should I do now? I couldn't search for my friends. Worse…why didn't I mind?

"Mm." He swallowed some fish. "Is your ship from—what do you call it?—Am–Amer–A—"

As adorable as his attempts were, I couldn't let him keep struggling. "America. No. Just me. We're from all over, but we traveled from Bandia."

Kai coughed, pounded his chest, then swallowed his mouthful.

"You've heard of it?" I sipped my water.

"You shouldn't have come here."

I nearly choked on my sip. Keeping a wary eye on him and checking the exit routes, I placed my mug on the table. Is this where he showed me his collection of dead bodies? "Why?"

"Your kind aren't welcome here. If they're found—"

"Found?" I stiffened. What threats had we washed up on? "By who?" You?

"My people. Of sorts."

I relaxed slightly. At least he wasn't admitting to being a threat…yet. "What people? We're not familiar with these lands. How do you know of ours?"

"Because once your kind finds our shores, they're imprisoned."

Panic seized my heart. "What? Why?"

"To contain the gachen-selkie magnetism problem."

"*You're* a selkie?"

"Mm." His gaze fastened on me. "Although many disagree."

"Why didn't you warn me?" I tossed the rest of my food onto the table. No longer concerned about poison, but no longer hungry. Was that what I felt? The gachen-selkie attraction? Would the pull affect me as if I were a full gachen?

"I've never seen a gachen. I've only heard stories. And I only considered the fact that a girl needed help."

"I'm only half gachen." Did that matter? I felt *something*. He should've warned me before getting too close. Would the selkie-gachen pull strike us and keep us glued here, together, all hopes of fulfilling my quest forgotten like Cairbre and Deirdra?

"What's the other half?"

"Human."

His eyes widened. Such beautiful dark eyes. "I thought humans were a myth."

As amusing as that was, the attraction concerned me more. "But…gachen. Selkie. Does that mean—?"

"I don't know." He rubbed his chin. "Although I enjoy my solitude, I'm here because my people exiled me." He gulped his water.

Could this get any worse? I watched him, waiting for him to confess his crimes, praying they weren't violent.

"When you reach your totem, you're supposed to turn into a seal. If you don't, they banish you from the villages."

Phew. "So…" I dared let my hopes rise. "You're not a full selkie."

"That depends on your definition. I say I am. But, despite being born to selkie parents and having a strange affinity to the water, according to my people, no. I'm not."

I let out a huge breath and relaxed.

"Well, since I'm part human, maybe we'll be fine. It's my friends I need to worry about. I need to find them."

"What's your plan?" He raised an eyebrow at me. "Walk into a selkie village to warn your friends? Have you listened to a word I've said? The potential magnetism won't matter. Once the authorities find them, they'll lock up your friends."

Attraction or incarceration. Both were imprisonments. But he had a good point. "What do you suggest?"

He shrugged. "For now, let's get you better. We'll find your friends. No fear."

Too late to do anything now. They didn't know to hide. And if they hid, I'd never find them.

I ate the fish, hoping it was safe. After I'd eaten my full, my eyes drooped.

Kai stood and reached out his hand. "Come, I'll let you have my room."

"No, I—"

"I often sleep out here on the lanai." He took a deep breath. "The fresh air is great for sleep."

Why argue? I was better off somewhere I could close a door. I grabbed his hand and let him help me to the room. The door didn't lock. A heavy table stood in the corner. I scraped it across the floor, careful not to put pressure on my ankle, and barricaded the door. Satisfied, I turned back to the room.

Blankets and a small pillow lay on a pallet. A ladder shelf lined with wooden figures propped against the wall. I hobbled over and picked up a dolphin. Heavy and smooth, the high-polished wood warmed to my fingers. I replaced it and studied the people. A man, a woman, and two kids. Remarkable detail. I ran my fingers over them. Had Kai made these?

"Ya!"

My body shot off the ground. Grinning widely, Kai leaned through an open window. I placed my hand over my thumping heart.

"You scared me half to death."

"Half is better than all." He nodded toward the door. "You blocked the door with the table. Good thinking." He tapped his head with his finger and winked.

My face grew hot.

"Thought you might want this." He held out a blanket. "And be sure to lock the window. You never know what might crawl through." He snickered. "Sleep well." With a jaunty wave, he sauntered away.

I hobbled over to the window and peered in both directions. Nothing. I slid the wooden shutters, in their rails, until they met in the middle. After latching them, I returned to bed.

Chapter Thirty

SLEEP MUST'VE FOUND ME amongst the tossing and turning. Once more, I stood in the field, with no pain in my ankle, watching Declan on the shore. Swirling lights formed a window to someone, offering the perfect opportunity to find out who followed us without giving away my location. *I* didn't even know where I was. "Who are you?"

"Ah. You are there." An unfamiliar voice rang in my mind. The window was a blank slate. Black. I needed to clear it for clues.

"You know me?"

"Aye. I do." I sensed his pleasure, and something else. Something sadistic. "But how are you entering my mind? Particularly since you don't seem to know on whose mind you spy."

I stepped back. What was he saying? "Me? I'm starting this?"

"Aye. You must be powerful. I see why Morrigan fears you."

He knew Morrigan? Well enough to know her fears? "Who are you?"

"Fallon!" Declan called though he still stared out to sea.

"Where are you, Fallon?" The voice in my head pulled me back to the swirling lights. "I want to meet you. To tell you everything. There's much you need to learn."

"About what?" I stepped back, glancing Declan's way. He still looked to the sea.

"About me. Your family. You."

"Me? What do you have to tell me about myself that I don't already kn—"

"Fallon!"

"Turn away from him, Fallon."

Was that Declan's voice? Twice? Speaking over each other? He had crossed the field. Like my mother, he bared fangs and lunged at me just as something crashed.

I jerked and slammed my elbow against the pallet. "Ow!"

Splintered pieces of wood littered the floor. Moonlight shone through a gaping hole in the shutters. I hobbled to the window. My heart pounded as I braced myself, ready for a monster to jump into the room. I slid open as much of what remained of the shutters aside as possible. They creaked and broke apart further. Something rustled the tree. Something big. Large wings flapped spastically as it took to the sky in a rush. An owl? That was the only large nocturnal bird, right? Perhaps not in Ariboslia. Whatever it was, I must've spooked it. I scanned the darkness for any other movement, straining to hear. Nothing. Silence.

Kai appeared in the window. "What happened?"

I jumped a mile, landing on my bad foot. "Ow!" I hobbled back to the mat. "I don't know. I was asleep. Something busted the window."

His straight brows narrowed together as he frowned. "Close it as much as you can. Rác and I will sleep outside your window."

Was that supposed to comfort me?

****

I sighed and watched the still lake reflecting its surroundings like glass.

Kai returned from cleaning our breakfast dishes. He'd fixed the window, made a delicious fried vegetable pancake, and cleaned up. I pinched myself. No way was this real. I must've hit my head in the storm, and my body lay somewhere in a coma.

Might as well learn more about this amazing guy. "So, if you're not a seal, what's your totem?"

He smiled and stood. "Want to see?" He tugged the bandage on my foot.

I yanked my foot away. "What are you doing?"

"I'm removing the bandage, so you can get your foot wet. Is that a problem?"

"I guess not." I unwrapped my own foot.

He inspected my ankle and touched a tender spot.

"Ow." I recoiled.

"My apologies. But the feamainn is working well. The swelling is going down. Hop on." He knelt for me to climb on his back.

Somehow, it wasn't as awkward today. He carried me down the stairs to one of the submerged balconies, then descended the steps into waist-deep water. It felt cool and soft on my feet. Kai placed me on a railing sticking halfway above the water. "Do you want to take that off?" He pointed to my chest.

"Huh?" My heart thundered. So, he was some sort of pervert after all.

"Your necklace. You don't want to lose it in the water, do you?"

"Oh." The amulet. I touched Drochaid and laughed.

"What's so funny?" He cocked his head. Then his eyes widened. "Did you think I meant—" His gleaming bronze face blanched.

"No." I hated to see him flustered…even if it made him look more adorable than ever. He'd proven himself trustworthy enough to tell him about Drochaid. "I need to keep this with me. I don't speak Cianese."

"Huh?" He scratched his head. "What do you speak?"

"English."

I could almost see the light turn on. "Your lips matched. That thing allows us to talk? You're speaking En–Eng—"

"English. Yes. I need to keep it, or I can't talk to you."

"It won't fall off if you swim?"

I'd carried Drochaid through worse. "It should be okay."

The water came midway up my calves. Careful not to injure my ankle further, I swirled my feet. The floor looked like tile. "Was this a balcony?"

"Aye. The lake has risen." He slipped his shirt over his head.

Unprepared, I sucked in my breath and stared at rows of tan, tight abs.

"I'll meet you on the other side." Kai flipped the shirt over his shoulder, hopped back up the steps, and disappeared behind the trees.

I swung my legs over the railing, so I faced the lake. An endless sparkling blue. I heard a splash and turned to look for Kai, but he was gone. He must've jumped into the lake.

A dolphin brushed against my feet. "Kai?"

The dolphin hovered before me, nodding its head, making cackling sounds. He dove, then reappeared and spit water at me.

"Hey!" I raised my hand and dodged, nearly falling off the railing again. "Are you trying to get me wet?"

He nodded and cackled again.

"You want me…in there?" I pointed at the lake.

He threw his head up and down again, sending his body rocking over the surface, then fell sideways.

How could I pass up a swim with a dolphin? Hopefully, it wouldn't hurt my ankle. I jumped.

Kai swam up beside me, his skin slick and rubbery. I grabbed his fin, and he shot off, his powerful body undulating through the lake, pulling me along for the ride. My heart screamed with pure joy. How great it must be to be a dolphin! God's waters my home, my plaything. This was the next best thing to flying. Kai dipped as if preparing me to go under. I held my breath, and he dove. I kept my eyes open, nothing but clear blue in every direction. Sun rays sparkled, cutting through the water in geometric lines. We reemerged on the surface. I took a deep breath and wiped my hair from my face while Kai's blowhole spouted. He replaced me on the railing, and I pulled myself up.

I let the sun warm my face and tried to hang on to the thrill. I never wanted to leave.

Kai returned, his clothes sticking to his damp skin.

"How was that?" He hopped on the railing beside me.

"That was awesome!" My heart still pounded from exhilaration.

He ran his fingers through his hair, shaking off the water, flinging droplets at me. Then he threw me a side smile, showing off his dimple. "Ya. There's nothing like it."

"It's like being in the sky." I looked at the clouds. "If only I were big enough to bring you."

"You're a bird?"

"A falcon."

He followed my gaze. "That must be incredible."

"It's the most amazing feeling in the world. Soaring above the trees. It's so quiet. So peaceful. And yet...so thrilling." I caught him gazing at me, a small smile twitching his lips. "Like being underwater." Suddenly shy, I watched my feet swirl the water.

"Ya. It's—"

A twig snapped behind us. We turned toward the sound in time to spy a large bird flying away. An eagle?

CHAPTER THIRTY-ONE

KAI'S TUNIC WAS LIKE a dress on me. I hobbled to the couch on the lanai, pulled my feet up next to me, and covered my legs with the shirt. A red-orange sky surrounded the sun descending on the far side of the ocean-sized lake. Never had I experience such luxury, taking in such a view from the comfort of Kai's outdoor living room.

Tiny multicolored birds flittered from the rafters. Rác lifted his head as a little bird dropped near. It twittered and flew away, and Rác settled his chin back on its resting place on his front paws.

All I'd seen so far were small birds. Did eagles exist around here? Did I know any other eagles besides Declan? But it couldn't be him. There was no way he knew I was here.

No. It was a bird. Sometimes a bird was just a bird.

I stared out over the water. Guilt gripped me, choking me, making it hard to breathe never mind think straight. How could I stay here, enjoying this view, frolicking in the water, admiring a guy I'd just met? I had a quest to fulfill and another guy I liked....

A guy I hadn't seen in almost a year. A guy who may or may not still be alive.

Was I using Declan as an excuse to keep other guys away?

Or was this a gachen-selkie thing? Was this what happened to Cairbre and Deirdra? Were we destined to fall for each other and never part? Was it my imagination or a magical pull that made me even consider it a real possibility?

But there was nothing I could do. Not without my friends. Not with a sprained ankle. Right?

"Dinner is ready." Kai reached for my hand.

Everything else melted away as I took his hand. I leaned on him and hobbled into the house. He smelled like trees and air on a cool summer day. I was doomed.

We transitioned from the stone deck to the tiled floor. Breeze swept through the open windows, and Kai brought me to a table and fish and vegetables.

"You did all this?" More guilt swept over me. I should have helped.

"Aye. I even built the table." He ran his fingers along the smooth surface. "You like it?"

"It's beautiful." Was there anything he couldn't do? He cooks. He's handy. The white fish flaked apart. I ate a forkful. "This is so good." He didn't just cook—he *cooked*.

"I saw how much you liked the fish last night and the vegetable pancake this morning, so I thought you'd enjoy this. No more feamainn." Winking, he took a bite.

If an evil force wanted to take me out of the game, luring me to this haven with this perfect specimen of a male was the best course of action. I never wanted to leave.

****

Kai played a stringed instrument on his lap as I sat, shifting my gaze from the stars to him. Wasn't this the life God wanted for me? Safe. Cared for. Happy. He couldn't want me to continue with my quest, putting my life on the line, spending my time hungry, tired, and afraid of what might happen next.

My head lolled forward. Then I snapped awake. Kai stopped

playing. He put the instrument aside and sat beside me. "You should rest."

"I'm not tired." I didn't want the night to end. With my luck, I'd wake to reality and find this was just a dream. I wanted it to last forever.

He let out a soft chuckle.

A shivery cry rang out in the night.

His eyes widened. "What was that?"

It sounded familiar. "You live here. Haven't you heard it before?"

He shook his head and stood, holding his hand out for me to be silent. We waited for the sound to return. Seconds ticked by. A minute. Nothing.

Where had I heard that cry? I'd seen the bird earlier. And now the cry.

Declan?

****

Something pinged on the ground, waking me. A breeze swept through. White curtains danced in the moonlight streaming through the window. Hadn't I closed that?

I caught a whiff of something. Was that—? No, it couldn't be the fasgadair scent. Not out here.

Another ping. Something small and dark bounced along the ground. It came to a rest on the floor beside me. I reached out for it, ready to pull back should the mystery object move. It didn't. I grasped it. Smooth, hard…a pebble.

I strained to see beyond the curtains. Nothing but trees swaying in the wind. My feet recoiled from the cold tile. Pulling the blanket around my shoulders, I inched toward the window. Like the people I yelled at in horror films, I crept forward until I leaned out the window and the sides of the house were visible. Nothing. I took a deep breath and retreated toward the bed.

"Fallon." My name came in a whisper from a voice that was familiar, yet amiss. The electric fasgadair scent followed it.

"Kai?" But it wasn't Kai's voice.

"Fallon." The whisper came again. This time farther away.

I pulled myself over the windowsill, chastising myself for being so dumb. Like those characters, I, too, deserved to die for my stupidity. Yet curiosity overwhelmed me.

I hobbled along a dirt path, following more whispers, then rounded a bend in the trees and stopped. The fasgadair scent assaulted my nose, and a figure stood in the moonlight. "Declan?"

The figure didn't speak. He emerged from the shadow.

I gasped. My heart quickened, and I edged forward, reaching out. "Declan."

He stepped back, and I lowered my hand. His eyes.

"No," I gasped, my own voice a low hiss.

"I won't hurt you." His voice…Declan's, yet deeper, darker. Venomous.

"You're a–a—"

"A fasgadair."

Those words…from his lips. And those eyes… His once beautiful green eyes were now freakish, the green overtaking most of his eyes. The moonlight made them appear to glow. Fighting the urge to run, I crept toward him instead. "Let me help you."

Declan retreated. "No."

"Why not?"

"You can't help me."

"My blood can. What is it? Are you afraid you'll die?"

"No." He hung his head, mumbling something like he'd welcome death.

Then why? Why wouldn't he let me help? Why would he want to remain this monster? Was it me? He didn't want me near him? What had I done? His rejection pierced my heart.

"Is it Kai?" I crept forward again, only for him to lurch back, keeping the same distance between us. "Because there's nothing—"

"No."

My prior guilt resurfaced. "Is it because of what I did at Bandia?

The ships? The fasgadair?"

"No."

I jumped at the sharpness in his voice. "Then why?" Anger burned within. "Why are you here? Have you been following me?" My mind assaulted me with strange memories: the bird following me from the megalith, the missing food on the ship—both times—the bird in my room with Rowan. "You *have* been following me. From the beginning… You followed us to Kylemore. You stole Rowan's food. Did you steal Valter's too? And everyone thought he was being obnoxious." I placed my hands on my hips and scoffed, shaking my head in disgust. All evidence pointed to Declan. "Why are you spying on me?"

"I found Pepin. I'll tell you where to find him."

Pepin? My mind swirled with mixed emotions. I'd have to resume my quest. "No."

"No?" His freakish eyes bored into my soul.

"Why should I go anywhere with you? You're a fasgadair. I can turn you back, but you refuse. Why?"

"It's complicated." He dropped his gaze to the ground.

"Yeah, I'm sure."

"Don't you care where Pepin is?"

"No."

Declan's bizarre eyes flashed. His jaw tensed, and his temples pulsed as if holding back inner rage. "What are you going to do? Stay here and play with the dolphin?"

"Maybe."

He huffed and shook his head.

Declan—a fasgadair. Evan explained what it took to become fasgadair. If he'd drank some monster's blood, he had no right to judge *me*. Unless he was forced. Either way, whatever he was going through, I could save him.

"Fallon, you have a duty. I'm offering help. Why do you refuse?"

" 'It's complicated.' " Mocking his response to me, I hobbled away.

****

"Did you sleep well?" Kai asked.

"Eh." I shrugged and leaned on my arm, resting on the table, and continued pushing food around my plate.

"After we eat, I'll check the north shore for your friends."

"Don't bother."

"What?" He narrowed his eyes. He looked scary when he did that. Fierce. Yet gorgeous. "You don't want to find your friends?"

"I'm sure they'll find me soon enough." I straightened in my chair. "Let's go for a swim."

He searched me as if seeking answers even I didn't have. "If that's what you want."

"Yes." I nodded with certainty. "That's what I want." Anything to avoid reality.

Chapter Thirty-Two

DAYS PASSED. KAI AND I spent most of the day in the lake until my skin puckered like a raisin. We fished or tended his garden and cooked. We spent evenings under the stars, talking about everything—like Declan and I used to—while Kai whittled away. Or I'd listen to him play the torman-ciùil. There were no fasgadair, no betrothals, no mysteries. Only peace and calm. If this was a dream, I prayed nothing woke me.

I scanned the beach and found a small hole. "Is this one?" I asked.

Kai inspected the hole. "Ya." He stomped near the hole, and water spurted out. "You found one. Dig it up." He flashed his crooked grin, then moved to another spot.

I sank my fingers into the mud and rooted around. "This is disgusting. Don't you have a shovel?"

"Who needs a shovel?" He stuck a hand into the ground and came up with a clam. Show off.

Mud oozed through my fingers. I felt something hard and grabbed it. A slimy shell. "I got one!"

"Well done." He pulled another clam from the muck and tossed it into the bucket. "Throw it in."

I added it to the dozen Kai had found. Then searched for more until the mud no longer bothered me.

"I think we have plenty." He tossed one more into the full bucket. "Come here."

"What?" I walked toward him.

"You've got something." He held his finger up, pointing to my face.

"Mud?"

He nodded. "Right…here." He swiped my nose with his muddy finger.

"Hey!" I readied a muddy hand to retaliate.

Laughing, he jumped back. When I pursued, he dodged. He stepped in a hole and stumbled. I mashed my hand on his face, smearing mud from his eye to his mouth. He swept my feet out from underneath me and caught my fall. We both landed in the mud.

Kai stared at me with those sparkling dark eyes. So intense. I sucked in a deep breath to calm my thudding heart as he leaned toward me. Was he going to kiss me? I held my breath.

A bird's cry rang out. The same cry I'd heard days earlier. Was Declan *still* spying on me?

Kai stopped advancing. "What was that?"

"It sounds like a bird." I shoved him aside and sat up. "I should wash off."

He didn't make another attempt to kiss me, assuming he almost had. Did I want him to? Yes. But was it a good idea? Things were far too complicated. And as much as I'd love to take a page from Cairbre and Deirdra's book, I'd have to give up this fantasy and return to real life. To God's work.

How would I live with myself if I didn't?

I pushed my concern aside as we cleaned up in the water, then returned to the house. Kai sat beside me, drying his hair with a towel. "Your ankle seems better."

I wiggled it. "Uh-huh."

"That's good." He frowned, giving his hair another shake in my direction, then wrapped the towel around his shoulders. "Does that mean you'll be leaving soon?"

"I guess so." Did he *want* me to leave?

"Why don't you come with me tomorrow and look for your friends?"

A lump formed in my throat. He was ready for me to leave. Was I a burden? Shame coursed through me for not considering what a disruption an extended stay from an unwelcome guest might've caused. As usual, I thought only of myself.

If only I'd gotten Pepin's location from Declan when I'd had the chance. I wanted to pack my things and leave. Now.

****

I climbed out the window into the dark and hiked down the path. Once I was a safe distance, I cupped my lips and called for Declan in a hushed voice. A fasgadair should have no trouble hearing.

I followed the path to where I'd found Declan last and continued calling his name. He didn't appear. My heart sank. What had made me think he'd stick around? I sat on a rock and threw myself a pity party. Invitation for one. No one wanted me. Kai was ready to get rid of me. Declan chose to be a monster rather than rejoin me. Were my friends even looking for me? Or had they given up and moved on with my quest without me?

Tears coursed down my cheeks, dripping onto my lap.

"What are you doing out here?" Declan asked in his evil-Declan voice.

I jumped up and wiped the tears from my face. "I–I was looking for you."

His eyes flashed. "Why?"

"Where's Pepin?"

****

I tossed and turned on the mat. Tomorrow I'd leave paradise and Kai. Why was that the last thing I wanted? My heart ached. My life had brought me nothing but trouble. For once in my life, I was happy. I liked Kai. And he wasn't betrothed. Unless fate was crueler than I imagined.

Or was I lying to myself? This happiness wasn't real. It was superficial…based on my circumstances.

And how would I stay happy avoiding my purpose? Avoiding God's plan? I'd experienced a deeper, more life-sustaining happiness before. It began with the meeting in Saltinat when I received Drochaid's gem. When I met God and received forgiveness, love, and purpose.

Peace washed over me at the memory.

I had to return to my quest, to God's will for my life. Who knew better what I should do and where I should go than the One Who created me?

I'll get back on track, God. Tomorrow…

Sleep crept in, and I stood in the field. Declan took his usual spot on the shore. Lights whirled into a window. Whoever lay beyond there knew me and my family. Or so he claimed. Was it a trap to get me to deliver myself into his clutches? Why not divulge whatever information he had to share here? Why be so mysterious? I peered into the window. A hazy image of a small room appeared, like the captain's quarters on a ship.

"You've returned." His voice rang in my mind.

"Are you on a ship?"

The hazy image went blank. Had he covered his eyes?

"Where I am is of no consequence." I sensed his irritation by more than his voice. It filled the space as if it existed all around me. "The question is…where are you? I will come to you."

"Yeah, right." I scoffed. "I'm sure chasing after us must be tiring. But do you seriously think I'll make it that easy for you? If there's something I should know about my family, tell me."

He chuckled. A sinister sound.

"That's not how this works. But, since you don't seem convinced that we should meet, perhaps I'll give you an opportunity to seek answers for yourself. Ask your mother about your birth. Every child should know about their birth, don't you think?" This time, his chuckle sounded bitter.

"Fallon!" Declan called.

I swiveled toward him on the shore.

"Once you have a chat with dear ol' mum, I trust you'll *want* to meet."

"Turn away from him, Fallon."

Just as I turned, Declan bared his fangs and lunged.

CHAPTER THIRTY-THREE

I GLANCED ABOUT THE small room. Kai's room. He must want it back. I hated to leave, but it was time to move on. I didn't want to overstay my welcome any further, and I had to get back on task.

Besides, now I needed to find Cataleen and ask her about my birth. Guilt washed over me. Was I more interested in finding out what the mystery person in the dream knew than ensuring my mother was still alive?

Everything around me belonged to Kai. The tunics he let me wear, the brush he let me borrow. Nothing was mine. I had nothing to pack or a bag.

"Take this." Kai threw a stuffed satchel over my shoulder, then pushed a package into my hands. "It's dried fish. In case you get hungry."

I blinked back tears. "Thanks for all you've done."

"What? You think we're parting ways right now? I know where the statue is you're looking for. I'll get you there." He grabbed another small pack and shoved it into a satchel. In one sweeping motion, he threw the satchel around his neck and shoulder. "Want me to carry you?"

"I can walk. Thanks."

"I'm happy to carry you, whether or not you can walk." There were those dimples again. Sigh. Why was he making this so hard?

Kai led me up the hill, past what had been my bedroom window, and into the woods where I'd met Declan. "I still don't understand how you know about the statue."

What was I supposed to say? *So, this guy I used to like is a vampire now, and he's been following me around. He told me about the statue and how to use it to find Pepin.* Yeah, right. Kai would never let me follow a stalker vampire's instructions. "It's hard to explain."

Raising an eyebrow at me, he released a defeated breath. "All right. I'll take you there." We walked down a steep trail. Kai had wrapped my ankle tight, but I had to maneuver around roots, rocks, and sloping ground with care to keep from reinjuring myself.

"The statue is up ahead." He pointed at more woods.

As we neared, a gray shape emerged amongst the spindly branches. The statue. A man. An angry man judging by his scowl. He clutched something in his left hand. He raised his right arm as if about to strike.

"Do you know where to go from here?" Kai surveyed the scene. Hard to read, he looked both relieved and concerned.

"Yeah."

"Let me take you there."

"No. It's fine. I know what to do."

Kai grasped my upper arms. Tight. He stared into my eyes. "I'm not leaving you until you're with your friends. Safe."

How was I supposed to respond? Would the pech be angry if I shared their secret with a selkie? Approaching Pepin this way alone was already risky. But Pepin should be able to explain me. But Kai? I dared look into his intense, dark eyes, still fixed on mine, intent on making his terms clear.

"Okay, okay." I shrugged him loose. "But you can't share this with anyone." I moved toward the statue, grasped the raised arm, and tugged. It creaked as I pulled it down.

He sucked in his breath. "What does *that* do?"

"I guess we'll find out." I lowered the arm as far as it would go, and a tremor pulsed through the ground from the statue outward. I held the statue to keep from falling.

Kai widened his stance and splayed his arms. "What was that?" He turned around as if trying to see where the tremor went. "I thought that was just another piece of ruins."

Something rustled in the woods.

"Is someone there?" I asked.

If it was pech that weren't expecting us, they might not show themselves. I had to lure them out. "I'm looking for a pech named Pepin. Is he with you? I'm his friend, Fallon."

More rustling. Hushed voices. Then nothing.

"Hello?" I stepped toward the woods.

Kai grasped my shoulder and yanked me back. "They're gone. But let's wait. Maybe they've gone to give Pepin the message."

We sat on the path and munched our dried fish while we waited.

"You don't have to stay." I reminded him.

"Yes, I do."

So, the guy had a stubborn streak. Why, if he was so eager for me to leave, did he refuse to let me go?

Trees rustled behind me.

"Fallon!" Pepin emerged. "How did you find me?"

I bent over to hug him. "It's a long story. It is so good to see you. I thought I'd lost you. Do you know where the others are?"

Pepin shook his head. "I'm hopeful Turas might help."

"Who's Turas?" I asked.

"Not who, but what." Pepin shrugged his stocky shoulders.

"The old rocks?" Kai ran his fingers through his wavy hair.

"Old rocks. Hmph." Pepin crossed his arms and scowled at Kai. "Who is this…" He waved his hand toward Kai, scrunching his eyebrows as if trying to come up with the right word.

"Person?" I raised an eyebrow at him.

Pepin tipped his head as if that word sufficed but wasn't what he'd been thinking.

"This is Kai. He took me in while I was hurt."

"Hurt?"

"I sprained my ankle jumping from a tree."

Pepin tugged his beard. "Thank you for caring for our Fallon. I'll take care of her from here."

Kai's gaze ping-ponged from me to Pepin, then rested on me, his soulful eyes searching me for certainty.

I nodded.

So he turned, threw one last glance over his shoulder, then headed home. Why did I want him to turn back and say he couldn't leave without me? A pain in my chest deepened with each step widening the distance between us. The connection stretched, attempting to keep us united as the growing gap threatened to tear it apart. I could almost see it writhing and bleeding as Kai disappeared around the bend, severing the link. I held my fist over my heart as if I could keep the ache from spreading. Did we suffer from a watered-down version of the gachen-selkie attraction?

"Follow me." Pepin waved and headed into the woods.

I followed, but it was tough going without a path. I had to push through shrubs, and I had no way of knowing if I was stepping on uneven ground.

He kept stopping and waiting. "Why so slow?"

"I'm trying to be careful of my ankle." I pushed a branch aside. "Where are we going?"

"We're almost there."

That wasn't what I asked, but whatever.

We stopped at a boulder. Pepin shoved it aside, revealing steps into the ground.

I groaned. How I hated small enclosed spaces! Why were there so many caves and tunnels in Ariboslia?

He directed me to enter first, so I stepped down the dirt stairs into the dank hole. He followed me down a few steps, lit a torch attached to the wall, then tugged a handle under the boulder to close the opening. The ceilings were so low, I had to stoop. The walls seemed to close in on me. Breathing became difficult.

God, help me. Don't let me have a panic attack. Not now.

The chorus of a hymn we'd sung a million times in church popped into my head.

Standing on the promises that cannot fail,
When the howling storms of doubt and fear assail,
By the living Word of God I shall prevail,
Standing on the promises of God.

I sang it over and over, letting nothing else penetrate my mind as we proceeded down the entombed hall.

My back and neck ached after only a few minutes. The ground sloped downward. More tunnels jutted off ours. Sometimes we made a turn; sometimes we walked past the openings. I might have been an ant in an ant farm.

We rounded a corner to a straightaway. At the end, light flickered, and gruff voices grew louder. We emerged in a room tall enough for me to stand with about an inch gap between my head and the stone ceiling. Something pulled at my hair. I grasped my head and ducked to find what got me. A shard poking out from the roof.

Standing on the promises…

Hands on my hips, spine still not fully extended, I took deep breaths. Where was I? Some pub with a bar, tables, and pech? Great. Only they weren't like Pepin's people in the Tower of Galore. Pepin's description of them anyway. Darker skin, black hair, and dark eyes blended into a blur that enhanced the underground feeling of no light. One by one, they swiveled and hushed until every gaze in the room fell on me and the steady hum declined to a few isolated words then complete silence.

Pepin cleared his throat. "This is Fallon—the girl I told you about."

Groans erupted as pech returned their attention to whatever held it before our entrance and conversations resumed.

Wow, what a welcome.

Pepin grabbed my arm and propelled me to a pech sitting alone at a table. His stubby fingers tightened around a stein almost half his size—at least it looked huge in his hands. As we approached, he took a deep swig, clanged his mug to the table, and wiped his mouth on his sleeve.

"Aldrick, this is Fallon."

"So you said." He swigged another gulp. "Where's Drochaid?"

Wow. These people were oozing with friendliness.

Pepin motioned to me so I revealed Drochaid from beneath my neckline and bent forward for Aldrick to inspect it.

Aldrick's eyes narrowed, then widened. He angled his stout body on the stool, facing Pepin. "You said an angel gave you these specifications?"

"Yes."

Aldrick released to Drochaid. "Interesting." He braced both elbows on the stone table before him. "Have a seat."

Pepin and I sat across from him.

"It might work," Aldrick said.

"What might work?" I bent my knees up by my chest as I crunched myself onto the short stool.

"Turas. Drochaid might be the key to get it working again," Aldrick whispered, scanning both directions.

"What's Turas?"

Aldrick gripped the table and leaned back as if preparing for a long story. His black braid slipped from his shoulder and swung behind him.

"The pech were the first intelligent life in Ariboslia. The gachen came later," Pepin said.

A pech at another table twisted toward us, his head hovering by Aldrick's shoulder. "You mean the pech are the *only* intelligent life in Ariboslia." He laughed and returned to his friends at his table who congratulated his wit.

Aldrick and Pepin rolled their eyes.

I stifled a yawn for fear of seeming uninterested.

"In those days, the pech had a special megalith. When it was whole, it formed a complete circle. Inside the circle was a semicircle." Aldrick gulped his drink. "It was our ancestors' masterpiece."

Pepin nodded. "As a child, every pech hears the stories of those days. Turas allowed us to tap into the spiritual realm. Once inside the spiritual realm, time and space were of no consequence. You could go wherever and whenever you chose, just by thinking about it."

"Seriously?" I sat upright, slamming my knees against the stone table. Ouch. Oops. I rubbed them. "What happened to it?"

Aldrick growled. "People in the human realm. Romans, I think they were called, tore most of it apart. They stole many of our stones to create roads."

"Such a sad sight." Pepin clicked his tongue. "To think there was a day when pech weren't separated by the sea. We traveled via Turas. But pech won't risk traveling the seas, so now the ocean keeps us apart."

"Except for one brave, little pech." Aldrick smiled under his facial hair. Did all pech have such white teeth? Despite the lack of a welcome, there was something about Aldrick I liked. He seemed to respect Pepin. Perhaps these pech weren't as bad as where he'd lived. According to Pepin's stories, the others had been so mean.

Pepin's face flared as red as his hair.

I reangled my feet to give my knees more space. "So, if Turas is broken, what makes you think Drochaid can get it to work?"

Pepin straightened. "I had a dream."

Suddenly, I didn't care about my physical discomfort. Every cell attuned to Pepin. "Like when you knew we had to flee from Ceas Croi?"

"Sort of. You kept repeating the date April 24, 1521 BC. Turas brought us to that time when it was whole. From there, we could travel wherever and whenever, as if it were still intact."

"So, when do we check it out?"

"In the morn."

"So soon? Aren't we going to look for our friends?"

Pepin frowned. "I've searched and found no evidence they washed up on these shores."

Guilt panged within my chest. "They might be in trouble. Selkie live on these lands. If they find our friends and learn they're gachen, they'll throw them in prison."

"All the more reason to get to Turas tomorrow."

CHAPTER THIRTY-FOUR

PEPIN PADDLED THE SMALL boat, grumbling whenever the breeze wafted water droplets his way.

Sitting back, I folded my arms over my chest. Though he hadn't said it, he didn't trust me to row. "If you hate water so much, why are we taking a boat?"

"It takes too long to circumvent this accursed, bottomless pool." Sweat dampened his hair and the sides of his beard. "It's too deep to tunnel under." More water droplets sprinkled his face. "Dah! Water is meant for drinking and bathing, not teetering upon."

Kai's home must be close. But where? Nothing looked familiar.

We nosed the dinghy up to a rocky shore surrounded by shrubs and tall trees. Pepin hopped out the front and lugged the boat ashore. I grabbed my satchel and followed him through the trees. We walked for hours over sticks and stones. Though my time with Kai involved little walking, I'd swam so much, I felt stronger. My ankle was much improved. I could've kept going when he suggested we take a break.

He leaned against a tree, panting, and wiped the sweat from his forehead. When I sat beside him, he tossed a meat stick at me, then chomped on his own.

"How far is this place?"

"Another day's walk. We'll camp tonight." He chewed with his mouth open. "We're far enough inland the selkie shouldn't be a problem."

"What about the fasgadair?" My piece of jerky was tough. I clamped my teeth and pulled, tearing it apart.

"Fasgadair?" He sniffed as if seeking hints of them on the wind.

"Aren't there fasgadair here? I mean, Declan…"

"What of Declan?" Pepin squished his furry caterpillar eyebrows together.

"I—He—" I took a deep breath. "Declan is here. He led me to you."

"What?" He sat up straight. "Where?"

"Doesn't matter. But—" Better just yank the Band-Aid. "He's a fasgadair."

His eyes bulged. Then he frowned. "Did you try to save him?"

"He won't let me."

Pepin returned to his slouch. "Why?"

I shrugged. "He won't tell me." I tore a piece of my jerky.

"Is he alone?"

"I think so. He's been following us all along—since we first came through the megalith."

"How is that possible?" He rubbed his beard, eyeing me skeptically.

"Remember the bird I thought was following me? And stole Rowan's food? It flew into our room in Bandia. Then it stole Valter's food."

"Valter wasn't lying to get more food?"

I shook my head. "No."

Pepin groaned. "Not to worry." He patted my knee. "We'll find a way to save him…after we find our friends."

****

The following day, as the sun was sinking in the sky, the forest cleared. Massive rocks in a circular pattern protruded from the earth before us. Some stood on end with others balanced over the tops while others lay resting on the ground. I sucked in a breath, full of awe at the enormousness and beauty that lay in the lush grass. "Stonehenge?"

Pepin beamed with pride as if this was his baby. "Is that its name in your realm? You know it?"

"Everyone who ever went to school knows it."

He seemed to grow a couple of inches. He closed the gap, reached out, and caressed the stone like an equestrian with a prized racehorse. "Such a beauty."

"I've always wanted to see it in person." I entered the center and twirled. "So, I could visit the time when Cataleen brought me back to Ariboslia and prevent her from going? My dad wouldn't die, and we could live together?"

His hands fell limp to his sides. "We can't change history." He touched my arm.

"Then what's the point?"

"From what I understand from Aldrick and the dark pech, when we use Turas to tap into the spiritual realm and visit the past, we're like shadows watching events in history unfold. People in history can't see or talk to us."

"I thought you said the pech used Turas to travel across the ocean."

"They traveled to other locations in the current time by removing the amulet from the stone."

"What's the point in going back in time if we can't change anything?"

"For one, we have to if we want to visit another location. We have to go back to when Turas was whole. For another, to learn. To watch events as they transpired."

So, rather than wait to talk to my mother about my birth and hope she told the truth, I could visit the day I was born and see for myself? "Can we go to the shipwreck and find out where our friends went?"

"Ummm." He scratched behind his ear. "That's my hope. But I'm not sure what happens on the sea."

"If we're not really there, we can't get hurt, right?"

"Probably." He moved to an itch on his forehead. "Better to test it out on something safer first."

"Like what?"

"Let's try to go to April 24, 1521 BC first. Here." He took Drochaid, still around my neck, and placed it in a matching depression in a rock standing near the center. He glanced at me. "Keep repeating April 24, 1521 BC. No matter what happens, don't move from this spot."

"April 24, 1521 BC. April 24, 1521 BC. April 24, 1521 BC."

He swirled his finger around the edge. Like a rusty machine, hesitant to move after years of neglect, the rocks surrounding us groaned and trembled, then roared to life. They moved in a circle without disrupting the earth. Their momentum grew to a full spin until a seemingly solid wall of swirling rocks thundered around us. They spun, disturbing nothing. As if they didn't exist. Within the circle, all was calm, like the eye of a hurricane. Not a hair twitched.

I looked at wide-eyed Pepin.

The whirlwind slowed as the rocks screeched to a stop. The wall disappeared as the stones returned to their stationary places. Only this time, Turas was perfect. Pepin sucked in his breath.

Gone were the broken and felled stones. The larger stones in the semicircle next to us stood in five sets of twos, with a rock balanced across the tops of the pairs. Beyond that, shorter stones, still many feet above my head, stood the same size and distance apart, each connected by a stone balancing across, forming a perfect circle. How did the pech make such an incredible monument in the 1500s ...*before* Christ?

Pepin and I left the circle to see the whole thing. A brilliant light descended upon us. As it grew closer, a human form took shape in the fiery glow. I fell to the ground and tried to scurry away while shielding my eyes.

Pepin dropped to his knees.

"Do not be afraid," the being said. "I am an angel sent by God."

An angel? I peeked between splayed fingers as the light dimmed and brightened, then dimmed again like a light with a faulty wire. The thing looked human but genderless with a glittering white robe tied by a golden cord. I trembled and lowered my hand as my eyes adjusted and stared at the creature.

"You are in between the human realm in 1521 and the spiritual realm which exists outside of time and space. Angels and demons travel this space. Remain within Turas's boundary at all costs and do not linger. Heed my warning. Should demons realize you're using Turas to enter the spiritual realm, they will do what they can to deceive you. Make no mistake, their only intent is for harm, always. Be careful how often you use Turas. Return now to its protective boundary and never stray from it again." The angel returned to the sky and disappeared.

We scurried to the inner circle. I never wanted to see a demon. Ever.

My over-firing brain cells took a moment to remember how to form words. "I—Uh—"

"I'll never get used to that." Pepin's movements waggled his braid.

"Huh?" Higher-level brain functioning returned. "Oh, yeah. You've seen an angel before. That's why you made Drochaid." I touched the amulet around my neck.

"Mmmhmm." He moved to the depression in the stone. "Now we test it. Got anything in mind?"

I nodded. "I know the date, but not the location."

"You may not need to repeat the date and location. Try to imagine what you know."

Imagine it? I thought about my mother, myself, and June twenty-first. I kept those cycling in my mind, as I had with the date, just not aloud. Pepin ran his finger over Drochaid. The swirling began again. A gray circle surrounded us once more, and blue sky appeared over our heads. As the circling stones slowed, I found myself in my farmhouse, only in better condition.

"I'm home?"

A woman's scream rang out from upstairs. Rushing feet creaked the floorboards. A baby wailed. Was it me?

I stepped forward, and my knee connected with something. "Ow!" I touched the invisible rock.

"What is it?" Pepin placed a hand near mine.

"The rock." I tried stepping away, but Drochaid caught around my neck, suspended in midair. "How am I supposed to get up there? I'm trapped by this invisible stone."

"Try imagining yourself there instead of walking there."

I pictured myself walking through the house, and the scene changed as if I were. Up the stairs. So weird! Like a controllable dream. But I was wide awake, visiting my personal history.

Light shone through a crack in my bedroom door. The baby's cry and voices came from the room. Moving shadows broke up the light. The door burst open, and my grandmother—Fiona, only much younger—charged my way. I tried to dodge her, but I wasn't quick enough. She walked right through me. Stunned, I inspected where she'd walked through me. I felt solid.

I imagined myself walking into the other room, and I appeared there, along with Pepin. The room wasn't as I remembered it. The walls were white. No wallpaper. But that was my bed, only newer…with Cataleen laying under a sheet. A man stood by her side holding an infant in a ducky blanket.

"He's so beautiful, Cataleen."

He?

"She's not done yet," said a woman, peeking between the sheets. "Okay, Cataleen. One more push."

My mother took a deep breath. Her face, already red, darkened a few shades as she strained. She cried out again.

I tried not to watch the woman with whatever she was doing. A few moments later, another baby cried out.

"It's a girl!"

The man whooped with joy. The father? *My* father? A tear ran down his cheek and dripped on the baby boy's head.

The woman cleaned up the girl, wrapped her in a flowered blanket, and placed her in my father's other arm. He froze as though petrified he might drop one before he adjusted both. Then he gazed at Cataleen. A smile overtook the fear, and he beamed.

Was that my father? Was the girl me? That meant… I had a twin? No way.

I'd never seen photos of my father. But my grandmother was here. And this was Cataleen. She'd never told me she had other children. Or that I had a twin.

"Okay, Cataleen. Last one. Are you ready?"

Another one? I was a triplet?

Cataleen nodded, sweat beading on her forehead.

I tried to ignore the birth-pain cries and imagined myself by the man who had to be my father. Black hair like me. Our faces were similar. My purple eyes came from Cataleen. His were hazel. I reached out to touch his face as he stared at his children with adoration. Just as I should have come in contact, my finger slipped through his face as if it were a mirage.

Another baby cried out from behind me.

"It's another boy!" the woman cried.

"Another son?" My father whooped again.

"Here, let me take one." Fiona walked through me and grabbed the boy in the ducky blanket from my father.

I moved aside.

"Sorry I'm late." Wolf barged in. A stout man followed.

Wolf looked younger. But not much. He must've become a fasgadair shortly after my birth.

"Faolan, you made it." My mother smiled.

My grandmother put the firstborn son in his arms. "They're all here."

"All? How many is *all*?" Wolf—shaken by the question?—jostled the babe.

"Three. Two boys and a girl." The woman helping Cataleen swaddled the last baby in a blanket covered in bears. She placed him in Cataleen's arms.

"Wow." Still cradling the first boy, Wolf rushed to my mother's side and touched her forehead. "Are you well?"

"She's fine," my grandmother said.

The stout man cleared his throat. "I'm sorry to be the bearer of bad news on such a joyous occasion. But we have disturbing news from Sully regarding the children's safety."

"What's he saying?" my father asked Cataleen.

"Here." My mother pulled Drochaid from her neck. "Take this. Faolan and I understand English and Ariboslian." She pointed to the strange man. "This is Declan Cael the third, an elder of my village."

Declan's father?

Once my father wore Drochaid, he returned to Declan's dad. "What were you saying?"

"Eh-hem." He gave his chest a couple quick thumps. "I said I have unfortunate news from Sully regarding your children."

"What's that?" My father scowled at Declan's father.

"They're not safe."

"That's why Cataleen is in America. It's safe. Aodan can't get them here, can he?" my father asked.

"Aodan isn't the concern. And, according to Sully, they're not safe as long as they're together."

Cataleen sucked in her breath. "What does Sully know?"

"There will come a day when you can no longer protect your children. They will still be young. If your sons are with you when this happens, all three of your children will die."

"What?" Holding infant me close, my father neared the man. "That can't be. Honey, tell him he's wrong." His pleading face broke my heart.

Tears slipped down Cataleen's cheeks onto my little brother. "I've never known Sully to be wrong."

"Then where is Sully? Bring him here. Let him give us this news directly. Why trust this man?" My father jabbed a thumb toward Declan's dad.

"As she said, I'm an elder of Notirr. Cataleen can vouch for me."

"Aye, my love. 'Tis true." She spoke through sobs. "We can trust him."

Declan's father moved next to her. "If you care for your children's safety, please allow me to take your sons. I promise to care for one. To raise him as my own. I'll find a good home for the other."

"You can't keep both?" Cataleen's voice cracked. She tried to pull herself up, then fell back onto the pillow.

Declan's father shook his head. "According to Sully, we must separate them for their safety and for God's plans to come to fruition."

"You can't be serious." My father's head ping-ponged between Declan's dad and my mother. A mixture of anger and pain—true anguish—twisted his face. "Please tell me you won't suggest I give up my sons?"

"I can't watch any more of this." My head reeled. I wanted to get away. I squeezed my eyes shut. The ground felt as if it had shifted. I opened my eyes. We no longer stood in the room, but in a swirling, gray vortex. The blue sky returned. As the circling stones stopped, the incomplete Stonehenge and the grassy field reappeared.

Chapter Thirty-Five

I RAN FROM THE broken circles, fell to my knees, pitched forward, and puked. When my stomach settled somewhat, I moved away from the stench. I sat, elbows on my knees, head down, resting on my arms, and tried to breathe. My heart screamed at the injustice, my parents' pain. My father's pain. He died when I was three. How miserable those years must've been, wondering if his missing kids were okay. I could've had a family, brothers. Why would God allow my family to be torn apart?

I screamed, and a flock of birds squawked and fled.

Pepin sat beside me and rested his hand on my shoulder. He didn't say a word. I was grateful for the silence.

Was this what the voyeur in my head wanted me to find out? Declan was my—my *brother*? Acid rolled in my stomach, threatening to rise again. I wanted to tear my clothes or lash out at something. I had been attracted to my brother? My stomach lurched, and my heart ached.

Did the voyeur know about my other brother as well? How did he know any of this?

I grew up in a broken home. No parents. No siblings. I had Bumpah until I was seven. Then I was left with my grandmother who turned mean after his death.

I could've had them all. Even for just a little while. And I wouldn't be here, regretting having had feelings for my brother.

My brother…

We'd almost kissed! I touched my burning cheeks. Thank God, Wolf had been there to stop us.

Wolf…

He knew we were siblings. Hot tears coursed down my face. I was so embarrassed. So ashamed.

But it wasn't my fault. Or Declan's. If people hadn't been keeping secrets from us, we wouldn't have made these mistakes.

The anger I once wore like a protective blanket reemerged. I picked it up, wanting to wrap it around myself again. Better to be angry than hurt. And I was hurt. And angry. At my mother for keeping these secrets. But more so at Wolf. He'd been with me through the entire journey.

But he'd been a fasgadair in wolf form. He never had a chance to tell me. And my mother was in captivity. There had been little opportunity to divulge these secrets before I left Ariboslia last year.

But what about now? Or in Bandia? Or bored on the ship? There had been plenty of opportunities for either to tell me. What else did they keep from me?

What about Declan? What would he think? Would he be too embarrassed to look at me again? Did he know? Was that why he wanted to stay a fasgadair?

Brother. He's my brother.

Who was my other brother?

Rustling in the bushes jarred me. A black-and-white blur dashed out from the trees and headed straight for me, ears flapping, mouth open, tongue flying.

"Rác!"

The dog barreled into me, nearly pushing me over, smothering my face in wet kisses. Just what I needed right now. Furry love.

If Rác was here, then…

Kai sauntered across the grassy plain. "I hoped I'd find you here."

I ran and hugged him, then sobbed into his shoulder.

"Wha—?" He held his arms up as if unsure what to do. Then he hugged me and patted my back. He led me to a stone to sit. He drew something from his sack and unrolled it. Cheese. "I was getting hungry, anyway."

"Huh?"

"Here." He gave me the cloth.

"Oh." I wiped my eyes.

"Why the tears? Are you *that* happy to see me?" He laughed.

"No, I—" I didn't mean to say I wasn't happy to see him. "I mean. That's not it."

"Then what?"

My heart caught in my chest. Part of me was psyched to see him. But another part was angry. He'd abandoned me. Just like everyone else. He wanted me to leave.

But had he? Or was I being overly emotional?

Kai threw me a shy smile, and his dimple appeared. So adorable. He shifted his gaze to Turas. "So, are these old rocks helping you find the rest of your friends?"

"Hmph." Pepin stood and walked back to Stonehenge.

"Not yet."

Kai sidled up close to speak into my ear. "I don't want to offend the little fellow. But I'm curious how those rocks can help."

"After what I've just seen, I trust they will." I caught a whiff of Kai's airy pine scent. Wanting to lean in, I backed away. "Why are you here?"

"What?" He straightened. "We're not friends anymore?"

"You wanted me to leave, so I left."

"Who says I wanted you to leave?"

"You told me to go."

His mouth widened in mock shock. "I did no such thing. Once your ankle felt better, I assumed you'd want to find your friends. I was trying to be helpful."

What *had* happened? My memory failed me. But he was right.

He never told me to leave. Not in so many words. I'd twisted whatever he'd said into an assumption. I had a flair for the dramatic. "That still doesn't answer my question. Why are you here?"

"You know how to make a man feel welcome."

"Sorry. You wouldn't believe what I've been through."

"Care to share?"

"Not really."

Pepin cleared his throat. "I hate to break up the reunion. But, Fallon, we need to find the others." He threw Kai a look that might as well have said, "get lost."

"Mind if I join you?" Kai clearly couldn't read facial cues.

"I don't think that would be wise." Pepin wrinkled his nose as if he smelled something foul.

"Why not?" Kai aimed his puppy-dog eyes at me.

"We can't reveal the pech's secrets to just anyone." Pepin folded his short arms over his chest—short *hairy* arms. Amazing how much body hair curled out of his rolled-up sleeves. "You know too much already."

Kai looked to me as if asking me to override Pepin.

But I didn't really know him either. Rather than come to his defense, I grew suspicious. "Why do you want to be here? Why now? Are you interested in helping me? Or are you curious about Turas?"

Kai shrugged. "I wanted to help, but it was risky. My village banished me, but at least I have my little piece of paradise. If I get caught near a selkie village, they'll throw me in jail. So, I returned home. It was quiet. Too quiet."

"So, you don't want to be alone?" I steeled myself, daring to hope for a better reason.

He drug a toe through the dirt, scuffing his leather shoes. "I guess I'd rather take a risk. Even if the selkie find me in their territory and lock me away. I'd rather risk losing my home, my freedom. Even if I never get to the sea again, which is the worst torture imaginable…even to a sub-selkie like me. Better to spend my life doing something worthwhile for someone I care about than enjoying paradise alone with no purpose."

Someone I care about? He cared about me? If he was manipulating me, he was doing a great job. I sighed. Perhaps I should take a risk too.

Chapter Thirty-Six

PEPIN KEPT SCOWLING. I hoped I made the right decision letting Kai tag along. I already had so many enemies. I didn't want to get on the pech's bad side too.

"Ready?" Pepin placed Drochaid in its depression.

"April 24, 1521 BC. April 24, 1521 BC. April 24, 1521 BC."

Pepin swirled his finger around Drochaid's edge. Once again, the rocks spun. Kai grabbed my shoulder as the rocks swirled into a seemingly solid wall.

When the spinning ceased, we stood in an unbroken Stonehenge. Kai walked around, gazing in the air at the massive stone perfection as he released random expletives of awe.

"This is unbelievable."

"Yes. Let's keep it that way. Particularly among the non-pech communities."

Man. What was Pepin's issue with Kai? I'd never seen him so snarly.

"Whatever you do, stay in the circle." The angel's warning sent a chill through me. No supernatural creatures appeared…yet. But what if a demon arrived while we lingered? I never wanted to face one. "We should go."

Pepin nodded. He scowled and viewed Kai askance. "You'd better stay close."

Kai returned to my side.

"Imagine the last thing you remember on the ship." Pepin shuddered, sounding as if he didn't want me to follow his suggestion. "Based on our last experience, I believe we'll be safe on the water."

As Pepin worked Drochaid, I imagined myself back in the captain's cabin, bracing myself, water sloshing on the floor. The rocks merged into one.

Turas slowed to a stop, and we stood in the cabin. I steadied myself as the ship tilted, then laughed at myself. I didn't need to worry about the ship's sway. No matter how the boat tilted, we remained still, unlike my past-self and the others who were tossed like passengers on a roller coaster.

The boat pitched back and forth. I watched my past-self, tied to the chair, stare in horror at Rowan. Everything not secured rolled from one end of the room to the other. The noise became deafening—winds howled, wood creaked, waves crashed, debris skidded. A wave pushed the door off its hinges and straight toward me. My past-self fought to escape, but the ropes held me.

That was the last thing I remembered.

Evan untied himself and fought the current and swirling debris to reach me. He felt my neck for a pulse. "She's alive. Unconscious, but alive. She hit her head."

The captain appeared in the doorway. "Abandon ship! We're being torn asunder. She's awash. Hurry to the longboats!" He disappeared. Abracham, King Aleksander, and Maili came free of their binds first and helped untie Rowan, Pepin, Cataleen, and Sully. Where were Wolf and Cahal?

King Aleksander clasped Rowan's face. "Save yourself, daughter."

"What are you saying, Father? We're going together."

"I must free Valter."

"No!" Rowan cried. "You can't risk going down there for him. He tried to kill you."

"I must."

"Your Highness"—Abracham grasped Rowan's arm, rooting her—"the lower levels are likely flooded."

"God willing, I'll survive." King Aleksander trudged through the water to the door.

"No!" she yelled and tried to go after him.

Abracham kept a firm grip. "He'll be all right."

"I've got Fallon." Evan threw me over his shoulder and joined the crowd.

I imagined myself trailing everyone out to the upper deck. Pepin and Kai stayed in the same vicinity everywhere I went.

The crew helped women and children into a longboat.

Wolf called out for me.

Evan responded, "She's here."

"I'll take her." Wolf cradled me. "Come. We need to evacuate."

"Valter?" Wolf stopped. His face blanched as if he'd seen a ghost. "How'd you make it out?"

"A–A—" Wet hair stuck to Valter's forehead. His blue lips quivered. "A fasgadair freed me."

"A *what?*" Evan asked.

"Seclusion's made the lad go daft," Wolf said. It sounded funny coming from a guy who looked so young.

"Where's my father?" Rowan asked. "He went to rescue you."

Valter shook his head.

"Get the ladies on a boat." Long strands of gray hair stuck to Abracham's face as he shouted over the din.

But crewmen lowered the full dinghy into the sea.

Someone whistled. "Over here!" A crewman stood next to an empty dinghy.

My mother, Sully, and Pepin climbed aboard. Pepin's skin had taken on a green tinge. He held the seat and the edge in a white-knuckled death grip. Only Sully appeared calm.

Wolf turned to Rowan. "Let's go."

Her eyes gravitated toward the stairs. "How can I leave without him?"

"You must, child." Abracham chucked her chin. "Go. I'll find your father."

"No. I—"

Cahal plucked her up and ran to the dinghy. The vessel pitched hard. Wolf lost his footing, and I slipped from his grasp. A wave caught me and carried me over the ship's edge.

"No!" Wolf screamed. He, Cahal, Rowan, and Evan ran to the edge where I'd disappeared.

"She has to be there." Cahal prepared to jump.

Wolf and Evan each grabbed an arm. Veins bulging in their necks, they tried to restrain him.

"Let me go! I have to save her!"

"If you go in there too, you could die. You won't save her," Evan yelled.

"Then I'll die trying. I can't leave another friend behind."

"She's alive." Wolf yanked Cahal's chin, forcing his attention. "I'm sure of it. God has plans for her. He'll see her through this. Trust Him. If we're to help her, we need to first save ourselves…and the others. Please, Cahal. Help us save them."

Cahal relented, but I've never seen such a tragic look on anyone's face. It twisted in complete agony. My heart melted. He cared enough to risk his life for me. That man had a special place in my heart. This scene secured it for life.

The crewman called to them again. They braced themselves while the dinghy teetered. Rowan and Maili hoisted themselves aboard.

"Where's Valter?" Rowan asked.

"I don't know, lass." Wolf's gaze roamed the ship.

Wolf and Cahal boarded last. The sailors lowered the dinghy, which swung and crashed into the side of the ship as it pitched. Pepin tumbled backward out of the boat.

My friends searched for him. But the sea swallowed him up, and they were helpless, trapped midair on the longboat.

The real-life Pepin shuddered beside me.

"I thought pech sunk like a stone?" I pivoted fully to him. "How'd you survive?"

"A seal."

"A selkie helped you?" Kai leaned closer.

Pepin shrugged. "Or a seal."

The crewmen lowered the dinghy a few feet. Then the rope stuck on one end. The occupants screamed and held on with white-knuckled grips as they dangled precariously on the other side. The rope loosened, and the boat dropped the last few feet, plunging into the raging sea. By some miracle, they didn't lose anyone else.

I stared at Pepin. "How many times can you defeat death?"

He threw me a meek smile.

"Well, I can't follow the boat and look for you," I said.

"Why would you? I'm here. Follow the boat."

Duh.

My first opportunity to walk on water...sort of. Whatever the waves did, they didn't toss Pepin, Kai, or me. Or get us wet. When they raged over our heads, they blocked our view, but otherwise passed through us.

The passengers tied themselves together and to the boat. They clung to each other, wide-eyed and shivering. Hours later, the waves calmed. Cahal's eyes were still wide, his body rigid. Evan's and Wolf's heads bobbed on their limp bodies. Their eyes half-closed. Sully, Cataleen, Rowan, and Maili slept.

This Stonehenge time-travel thing was like being in a virtual reality that didn't allow for movement or touch. Just tracking history as it played out by following it with my mind.

How freaky to control this alternate view of life? Wherever I thought to go, I appeared with Pepin and Kai in their same places wherever I led. They changed their positions from standing straight on two feet, to shifting their weight to another leg, to sitting. At Stonehenge, were we visible in whatever positions we were in now? But then, we'd return at the same moment in time. Should anyone arrive, they'd see us at the exact moment we'd left as if no time had passed. But then, no one had been there when we left, so no one would be there when we arrived. So, it was a moot point. Right?

But what about what the angel said? Were we sitting in the spiritual realm, outside of time and space, where angels and demons may or may not be? Were we sitting ducks there? But when we returned, it was always in the present. So where were we?

My mind exploded. I couldn't think about this anymore.

My legs tired of standing, endlessly following the longboat without moving. I'd rather walk. I tried to follow Pepin and Kai's lead and sit down, but Drochaid tugged against my neck. I couldn't sit and keep Drochaid in the depression unless I took it off and held it. What would happen if I let go? So, I remained standing, leaning against the invisible stone in which Drochaid rested. My legs ached. How much longer would I have to do this?

CHAPTER THIRTY-SEVEN

M Y FEET HURT. MY legs and back ached. Standing still was the worst. Why was I putting myself through this torture? The last time we'd returned, we were refreshed as if no time had passed, because no time *had* passed. Here, wherever we were, probably the spiritual realm, the aches and pains of time passing strengthened the longer we remained. But I didn't have to put myself through this. We had a time machine. "I need to go back. Just for a minute."

"No!" Pepin jumped to his feet and darted to me. "Don't."

So close, I'd just been about to imagine us home. "Why not?"

"You heard the angel's warning about the demons," Pepin said. "We can't go back and forth as often as we want."

"But I'm so tired. At least you guys can sit and rest."

Pepin wiggled his fingers as if beckoning me. "Give me Drochaid."

I grasped the strap.

"It will be all right, Fallon. As long as Drochaid remains in the stone and one of us has a hold. Just don't let go until I have it."

I pulled the cord off my neck and, desperate not to drop it, helped him get it around his. Pepin was so short, the cord angled up, and I feared it might slip off if he slumped. I remained next to him, hands ready.

"Rest. Kai can take a turn if I tire. Isn't that right, Kai?" Pepin threw him an icy stare.

"Gu dearbh," Kai said.

Oh great. Even here, I couldn't understand Ariboslian or any other language without Drochaid. That complicated matters. I returned to Drochaid and grabbed the cord. "What did you say? I can't understand you."

"She doesn't speak Ariboslian or Cianese. Drochaid allows us to communicate with her. But—" Pepin tugged on Drochaid's cord.

Kai nodded and smiled. "I said 'indeed'." He waved me off. "Go rest. I won't talk." He stretched out, resting his head in his hands.

Wait. Pepin had been speaking with Kai all this time. "Pepin, you speak Cianese too?" Was there nothing Pepin couldn't do?

"I travel. Remember?"

"Yes. I remember." His standard answer. Then again, his English wasn't strong. It was probably all he could think to say in few words.

"Kai speak Ariboslian too."

"Yeah, he mentioned that." I glanced at Kai, who raised an eyebrow at me. To be fair, I probably shouldn't speak English without Drochaid. I sat and rubbed my legs. I'd still have much preferred going back and getting refreshed, but Pepin had a point. And this seemed to be working okay. Now it was Pepin's turn to imagine us to the right places. My mind relaxed. I reclined and closed my eyes.

"Tha fios agam càite a bheil seo." I couldn't understand Kai's words, but his enthusiasm was clear in his excited tone.

I opened my eyes and groaned while Kai carried on in Ariboslian. The sun was peeking over the horizon, and the dinghy had washed up on the shore with all its passengers passed out.

"Wait." I hopped up, stretched, and trudged to my post. Pepin slipped Drochaid's cord over his head and put it on mine. I turned so Drochaid was behind me and slumped against the invisible stone. "What were you saying?"

"I recognize this place. That's why I couldn't find them. I didn't even consider traveling this far north. How did they end up so much further north than you?" Kai rubbed his shoulder. "The water current should have brought you much closer together."

"It must've been God's plan to separate us," Pepin said. "Had I not found the dark pech, I wouldn't have learned about Turas. Had you not found Kai, we still wouldn't know where we are." Pepin twisted his back one way, then the next, causing staccato pops that made me shudder.

Did I just hear Pepin say something positive about Kai? Progress. "So, where are we?" It just looked like a beach, similar to where Kai found me.

Kai grimaced. "Selkie territory."

"Oh no."

"Why?" Pepin squished his caterpillar eyebrows together. "What happens in selkie territory?"

"If they're found, the selkie will lock them away… Forever."

****

Once the sun was high in the sky, Cahal woke. His body jerked, eyes wide, as he took in his surroundings. I was glad Kai suggested taking a turn at the helm since we had a long wait. I relieved him of his duty.

Cahal shook those closest to him and told them to wake up. He untied himself, stepped around their splayed bodies, and jumped free of the craft.

One by one my friends stirred, each face masked in pain as their senses returned to them. Like zombies, they rose, untied themselves, and escaped the boat. Once the boat was clear, they pulled it further up the beach.

Wolf surveyed the beach. "We need to find Fallon."

"Aye," Cahal agreed. "You, Cataleen, and Maili search that way." He pointed up the beach to the north. "Evan, Rowan, and Sully, follow me this way." He nodded toward the south.

They assembled themselves per Cahal's orders and headed out. Sully ambled behind his group.

"Which group should we follow?" I glanced at each group increasing the distance between each other.

Pepin's head ping-ponged back and forth between each group. The bewilderment on his face offering no insight.

"Pick one of us."

Jolting, I whirled toward Sully.

He looked over his shoulder in our direction. "If you need to, return here and follow the others." Then he faced forward once more.

Evan turned back to Sully. "What's that, Sully?"

Sully snickered. "Just thinking out loud."

Pepin, Kai, and I stared at each other, mouths agape.

"Can Sully see us?" I raised an eyebrow at Pepin.

"I've never understood Sully's abilities. He sees in ways I can't understand." Pepin scratched his beard. "Now I wonder about the times I've caught him talking to himself."

I chuckled. Sully's surprises were endless. "Should we follow Sully's group?" I wanted to learn more about him and his abilities and talk to him.

"Perhaps we should follow Wolf's group." Pepin spread his hands, palms up, as if offering no choice. "I think they're safer with Sully."

"Good point." Disappointing, but smart.

"I agree," Kai said. "The group heading north isn't far from Taobh Na Mara, a seaside village. They're more likely to run into trouble first."

While Wolf's group grew smaller in the distance, I imagined us behind them, and there we appeared, like magic.

****

The landscape grew rocky. We trailed Wolf and the others weaving up a path along a cliff. Waves crashed below us. Seals sunned themselves along the rock face.

"I hope those are just seals," Cataleen whispered. "If not, this is selkie territory we're heading into."

"Aye." Wolf halted, forcing his troupe to stop short to avoid running into him. "How do ye suggest we proceed? Fallon might've come this way. She wouldn't question if this was a selkie village. She'd be alone. Possibly hurt. Hungry. She'd be more concerned about getting help and finding us than the consequences of meeting a selkie."

The group murmured agreement.

"Let's veer from the path and seek someone in human form. If it's a male, we'll send a male. If it's a female, we'll send a female," Maili suggested.

Of one accord, the others followed Wolf into the woods. They pushed through brush while Pepin, Kai, and I floated right through the branches. We were the perfect spies. Unless you were like Sully, we were undetectable. A creepy feeling washed over me. Was I ever watched unaware? I shivered.

"Are you cold?" Kai put an arm around me.

I wanted to wrap my arm around him, but I couldn't. Instead, I shrugged his arm off. "I'm fine."

They ventured into someone's backyard. Sheets hanging on a clothesline billowed in the breeze. A young girl with long black hair sat in the grass, playing with dolls.

"I'll go." Cataleen stepped from the cover toward the girl.

The girl stopped her chatter, her doll in hand, frozen in midair as Maili approached. I pursued with Pepin and Kai.

"Hello," Cataleen called as she neared the statue of a girl. She crouched down to her. "Have you seen a young woman with long black hair and purple eyes, a little taller than me?"

The girl blinked. Her mouth still open, her hand still suspended in midair, holding her doll, she shook her head.

"How about a small man with long red hair and a beard?"

"Ahoy!" a woman's voice called.

A woman appeared from behind the hanging sheets. She ran toward the girl, probably her daughter. "Who are you?"

Cataleen straightened. "My apologies, ma'am. I'm looking for my daughter."

The woman kept a suspicious eye on my mother, but most of the alarm had faded.

Cataleen repeated her description of me.

"I'm sorry. We've not had any visitors to this village in months." She grabbed her daughter's hand and pulled her away. "We can't help you."

She walked toward the house, her daughter tripping behind her as she tried to look back.

After they disappeared into the house, Cataleen returned to the woods. "We should return to the boat. Perhaps the others have found her."

"They should be more careful approaching people. Don't they know what selkie look like?"

"What do you mean?" Selkie had a certain look?

Kai motioned to his face. "Dark hair, dark eyes, tan skin. We all have these features. That woman and her daughter have probably never seen light-colored hair in their lives. But they know gachen have that coloring. We all do. Which is why I didn't know you were gachen. Your skin is pale, and you have purple eyes, but I didn't realize gachen could have black hair."

"My father had black hair. But he was human," I said. "But Wolf has black hair too. And Evan. And everyone I've met from Kylemore. And what about the selkie woman from Saltinat? She was blonde."

"Saltinat? The underwater city?" Slack-jawed, Kai grasped his chest as if his heart might stop. "It's not a myth?"

I shook my head. "I've been there."

Pepin sandwiched himself between us, facing Kai. He pointed a stubby digit in Kai's chest. "You're a selkie?" He turned to me. "And you knew this? Yet you still insisted on bringing him along? Have you learned nothing?"

"We're not Cairbre and Deirdra. He doesn't appear to be a full selkie, and I'm only half gachen. And I'm here…fulfilling my duty. I didn't push it aside like Cairbre did." Though I really, really wanted to.

"Hmph." Pepin moved away and dropped down to sit, mumbling under his breath.

Kai sidled up next to me. "So, tell me about Saltinat."

****

Evan and Wolf collected crabs and cooked them over a fire. Maili seemed rather disgusted but ate anyway. My stomach growled. Too bad we couldn't eat some too.

Kai reached into his pouch and handed Pepin and me some dried fish. Not much, it was better than nothing.

"Thank you." I bit into my piece.

"Yes. Thanks." Pepin pinched his fish between two fingers and inspected it, his nose wrinkled in disgust.

I swallowed. "Perhaps we should have followed the other group."

"Let's stay a bit longer." Pepin nibbled the fish and gagged.

"There they are!" voices called.

Everyone stood and watched the approaching men, swords swinging from their hips. Wolf and his group sought escape, then looked at the men, apparently deciding to talk to them rather than run.

"Ahoy!" one called out. "What purpose have you on these shores?"

Wolf neared the men, holding his arms out while Maili and Cataleen backed away. "We've been shipwrecked, sir. We're looking for missing friends."

"They haven't appeared in our village."

"We understand that. We're planning to sleep here and resume our search in the other direction tomorrow."

"Where are you from?"

"We've traveled from Bandia."

"You're gachen then?" The man's right eyebrow rose.

"Aye." Wolf sighed.

"Come with us."

Wolf backed away. "As I said, we're going to wait and continue our search. We won't intrude on your village."

"Regardless, we can't chance you coming upon any selkie. Come with us."

Wolf shook his head. "I don't think so."

The men drew their swords.

"I do." The lead man waved his sword. "If you don't want your women to get hurt, make sure they follow close behind. Otherwise, my men's orders are to kill."

Wolf looked at Cataleen, then Maili. They both nodded and bowed their heads.

CHAPTER THIRTY-EIGHT

THE MEN BROUGHT WOLF and his group to a vacant home. They put the girls in one room. The men in another. Pepin, Kai, and I stayed outside in the hallway. Where a man stood guard.

Another man approached. "I've spoken with the castle guard. They will be here tomorrow to take the gachen into captivity. They're combing the beach for the others now."

The man standing guard bowed, and the one who spoke turned and left.

"I can't believe this is happening. Kai, how will we rescue them?"

Kai shrugged. "We'd have to get into the castle somehow, but it's impenetrable without an army. We're no match for them."

"But our God is," Pepin reminded us. "There's a way."

"Should we keep following them? Or should we leave and figure out a way to free them?"

"When we get back to Turas, will it be as if we'd never left?" Kai asked.

"That's what happened last time." Then again, I didn't have a watch. But Pepin had an internal clock. "Right?"

"Right. And if we stay, we don't risk attracting the demon's attention," Pepin said.

"Then we have nothing to lose if we keep going. I say, let's follow them to the castle and see what we can find out," I said. "As long as you're willing to take turns with Drochaid so I can rest."

Pepin and Kai nodded.

But what about food? I was starving. We may have been outside time and space, but my body was aware of passing time without proper rest or food. If only we'd planned for this and packed more to eat.

****

The next morning, guards arrived to escort my friends. The guards stuffed them in a carriage with an armed guard. Two more armed guards followed on their own horses. We traveled inland a little. Then the road turned back toward the sea. We rode along the cliff side, the ocean to our left. Another village emerged. White rectangular homes lined both sides of the street, up and down the cliff side. A massive castle loomed in the distance. From here, it appeared like a mass of rectangles and cylinders with jagged and pointy tops jutting into the sky to differing heights. We halted at a gate. The driver spoke to the guards, and the gate lifted. We arrived in a courtyard, passed the massive front door, and rounded a corner.

"I guess the front entryway is too good for them," I said.

The carriage stopped, but the horses continued to stamp their feet on the cobblestones. Wolf and everyone else filed out. The guard led them into the castle down many winding steps and halls, tossed them inside a cell, and locked the door behind him.

"Wolf?" Cahal emerged from the shadows.

"Cahal!" Wolf hugged Cahal, then the others. Everyone was there.

I breathed easier knowing everyone was together. But we had a much bigger problem. *How* could we get them out without ending up behind bars ourselves?

"We've seen enough," Kai said. "Time to make plans."

"Wait." I had an idea. Sully. His gray eyes glanced in my direction, then to the others. They were busy filling in the gaps of what had happened to one another. Sully crept along the wall to where he'd be less likely to be noticed.

"Sully, can you hear me?"

He nodded.

"What can we do? How can we get you out?"

"Use Turas," he whispered.

"How? We're not really here. Only you can see us."

"That is because you're in the past."

"But we need to go back in time. Turas is broken. We have to travel to 1521 BC to when it was whole to get it to work."

"But then you can travel to any time."

"Right, but…" I paused. "So, you're saying we could meet you here in jail, in the present time? Will everyone be able to see us?"

"God will free us. In the present time, connect everyone to Drochaid to pull them into the spiritual realm."

"What?" Evan approached Sully. "Did you say something?"

"Bah." Sully waved his hand. "Pay me no mind."

Evan shook his head and returned to his prior conversation.

I turned to Kai and Pepin. "Let's go back." With that, the cell disappeared. The swirling resumed. Gray circled us, and the blue sky reappeared. The stones stopped, delivering us to the incomplete Stonehenge. I exhaled, relieved to be in the present. The aches and hunger I'd experienced disappeared.

"Hmm."

"What?" I asked Kai.

"I was starving. But now I'm not." He rubbed his stomach. "I guess I shouldn't have wasted that fish." He reached into the pouch. "Ha! It's still here."

"Wonderful."

I didn't know Pepin could be so sarcastic. "I guess that's because we never ate it. Not in this reality." Bizarre.

"I'm not tired either," he said.

"I think we're agreed." Pepin rolled his eyes. "Time for our rescue mission. Since we don't know what to expect, let's proceed with caution. Fallon, no matter what happens, don't let Drochaid disconnect with Turas."

We'd become adept at returning to 1521. With the angel's warning in mind, I didn't dawdle. I conjured the image of the jail cell we'd returned from, where my friends were captive while I enjoyed my little reprieve in paradise. A cloud of guilt rained down on me.

When Turas stopped spinning, the jail cell materialized.

"Pepin?" Cataleen rose and moved toward him. "Where'd you come from?"

Pepin cleared his throat. "I, uh… Well, that's…"

That was unexpected.

"'Tis good to see you, mate. But yer on the wrong side of this cage," Wolf said.

Right. I imagined myself outside the door. Pepin and Kai stayed where they were behind bars. Were they now outside the spiritual realm?

The others stirred. Murmurs erupted among them.

"How are you here?" Maili asked.

"Who's the lad with you?" Cahal asked.

"Have you seen Fallon?" Evan asked.

"How did you get in here?" Rowan asked.

Pepin's head bounced from one person to the next with no opportunity to answer before the next question hit him. "Fallon is here." He turned to me. His eyes bulged, and he searched around.

"Pepin." I waved my hand. Didn't he see me?

The others followed his gaze, but their faces remained blank as if I didn't exist. "Where?"

Kai walked to where I had been standing, feeling the air.

"Kai." I waved my hand in the air.

His blank stare continued to search where I'd been. Oh no. My stomach sank like Pepin. This was bad. Very bad. Had I just delivered them to jail?

Kai reached through the bars as if he knew I was nearby. I imagined myself beside him, and we entwined fingers. His face relaxed, and his crooked grin appeared.

"Where'd the lad go?" Wolf asked.

"Kai?" Pepin kept looking around. "What is happening? Fallon?"

I gripped Kai's hand tight, moved to Pepin, and put my hand on his shoulder.

"Fallon!" Relief flooded his face. "What happened?"

"I guess travelers not attached to Drochaid get delivered. Tell them to hold hands. When they're ready, I'll grab your hand. Hopefully, I can pull us out of here." I lifted my hand from Pepin's shoulder, and everyone gasped.

"Everyone, link hands," he said.

Everyone moved to ensure they were holding hands. Then Pepin reached out to Cataleen. "Whatever happens, don't let go."

I grabbed Pepin's hand. *Please let this work.* Excited whispers filled the chamber. I imagined us outside the barred wall. We emerged on the other side in the same formation. More gasps.

"Nobody let go." I returned to the current Stonehenge.

Chapter Thirty-Nine

"We need to go back." Kai stared, unblinking. He seemed to vibrate as if he was plugged into an electrical charge.

"To the dungeon?" Was he insane? Risk capture? Risk demons? "Why would we go back? My friends are all here. We can resume our quest."

"What is your quest exactly?"

"To kill Na'Rycha."

"What if God brought you here for another purpose?"

"What purpose?"

"Free my people?"

"What are you talking about?"

"Remember, I told you about my banishment."

I nodded.

"And what happens if I get caught in selkie territory."

"You get jailed." The light turned on. "But we need to stay under the radar if we're going to get out of here."

"Under the what?"

"The rad—We need to get in and out unnoticed."

"You traveled all this way to get in and out? You're going back to Bandia because all is well there now? *That's* your plan? Just to get away until the vampires got bored and left?"

I hadn't spent that much time with him in the grand scheme of things. But I had no idea he could be so sarcastic. First Pepin. Now Kai. Was it me? "I see your point."

"Perhaps, this is what you're here for…to free my people."

"What good would that do?"

"Well, it might start a civil war, but you would gain support. Perhaps an entire army of support." He moved his head closer, dark eyes staring so intently they seemed to penetrate me. "Wouldn't that be helpful in your quest?"

"Possibly." Okay…definitely. "But how can we help? Won't it end in disaster? Selkie and gachen can't coexist, remember?"

"'Tis a lie," Rowan said.

I snapped my head toward her. "How do you know?"

"We encountered some selkie. They tried to help us before the authorities caught us. They told us everything." Rowan leaned against a rock. "Ships sail to this land and never return because the selkie capture and jail them. Some elders, selkie elitists, in Cairbre and Deirdra's day took advantage of the situation and made up the lie about the gachen-selkie attraction to keep the races apart. They want nothing more than to keep their isolated society of gachen who turn into seals. But that's all they are—gachen who turn into seals. Nothing more."

Was that true? "How can you know they're telling the truth?"

"They were selkie. None of us felt an attraction."

"Maybe it takes time to develop?" I eyed Kai.

"Fallon." She said it in her princess voice, so full of authority and disdain as she clasped her hands. "Why else would they capture gachen and never set them free?"

"But they set me free…from Saltinat."

"That was a different society of selkie. Had you come across any selkie men?"

"No."

She crossed her arms. "You had nothing to expose."

Was that why they threatened those who were banished, like Kai, with imprisonment if they ever returned? Because they might fight a system that wanted to remain a specific way? Offering them the choice between paradise or captivity?

"What choice do we have?" I lifted my empty hands as if demonstrating our lack of options. "We don't know where to go from here. Perhaps Kai is right. Perhaps this is why we're here. Let's free these people and see what happens."

"Is everyone agreed?" Wolf asked.

Nods and ayes came from the ranks.

Pepin grasped my arm. "Don't forget the angel's warning. The more we tap into Turas's power, the more likely we are to attract unwanted attention."

"I'll move quickly, Pepin. It will be okay."

He released his grip, but his stony expression didn't change. I hadn't convinced him. But he dropped his shoulders in defeat. "Don't let go of Fallon until it's time to reveal yourself to those we're rescuing. To be safe."

Kai grasped my hand and threw me a huge grin. His dimples deeper than ever, sending a thrill through me. I didn't get an electric zap as I had with Declan. I seriously hoped that had something to do with the fact that we were superhuman bizarro twins. Or, well, triplets. But there was something in Kai's touch. In that smile. Something comforting, a sense of what home should feel like.

Pepin grabbed my free hand in his thick, stubby one. "Again, don't let Drochaid free of its place in Turas. And be quick."

We returned to 1521. The moment we arrived, I imagined the cells we'd rescued my friends from. I couldn't see anything but a flickering light at the end of the hallway. Something thumped, followed by clicks and clanks. Footsteps and heavy breathing came my way, growing louder and louder, in synch with my ever-deafening heartbeat.

Guards rushed into the cell where our friends had been.

"Find them," the tallest called out. "They can't have gotten far."

Uh. Actually, they did. I chuckled.

Kai and Pepin's grips tightened. Kai waved me forward, down the hall.

We came to another cell and went inside. Many of the occupants peered through the bars. King Aleksander and Abracham among them. Others remained on the floor.

I imagined us into their midst. Kai let go. One by one prisoners noticed us, tugged on others, and pointed.

"Kai?" one old man cried in a raspy voice.

"We're here to free you. But you must grasp hands with one another and don't let go until we say."

Many bedraggled gachen and selkie with matted hair rushed toward me, squeezing me in. Stifled cries rang out as they clasped hands and noticed me and Pepin. They clung to one another, checking the line to ensure everyone connected to me.

"Fallon?" King Aleksander said. "How—?" He looked to Abracham as if to confirm he saw me too.

"I'll explain later," I said. "Just hold tight."

"This way!" Came a voice from down the hall. Shuffling feet grew louder.

I sucked in my breath. *Please don't let them see us.* "Where now?"

"Down the hall. Check all the cells." Kai motioned toward the guard's voices, his hand waved with impatience.

"This cell is empty too," a guard called.

I released a trapped breath. Good. Everyone is linked. I imagined us in the direction Kai pointed.

We repeated the process in the next few cells, and there were far too many people. "How many more cells are there?"

"I'm not sure," Kai said. "Let's get them to safety and return to check for more."

"We can't keep going back and forth. It's too risky," Pepin cautioned, his voice sharp.

"So is trying to bring too many people with us," Kai said.

"How about a few more, to lessen the number of trips?"

Pepin consulted the heavens and sighed. "As you wish."

We cleared out another cell. Then I imagined us back, delivered the gachen and selkie—whoever I'd rescued—and left them to my friends for explanations. Pepin, Kai, and I returned to the castle dungeons.

By the third rescue, my body felt heavy, like I could sleep for a month. Why was traveling within our current time so exhausting?

Pepin grew more annoyed. With each trip, the wrinkles on his forehead carved deeper.

The final cell we cleared out appeared to be the last. We'd reached a dead end at the lowest level.

"This must be it," Kai said.

Finally. I got us home and left the circle. I sat on the grass away from the crowds.

My mother sat next to me. "Turas is remarkable. You and Pepin step in, the rocks spin, blocking you from view, and when they stop, the place is full of people. So strange. Yet amazing. God is amazing."

I nodded and slid away. How could she give up her sons? How could she never tell me about them? She had plenty of opportunity.

Rowan hugged me. "Thank you for rescuing my father. I'm forever in your debt."

A man approached and grasped my arm. "Thank you." He planted a kiss on my cheek. "May I ask the name of my rescuer?"

"Uh." I pointed to Kai talking to a small group of people. "That's Kai. The tall one with the dimples." Pepin sat beside me. "And this is Pepin."

"And your name?" he asked.

"Uh. Fallon." Why was I so uncomfortable?

The man grasped my hand. "From the depths of my soul, I thank you." He lifted my arm into the air. "All hail Fallon!"

Choruses of "Hail Fallon!" rang out followed by more shouts and cheers.

My face grew hot, and the stranger lowered my arm.

"It was God who saved you," I said. That should have been my first response. But it was too late. People swarmed me, grasping my hand, swearing their undying allegiance.

What had I done? And what were we going to do with all these people?

****

As expected, the excitement dwindled. People lounged about, wondering what would happen next.

Kai kept viewing me askance. He seemed ready to end his conversation but had difficulty getting away. He put a finger up as if holding them off for a moment and headed my way.

"So, what's your plan?" I asked as he approached.

"*My* plan?" he asked.

"Of course. I understand you wanting to rescue them. How could we not? It was a great opportunity. But now what? We have no place for them. No food. No water. To your government, they're wanted criminals. They can't return to their homes. What do you intend to do?"

He ran his fingers through his hair and grabbed a clump, giving me a longer glimpse at his unveiled forehead. "What am I supposed to do?"

"We could use Turas to transport them to someplace else, but where? With the fasgadair, our homes aren't safe, and with the selkie, these lands aren't safe here either," I said.

"And everyone is hungry," Cataleen added.

"I suppose there's no way to keep Turas's secret after this." Pepin wagged his head, his bushy eyebrows drooping.

"Is that your biggest concern right now, Pepin?" I slammed my hands on my hips. "You could help us figure out how to care for these people."

"I may have an idea."

CHAPTER FORTY

THE SUN TOOK ITS sweet time setting. I itched for Pepin's return. Most everyone was grumbling about how hungry they were. Some even commented that they were better off in jail. At least they were fed, even if it was maggot infested. If I heard one more person gripe about food and want to return to their cell, I'd drag them back.

One thing was for certain—the selkie-gachen magnetism was a lie.

Did that mean what I felt for Kai—whatever that was—was real? Did he feel anything for me?

I shook my head. I had to stop thinking like this. I couldn't get attached. Besides, I had more important things to do. I couldn't be like Cairbre and let someone keep me from fulfilling my mission.

A figure emerged from the tree line. Pepin. He looked especially small from this distance. He ran a few steps, slowed, then picked up his pace again.

I sprinted to meet him. "That was fast. We took two days to travel last time."

"The pech have underground lairs everywhere." He caught his breath. Sweat beaded his forehead. He must've been running. "I sought help from pech on this side of the lake."

"So? What happened?" I glanced at the crowd. "The natives are getting restless, and I can't take much more."

"The pech have agreed. If the refugees will promise to keep Turas's ability and the underground lairs a secret, they will help."

"How long will they be able to help?" Kai stepped closer. "These people need a permanent residence. That might require overthrowing the government."

Pepin shook his head. "For now, they have a place to stay. I don't think you'll get their help in overthrowing the government. But we can discuss that later. For now, gather them up and have them follow me."

****

We followed Pepin for what felt like hours—hard to say, though, without the sun. I praised God that everyone was tired. It kept them quiet except for occasional grumbles. But it was slow going. They kept stumbling. Even Pepin was exhausted. A grimy elderly woman who reeked of body odor and death leaned on me. She was all I could handle. Kai and the rest of my friends supported some. But many prisoners had been locked up for too long. They tried to help each other, but their efforts were futile.

By the time the sun made an appearance, pech ushered us underground. I waited to go in last. I couldn't be too close to these people in those tunnels. And I felt better having no one behind me should I need to turn back.

We stooped as we wove through pech ant-farm tunnels. Poor Cahal nearly bent in half. Pain masked his face, and he braced his back with his right hand. But he never complained.

Standing on the promises…

Pepin led us to a large room with a stone floor and ceiling where we could all stand without hitting our heads. Tables had been pushed aside with chairs stacked on top to make room for everyone. Dark pech swarmed in delivering blankets. Too small, but better than nothing. If people curled up, they provided protection from the floor and the cool air. With space limited, some people ended up under the tables, but they all fit.

More pech entered with bowls of hot soup. Since there wasn't much walking space, those closer to the entrance took bowls and passed them until everyone had been served.

"Ahem." Sully craned his neck to stand. "If you don't mind, I'd like to say a prayer before we eat."

The crowd shuffled—some in agreement, others appeared uncomfortable—but none protested.

"Father, Almighty God, thank You for rescuing me and my friends, both old and new, from imprisonment. Thank You for bringing us to this place and providing this meal. Thank You for the pech's generosity, hospitality, and trust. And thank You for being with us. I know You will see us through these difficulties, and I thank You in advance for what You're about to do. Please bless us all. Amen."

Sully sat, and all was quiet. Then chatter and slurping echoed in the cavern. One by one, bowls were tipped and emptied. We passed them back to the entryway where pech collected them.

I tried not to think about what might happen in the event of a fire. Or if the roof collapsed. With us packed in like sardines, there was no escape. Was there even enough air in here for all of us? I couldn't breathe. I gulped air as if it might be my last.

Kai stared at me. "What's wrong?"

"Can't." I gulped air. My chest heaved. "Breathe."

"She's afraid of confined spaces," Wolf said. "She's panicking."

Kai gathered me into him. My head against his chest. He wrapped his arms around me. "You're okay. Close your eyes. Imagine the view from my home. The water sparkling in the sunlight. The bright sky. Feel the breeze sweeping through."

I obeyed, listened to Kai's heartbeat, and tried to picture it.

"You're flying through the open air," he continued, his voice through his chest soothing.

My breathing slowed. I could almost feel the breeze. The dank air lightened. My heart slowed, syncing up with his.

"Listen to the gulls."

Kai shifted. I could hear the seagulls in the distance. I flew, but in human form. My arms splayed, carried by the wind. Kai appeared beside me and grasped my hand. We flew together. He threw me his dimply smile, then morphed into a dolphin. I grabbed his fin, and the air transformed to water. We swam without getting wet. Kai brought me to the bottom. I stood on the grass and let go. He swam away. The water dissolved to air.

I was back in the field of my typical dream with Declan in his place on the shore. The lights appeared, and the hazy image cleared, revealing a ship's deck. A row of people stood at attention, facing the window. Their eyes. Fasgadair.

"You're a fasgadair," I said to whoever's mind I linked with, only half aware I'd spoken.

"I suppose there's no point in blocking the image." He didn't sound too bothered that I'd found out. He dismissed his fasgadair crew and headed below decks.

"But who are you that you're able to share a mind-link with me?"

"I'd love to discuss that with you. Let's meet."

"You're on a ship. How are you going to meet me?" Oh no. Was he on his way here?

"Indeed. That's the plan. Why do you think I keep asking to meet you?"

Could he read my mind?

"I'm *in* your mind. Of course, I can read it."

I shivered. I'd have to keep any thoughts I wanted to protect hidden.

"Good luck with that. But out of curiosity, what are you trying to keep hidden from me?"

Nope. He wasn't going to trick me. I had to take control of this. "Why did you want me to find out about my birth?"

"Did you have a chat with your dear ol' mum?"

"I found out about Declan. But why would *you* care about that?"

"That's all? Just Declan?"

"There was another. We're triplets."

"And what of the third?"

"I don't know."

"Perhaps you should ask her more about that."

Would my mother tell me? Or should I go back to Stonehenge?

"Stonehenge?"

Oh no. I turned toward the Declan, hoping he'd wake me.

"What is Stonehenge?"

Come on, Declan. Come on, Declan. Get me out of here.

In a split second, with imperceptible movements, Declan charged.

****

I woke to steady breathing and a heartbeat. I'd fallen asleep on Kai's chest? My memory of the night before overwhelmed me. My panic attack. Heat warmed my face. I peeled myself away, careful not to rouse him. Too late. We locked eyes. He smiled. Inexplicable feelings coursed through me.

I lowered my gaze, stretched like it was no big deal, and put more distance between us. A breeze rushed by.

"How'd we get outside?"

Kai sat up. "You passed out. I carried you."

It must've been tough to carry me through those tunnels. I wanted to hug him, but I kept my distance. "Thank you."

As if my panic attack and Kai's rescue weren't bad enough, there was also last night's dream. I groaned. Fasgadair were on their way. How did a random fasgadair connect with my mind? Actually, I'd used the mind-link on him. How? I had no idea who this Freakshow was. I shook my head. However it happened, I messed up thinking about Stonehenge. I had to be more careful. I had to keep him from finding out about its power. Somehow, I'd have to block my thoughts.

Then again, everyone around here called it Turas. Even if he asked, would anyone know what he was talking about?

"Is something wrong?" Kai asked.

"The fasgadair are on their way. I don't when or how many, but they're coming."

****

My friends and I sat in a dark room with nothing but a long low table—a stone slab. The pech present sat at one end on low stools. The rest of us on the ground. Even on the ground, Cahal kept banging the table with his legs.

I kept my focus on the faces around the table, not on the smallness of the room.

Hreidmar, the dark pech's king, drilled us about the fasgadair. He pulled on the three braids dangling from his chin. "So, on your lands, the pech stayed out of the fight?"

Pepin nodded. "But the threat started small and grew over centuries. The fasgadair were satisfied to control Diabalta at first. When Aodan came into power and organized them, they stole Ceas Croi from our people. The pech should have gotten involved then, but they abandoned their homes and escaped through the underground passages. Not one sword was drawn."

Hreidmar shook his head and clicked his tongue. A good sign. Perhaps he wouldn't make the same mistake.

"Aodan's death last year fueled Morrigan's anger. She brought Na'Rycha to power with the sole intent of capturing Fallon...and killing every—"

Hreidmar jumped from his seat, toppling his stool and interrupting Pepin, and pointed a sausage finger at me. "She's the reason this threat is headed for our shores?"

"Does it matter?" Pepin spread his pudgy hands. "This threat was inevitable. And according to prophecy, Fallon's part of the solution, not the problem."

Hreidmar righted his stool and threw me an accusatory look as he settled back down.

Pepin cleared his throat. "Morrigan is the problem. She always has been. Through it all, the pech remained hidden. They're willing to join the battle now. But they waited too long. The fasgadair army is too powerful. The pech can't fight on their own. They no longer have the freedom to move around as you have."

"Hmph." Hreidmar scoffed. "We're not exactly roaming the lands freely."

"My people waited too long. Given our experience, I don't believe it's wise for you to stay out of the fight," Pepin pressed his point.

"I should have joined the fight when it was winnable," confessed King Aleksander. "If I had, we might've stopped the infestation."

"But you don't know how many fasgadair will reach our shores." Hreidmar smacked the table.

"True," Abracham agreed. "Regardless of how many there are to start, they'll increase their numbers by turning selkie into fasgadair. They'll overtake the selkie lands in a matter of days. King Aleksander compared it to an infestation. He's correct. The best time to eliminate an invasive species is when they first appear. Don't wait until they spread."

"Right." Pepin's head bobbed, bouncing his braid. "The pech have numbers the selkie aren't aware of."

"How do they spread?" Hreidmar asked.

Abracham grimaced. "'Tis rather unpleasant. The fasgadair drinks their victim's blood, then, if the victim drinks the fasgadair's blood in return, they become a fasgadair. When the fasgadair want to grow their numbers, they can do so rather easily. I don't know about selkie, but most gachen would prefer to live as a fasgadair than die. And sometimes they're forced."

"Hmmm." Frowning, Hreidmar tugged his braided beard.

"But we're not warriors. We've had peace for centuries," another dark pech said.

"Peace?" Wolf asked. "Or avoidance?"

"It has served us well." Hreidmar shrugged. "If the selkie are aware of our existence, they don't know our whereabouts."

"They do now," I said under my breath.

Unimpressed looks came at me from those within earshot.

"We should never have agreed to help," the smallest pech whined.

"We don't stand a chance against the fasgadair," another said.

"Do you continue our ancestor's traditions?" Pepin asked. "Do you still forge swords and knives? Do you compete in the annual Turnering av Stryke?"

The dark pech nodded.

"Then you have skills," Pepin said. "And weapons."

"In theory," another dark pech said.

I glanced at all my friends, wondering if we should pull the God card. Perhaps it was best not to say. That tended to make people abandon us.

"We're trusting God to come to our aid. He will help us," Pepin said.

Way to stand for your faith, Pepin. Let's see how this plays out.

The pech grumbled amongst themselves. Every few moments, they'd peer our way, then return to their conversation. They straightened and turned to us.

"We are not familiar with this God you speak of, but we've seen what you've been capable of thus far. You made Turas function. Something we've failed to do. You credit your God with this work. If your beliefs are correct, your God used Turas to rescue a great number of people from imprisonment and lead you to us. Therefore, we will assist with weaponry and on the battlefield. We'll see if this God of yours shows up." Hreidmar stroked his braids and motioned to the others who nodded.

Although I believed God was always with us, I, too, prayed for Him to show up and intervene on our behalf...somehow.

I believe, God. Help my unbelief.

****

"Good morning, refugees," Hreidmar called.

I rubbed my eyes and sat up on my mat. Hreidmar, bouncing on his toes, held his hands behind his back. My friends roused and sat up on their mats. I was grateful they'd agreed to sleep outside. I never wanted to go back in those tunnels if I could help it.

"We've heard news of your escape but have no fear. The selkie will not organize a search for you or the escapees." Hreidmar coughed.

"They have a much bigger problem." He surveyed the crowd. "Human-like creatures have reached our shores. Last night they attacked Taobh Na Mara, and they're seizing the castle as we speak. These creatures are draining victims of their blood. These creatures, I assume, are the fasgadair you spoke of."

Let the battle begin…

CHAPTER FORTY-ONE

K AI HEADED OUT TO rally those who'd been banished around the island. Maili got to work making bows and arrows and teaching archery. Cahal and Wolf taught the refugees how to fight with weapons and in hand-to-hand combat. Evan and Rowan educated the refugees and the dark pech on the fasgadair, their strengths, weaknesses, the power they have over unbelievers, and how to kill them. We'd become a fasgadair-exterminator academy.

Maili showed me how to handle a bow, but the arrows kept flopping to the ground. Either I didn't nock it in the right place, or I didn't anchor it to my mouth correctly. Or I released the tension incorrectly. Amazing how delicately you had to release it, but I got the hang of it. The arrow shot ahead every time. Now if only I could hit the target.

"You're doing well. Your body needs to get used to setting up and releasing the arrow first. The aim will come. Just keep practicing." Maili retrieved an arrow from her quiver and shot it across the field into the center of the target in one swift movement.

Show off. She probably learned to shoot a bow when she was three. That was her village's weapon of choice. It made sense. They were a bunch of tree dwellers.

My mind kept returning to the prior night's dream. Who was my other brother? Why did this fasgadair care? Theories tumbled in my mind. I could ask Cataleen. But then she'd wonder how I knew about them at all. I didn't feel like explaining my travels back in time. Truly, I didn't feel like talking to her at all. How could she keep all this from me?

I nocked an arrow, anchored it to my cheek, focused on the stuffed sack with the giant *X*, and released. "Ow!" The string smacked my forearm…again. The giant red blotch had deepened in color. What was I doing wrong?

My arrow stuck in the bag far southeast of center. I'd overcorrected from the northwest. But at least it hit the bag and didn't go sailing past. Again.

Enough of this. I rubbed my sore forearm as if that helped. Time to find out who my other brother was.

I pulled Pepin aside. "I need to go back to Turas. Will you help me?"

He tugged on his beard. "For what purpose?"

"There's something I have to do."

Head cocked to one side, he continued watching me.

I glanced around to ensure no one was listening. "It's a family thing. You saw my birth. I have to go back. I have to find my other brother."

The braid swung like a slow time keep as he shook his head. "You heard the angel's warning. We've tempted fate too many times. We need to reserve Turas for emergencies only. And we've a battle to prepare for." He nocked his bow. "I'm sorry, Fallon."

I sighed. Time to have a conversation with my mother. "Do you know where Cataleen is?"

"I think she was gathering water from the lake."

I headed down the path. My mother was coming up with two pails.

"Are you headed down to fetch water?" She glanced at my empty hands. "You seem to have forgotten your pails."

"No, I–I wanted to talk to you."

"Oh good. Here." She handed me a full pail.

I heaved the sloshing bucket and stepped in line with her.

"So, what did you want to talk about?"

"I wanted to ask about my brothers."

She dropped her bucket. "Oh!" She picked it up before spilling its entire contents. "Well, the buckets are only about half full every time I return anyway. Here." She grabbed my bucket and dumped some water so both buckets were a little more than half full. "Should make the walk back easier."

Folding my arms across my aching chest, I left my bucket on the ground. "So, what about my brothers?"

She set her bucket down. Rubbed between her eyes and sighed. "Did Sully tell you?"

Nope. Didn't want to get into that. "Why didn't *you* tell me?"

"I–I just—It's been eighteen years. I didn't know what to say…or how to say it." She reached out to touch my face.

I backed away. "Tell me now."

"Tell you what?" Tears welled in her eyes. "That I had three children and two were taken from me?"

A pang stabbed my chest. I wasn't trying to make the woman cry. "I—" I tried to force words past this horrid thing attacking my chest. "I just want to know about my brothers."

"I saw Declan again after I returned to Ariboslia when you were three." She smiled, her gaze somewhere else. "He looked just like your dad." She shook it off and picked up her bucket. "But I still don't know what happened to my other son. I tried to find out, but…no one seems to know. Not even Declan's father, and he's who left with them that night."

So, I'd need Turas. I needed to know. Not because the fasgadair in the mind-link wanted me to. Somehow, my brother was an important piece in this battle.

But Pepin wouldn't help me. Perhaps I didn't need him. I'd seen the motion he made over Drochaid's face once embedded in Turas many times. Did it have to be a pech? Perhaps I could try.

I helped my mother carry the water to the camp, then returned to my things for my water bag and a roll I'd saved and headed into the woods toward Turas. At least I hoped I was headed toward Turas. It had been dark when we arrived, and I couldn't be sure. But I had to try.

"Going somewhere?" Kai's voice came from behind.

I jumped and turned to him. "I—uh—When did you get back?"

"I just arrived. Are you going back to Turas?"

"Uh."

"Why?"

"I–I just—"

Kai laughed. "Just let me join you, and you can explain along the way."

****

Good thing Kai came with me. I wouldn't have made it back on my own. After a few hours trudging through the woods, we came to a clearing, and Turas rose before us. We crossed the green hills to the stones.

"I'm not sure if this will work without Pepin." I placed Drochaid in the depression. "But I'll try." I touched Drochaid as I'd seen Pepin do and swirled my finger over its face in the same manner. Nothing happened. My shoulders sagged. "I guess it does need a pech to operate it."

"Don't give up so easily," Kai said. "Don't you have to say the date to get back to 1521?"

Duh. I took a deep breath. "Let me try again."

Swirling my finger, repeating the date aloud, and imagining Turas whole was challenging. Like patting my head and rubbing my stomach at the same time. A brain tweak. It took longer than normal, but the stones groaned and twitched.

"It's working."

I wanted to shush him but needed all my concentration. The stones gained momentum and converged into a wall. When they stopped, Stonehenge was complete.

I released the breath I'd been holding.

Stonehenge was whole. We made it. 1521. A baby's cry rang out through the air, and the sensation of being in a thick fog of pure evil swept over me. It filled my lungs with each breath and coursed through every blood vessel, both exciting my senses to act and lulling me into a deep depression.

"What was that?" Kai ran toward the sound.

"No! Don't leave the circle!" I fought the desire to drop to the ground and cry myself to sleep.

Kai stopped short, arms windmilling. He'd almost crossed the outer wall. He regained his balance. "But there's a baby here." He pointed outside the wall to a wriggling blanket. Arms poked out, fingers spread. The cry intensified.

A wolf growled.

Kai stepped back.

The wolf neared the baby.

"I have to save it."

"No! Get back here. We have to leave."

"But—"

"It's not real. It's a trick. We have to go. Now!"

Kai returned to the inner circle. Close enough. I swirled my finger over Drochaid and imagined my room in the farmhouse in the past, my mother, the babies.

We arrived as Declan's father loaded the boys up, one in each arm. The evil spirit disappeared and seeped from my system. I shuddered as my spirit detoxed. My mother held me close, sobbing. Tears slid down my father's face. He sat on the bed next to Cataleen and gathered her into his arms.

Without a word, Declan's father walked away. I shut out the image of my parents in pain and followed him down the stairs, out of the house, and into the night. He traveled the path to the megalith. Declan senior pulled out an amulet, not Drochaid, and laid the crying babies in the grass. He crawled through the megalith, his head and upper torso vanished. He paused. Then the rest of his body followed. His arms reappeared, grabbed one baby, and dragged him through, then the other.

I imagined us going through the megalith. It worked. We arrived on the other side where Declan's father was gathering both babies back into his arms. He resumed his trek through the field of retreating grass. Each step he took the grass disappeared, then reappeared as he passed. The grass didn't move for Kai and me.

He must've taken a more direct route to Notirr. It didn't take as long for him to arrive as I took when I arrived in Ariboslia last year. Then again, I had no idea where I was, where I was going, or what I was doing. Declan's father was on a mission. Despite the delicate bundles he carried, they must've felt like weights growing by the pound, weighing his arms down. Regardless, he kept to a good clip.

Just before the sun came up, we arrived at Notirr. But rather than go inside, Declan's father hurried along the road, past the village. He ducked behind a clump of bushes, put the babies down, and retrieved bottles from his sack. He fed each baby, took a few bites of jerky, then lay on the ground to rest, pulling the babies close.

Should I hang out here while they sleep? Couldn't I skip this part?

Couldn't hurt to try. I noted the sun's height rising in the sky as a point of reference. Then I imagined it a little higher. It moved. Declan's father and the babies still slept. Just a little higher. Then, they were gone.

I swiveled around, panicked. Then chastised myself. All I had to do was imagine the sun lower and find them. But a baby cried not too far away. Declan's father crept through the woods along the road.

When the sun reached its full height, clomping hoofs came up the road. Declan's father crouched. Then he stood and rushed to the carriage. The man clicked his tongue. Something about him was familiar. The horses shook their heads, snorted, and came to a stop.

"Achaius!" Declan's father called out.

It was the same guy I met last year? Only in this time, he was closer to my age. His hair was still unkempt, but his face was smooth, his teeth white as he smiled.

"Are you on the way to Notirr with Treasach?"

"I am." He craned his neck to see what Declan's father carried. "What have you there?"

"I apologize. For the safety of these babies, I can't tell you where they're from. Just know I'm trying to protect them. In fact, I wish to keep one as my own. But I need it to appear that they came from Gnuatthara."

Achaius had been transporting babies and elderly when I met him a year ago. I had no idea he'd been rescuing Treasach for so long. Not that I'd asked. Or cared.

After raising an eyebrow, Achaius nodded. "Place them in the baskets in the carriage. There are no adults this time, just babies. But they'll be okay. They're almost there. And better off than how the Treasach left them." He muttered that last part under his breath.

Declan's father adjusted the babies in his arms. "We need to keep the boys separated."

Again, Achaius raised his eyebrow.

"'Tis a long story. Please trust me, Achaius. They both wear matching blue ribbons around their wrist. Please ensure one is delivered to Notirr, to my family. The other must go to another village."

Achaius sighed. "Very well. I'll bring the next one to Ardara."

After he placed the babies into the baskets inside the carriage, Declan's father waved and retreated to the woods. Achaius made clicking sounds at the horses and held their reins. The horses resumed their walk.

I imagined us inside the carriage with the babies. The rocking must have lulled them to sleep. As I tried to determine which ones were my brothers, the carriage moved on without us. We hovered above the road outside. I imagined us inside again, found one of the blue ribbons, then wound up outside again. Enough of that. Following was easier than staying inside…just like with the dinghy. This was the past. Even if something happened, there was nothing I could do.

We waited while Achaius dropped Declan off at Notirr. So, Declan was the one in the ducky blanket. He and the other baby were identical. But I wasn't one to judge. Most babies looked the same.

Achaius returned to the carriage and took off to the northwest. A direction I'd never been. We continued to follow the carriage up a slight, yet steady incline.

I wanted to fast-forward all of this, but I might lose them. I didn't want to waste time. Although, that wasn't possible since, no matter what I did, I'd return to Stonehenge at the same time I left.

But the demons now knew we were messing with Turas. And now they were messing with us. Knowing what kinds of stunts they'd pull to get us to leave the circle made me feel better. But what if something they found worked? What would happen if a demon got a hold of us in the spiritual realm? I shuddered.

The sun had disappeared behind the distant mountains when we came to a quaint village atop a steep hill. Homes like those in Notirr ringed the space, but these were compressed, side by side and atop one another. Down the slope, more homes and paths lined the hill. The road on which the carriage came to a stop was probably someone's roof.

Beyond the layered homes lay miles of open fields and a lake surrounded by trees. Mountains loomed above the tree line. Not a bad place to grow up.

A man approached. "Achaius!"

"Hello, Greer!" Achaius hopped down, greeted Greer with a quick hand grasp, one back pat, man hug. He then turned to the carriage and fetched a baby without the ribbon. He gave the baby to Greer. "We have two babies this time. Do you have room for them?"

"We'll make room for them. Not to worry."

Achaius lifted my brother from the carriage and placed him in Greer's other arm. "Do you need help with them?"

"Oh. I can manage." Greer smiled at the babies. "Come. Let's feed you." He sniffed and wrinkled his nose. "After a wash and clean clothes."

"I apologize." Achaius bowed. "The goal is to get them here safely."

"I understand." He jostled the little ones, cooing. "You're near the end of a long journey. How about a meal and a warm bed for you too?"

"That's kind, Greer, but I must be going."

"If that's your wish."

Achaius dipped his head. "I wish you well, my friend."

Greer dipped his head in response. "You as well." He tightened his grip on the babies and bounded up stairs between two homes, came to the next tier of homes, walked down the left path, and entered a small door.

A woman gasped and grabbed the baby in the bear blanket. My brother. "I've never seen a blanket like this, have you?"

Greer shrugged, and two older children came running.

"Can I see, Mama?" The littlest, probably five years old, stood on tiptoes to see the baby in her mother's arms.

Her mother stooped so she could see.

"Oooh." She smiled. Big eyes full of hope gazed up at her mom. "Can we keep it?"

"Well, I don't know…" The woman sighed and hugged Greer's arm. "We've plenty of children to feed around here."

"I was thinking, perhaps one more wouldn't be too much," Greer said. "I received that promotion to the council."

"What about the other baby, Da?" the older brother asked.

"We'll find him a good home."

The woman smiled. "Well then, what shall we call…?" She gazed at Greer. Her face a question mark.

"Him."

"What shall we call him?"

"How about Alastar, after my father?" Greer suggested.

The woman smiled. "Alastar it is then." She held the baby so he faced his new siblings. "Kids, meet your new brother, Alastar."

So, my brother's name was Alastar. The smells coming from the kitchen made my stomach growl. Yet again, I felt the passing time and was getting tired and hungry. But I didn't want to give up now. I had to know what happened to my brother. Who was he now? Was he still alive?

The bread. I had bread in my satchel. *Good thinking, Fallon.* I reached in and removed a roll. I might need the other later. This might take a while. I broke the roll in half and offered one to Kai.

"Thank you." He took a bite. "So, your other brother is called Alastar?"

"I guess so. Are you okay to keep going? I want to know who he becomes."

He lifted his remaining bread in a salute. "Now I am."

I imagined the same home and the same boy only at around five years old. The scene didn't change much. The same furniture still sat where it had five years prior. Fabulous smells still came from the kitchen. My stomach growled once again. I tore off a bite of my bread.

Something crashed in the other room, followed by a loud thump.

I pictured us in the other room. A small boy wearing an apron, covered in flour lay in a heap on the floor. He looked like Declan must've looked at this age, but his eyes were purple, like mine. Pain twisting his face, he pulled himself up.

Greer raced into the room. "Alastar." He ran to the boy. "Are ye all right, lad?"

"Aye." He nodded, allowing Greer to help him up.

"What happened?"

"I needed more salt."

Greer brushed his son off then moved to the cabinet and hauled out a bag of salt.

"How many times have I said not to climb the cabinet? If something is too high to reach, ask for help."

"I know, Da."

"What are ye making for us tonight?" Greer sniffed. "It smells wonderful."

"Lamb stew." Alastar grinned. "And biscuits."

"And biscuits?" Greer ruffled the top of Alastar's head. "Yer becoming quite the little chef, laddie. Where's yer mum? Is she helping ye?"

"Aye." Purple eyes full of adoration for his dad, Alastar smoothed his hair. "She's fetching more wood for the stove."

As cute as this was, I needed to get moving. I imagined the same place in another five years. We arrived in their blackened kitchen.

"What happened?" I jolted.

"This is the same place, right?" Kai straightened, hopping to his feet.

We moved to the other rooms. Char everywhere. We went outside. The whole village had burned. Aodan. He must've done this. But how would I find out what happened to Alastar? I had an entire five years to check.

Chapter Forty-Two

I WENT TO WHEN Alastar would have been six. The place was fine. Seven. Burnt. Six and a half. Burnt. Six and one quarter. It was fine. So, I kept imagining each day at the same time until all wasn't well. Like trying to isolate a crime on surveillance footage. Then I found it. The fasgadair attack.

Fasgadair ran through homes, throwing torches inside, forcing occupants out. They captured women, children, and men. They killed most of the men. Biting them. Draining them of their blood. A group of men took down a few fasgadair, but most didn't.

I wanted to block out the evil. Or do something, save them. Their cries pierced my soul. Hate coursed through my veins. I wanted to murder every fasgadair, set them all on fire. But I was helpless. Less than a shadow.

I found Alastar huddled with his sister and mom. His dad and older brother were gone. A fasgadair grabbed Alastar and his sister, one under each arm. Their mother followed, screaming, yanking on the unfazed fasgadair. He threw the kids in a wooden cage drawn by horses, then shoved their mother in after them.

I wanted to search for his father, but I couldn't leave Alastar. And they were moving out. A caravan with hundreds of fasgadair before, behind, and between cages full of gachen. Their cries filled the night sky. I stuck by my brother's cage to Ceas Croi. No amount of hunger or tiredness would keep me from finding out what happened to him.

I grew exhausted and slumped against the stone.

"Do you know where they're going?" Kai asked.

"Probably Ceas Croi."

"Can you get us there, then let me take over?"

"I can get us there. But if you take over and they speak, I won't have Drochaid to understand what they're saying."

"I can translate."

I shook my head. "No, I'm okay. But you're right. I should imagine him at Ceas Croi and spare us all this travel. We can always return if we lose him."

I imagined Ceas Croi and Alastar at this age. We appeared in a room in Ceas Croi. It reminded me of a witchcraft shop in my realm. A foreign, musky smoke burned my nose. Incense. Old books, creepy statues, jars, and canisters lined the walls. Morrigan stood at a table, her fingers gliding over the words in a book. She then checked the items in bowls before her, pulled something that wriggled in her pinched fingers out of one, and dropped it in the bowl next to the book.

Alastar sat in a corner, crying.

Morrigan glided in her inhuman way, her feet never seeming to move or connect with the ground. She glanced down and cocked her head at the boy as if he were a strange creature. "Stop your incessant crying. It's tiresome."

"I want my mum. My da."

"Your mum and da are dead." She clipped her words. "You live here now. I'm your new mum." A serpentine smile coiled her lips.

The boy cried harder.

My heart broke. Alastar. My triplet. My little brother. Taken from his mother at birth, then from the family who loved him, and now... Morrigan raised him? As his mother? A desperate urge to protect him flowed to my clenched fists. I had to find him. There *had* to be a way to help him. But he was my age now. I couldn't prevent this. Tears spilled down my cheeks.

I reached out for Kai's hand. "You better hang on, so no one sees you. I'm coming back in the present to see if he's here."

Once Kai grabbed hold, I imagined Alastar in Ceas Croi in the present. Only Morrigan was here, poring over spell books. Her clothes and jars were different, but everything else as it had been all those years ago. Where was Alastar?

Perhaps I should imagine us earlier.

Morrigan jerked her head up and stared into my eyes from across the table. "You!"

I sucked in my breath. *God, help!*

She materialized before me as if she'd gone right through the table. Just as her hand rose toward my neck, she vanished.

I touched my neck. Reassured there was no hand there, I sucked in a breath. But we were still in the same room. Were we in an earlier time as I'd been about to imagine? We must be. The books and items on the table were different. Everything else appeared to be the same. But then, I was never good at those "What's different" memory games.

Morrigan entered, Alastar at her heels. He stood a foot taller than her and looked just like Declan. But now he had grotesque fasgadair eyes in which the iris took up most the eye—like Declan's only purple.

I shivered and backed away. Morrigan had seen me before. But she didn't seem to see me now. This must be the past.

"My son." No affection penetrated those words. She wrinkled her nose.

"Is something wrong?" Alastar asked, pulling the door closed behind him. His tone couldn't be more uninterested.

Morrigan floated toward me and Kai. "I sense…a presence."

I imagined us out of her path. Her eyes followed.

"Want me to help you with a spell?"

"No." She waved a hand, giving Alastar her full attention. "You are becoming a great leader. You will do what your father could not."

Father? Who? Aodan? Had our uncle raised Alastar as his son?

A knock thudded the door.

Morrigan took a deep breath. "Enter."

"Na'Rycha, the soldiers are ready for your orders."

My blood grew cold as my brother turned. "I'll be there in a moment."

Icy blood traveled along my spine as I trembled. My brother. A fasgadair. The most heinous leader anyone has ever seen.

I needed to stop seeking answers from those rocks.

****

Can a brain puke? If there was a way to purge this information, I would. How much more of this could I take? I had brothers. We were triplets. Both were fasgadair. One was the leader. What would I do when I faced him? How had this happened to the sweet little boy who liked to cook?

Morrigan.

Every ounce of my being seethed. Morrigan was the problem. She destroyed everything, starting with my uncle, then my brother...my entire family. It wasn't God's fault. He was the only reason there was any good in this world. Morrigan was to blame.

My mind was a whirlwind. Kai was right to want to go back. Even if I could have kept traveling through time, my mind couldn't take much more. I had to think. Process. Then determine the best action. If I kept going, I'd end up endlessly traveling through time on a futile mission, like searching the internet. Every revelation led to another path until you were lost in the vortex.

And I still had the truth about my brothers to contend with. How was I supposed to share this news with everyone? Oh hey, guess what? I have two brothers. We're triplets. One is the guy I hoped to be my boyfriend, and, oh yeah, he's now a fasgadair. The other is Na'Rycha, the most feared tyrant in Ariboslian history aside from Morrigan. Oh, and my evil uncle and Morrigan raised him as their son.

Yeah. Sounded like a great conversation.

****

The next day I took my frustrations out in mock combat. I eyed the scarecrow as if it was Morrigan. I channeled all my anger and stared at my enemy as I nocked my arrow, aimed, and released. A direct hit into the beast's heart.

I shot another and another. All came within inches of each other. Hyper-focusing on the target and wanting it dead dramatically improved my aim. But I was like an angry bull locked in a pen. I needed to unleash my rage.

I picked up a sword to practice maneuvers on the sticks wrapped in rope. It took a moment to balance myself with its weight. Then I swung, slamming the sword into the rope, sending a shock up my arm. I yanked to pull it out, then slammed it again. And again. And again.

I grew tired, but my anger hadn't dissipated. I headed toward the lake for a drink.

"Mind if I join you?" Sully came up behind me.

"Sure."

"You seem distracted, lass. What's on your mind?"

Oh, nothing. I found out Declan and the leader of the fasgadair are my brothers. But you know that already. And I have no idea where to go with this quest. And God? Where is He in all of this? I haven't heard from Him. Although, I think He saved me from Morrigan who, like you, can see me in the spiritual realm—although it seems she can only see me when I'm in real time. But maybe He didn't save me. Maybe I just managed to get away in time.

In any case, it had been a long time since I felt connected to God. Perhaps He didn't forgive me for all I'd done. I'd messed up so much. "What do you do when you don't feel God?"

"Hmm." Sully walked with his hands clasped behind his back. "Don't let your feelings fool you. Always remember God *is* with you. You remember what it's like in the spiritual realm?"

"In what way?"

"You've experienced it. So, you know it's there even though you're no longer traveling in it, correct?"

"Yeah."

"God is like that. He's always there, but you can't see Him. But eventually, you become more aware that He's there, even if you can't see Him. He'll make Himself known, but it's up to you to look for Him, to remember He's always there. And talk to Him. Always. Even if you don't think He's listening. He is. Don't stop talking to Him."

When was the last time I'd talked to God? I mean, other than to ask for help after I'd already stepped in it? I used to talk to Him all the time. "But what if you've done awful things?"

"What would you do if you hurt a friend?"

"Apologize?"

"Is that a question or an answer?"

"An answer. I'd apologize."

"Then what do you think you should do with God?"

"Apologize?"

"Is that a question or an answer?"

I snickered and shook my head. "So, I just need to tell God I'm sorry?"

"Aye. Forgiveness is always just a prayer away." He patted my knee. "And remember, dear one—you are loved."

CHAPTER FORTY-THREE

I TOSSED AND TURNED on my mat. The past few nights, the deep breathing from those surrounding me had been soothing. Tonight, it kept me awake. Any time I felt myself dozing, Pepin snored and woke me. I wanted to shove a sock in his mouth.

Sleep overtook me, and the field of my dreams materialized. Declan stood in his usual spot at the shore. The window of lights was already there, waiting, with a crystal-clear view of another window. The large window overlooked the ocean—a breathtaking view. But it was strange, peering through a window through another window. Like watching television on television. "What are your orders, sir?"

Orders?

"So, you've returned." Whoever's head I was in seemed sad. "Were you able to talk to your mother?"

"About my brothers?"

"Aye. About the other one."

"What is it to you? Why do you care?"

"You haven't figured out yet who I am?"

"No." Wait. Was this…? No way. I've been talking to the devil himself all this time?

"I take offense to that. Perhaps 'tis time for a family reunion…Sister."

I don't care what I'd seen or what he was trying to tell me. This parasite, Morrigan's lackey, was not my brother.

"Parasite? That hurts. But 'tis true. And I'm here on the island ready to meet my sister. And trust me when I say it's in everyone's best interest that you come quickly. And alone. You don't want to know what will happen to these people if you don't. Those who are still alive and unmaimed that is."

"What have you done to them? What will you do after you've gotten what you want from me? These people aren't safe either way."

"What choice do you have? Come to the castle. I will assure you safe passage. You have twenty-four hours." He sighed. "Oh, and our dear brother is with me. I do so look forward to our reunion."

Declan lunged at me.

****

I couldn't eat my breakfast. I sat outside on the grass, cross-legged, with a bowl of porridge in my lap. The porridge wasn't terrible. It also wasn't good. But my stomach wouldn't have been able to handle ice cream.

Actually, a bowl of ice cream sounded fabulous. Too bad there was no Ben & Jerry's I could drown myself in.

What was I going to do? Would Alastar harm Declan? What good would it do to show up? Then again, going to Aodan had been the right call last time. But was it this time? Alastar knew better than to drink my blood. If he wanted me dead, he'd kill me another way. Would I escape this time?

If only I had someone to talk to about this. Someone who could give me advice. Better yet, tell me the right thing to do. Anyone I'd talk to here would tell me not to go.

I could ask Sully. He had an in with God. Then again, he didn't always know what God wanted and meetings tended to be called when Sully had something to say. Better not.

I could go to God. Sully had suggested I talk to Him.

God, I could really use Your help right now. I'm sorry I haven't been talking to You much. And I only come to You when I need help. And I'm sorry I keep messing things up. I shouldn't have let my curiosity get the better of me. I should have stayed away from the window in my dreams. I shouldn't have burned up that boat with the fasgadair. Or turned away from Declan. Or stayed in paradise while my friends were in jail. Or let the demons find us at Stonehenge. It seems I do the wrong thing all the time. But I can't make a mistake with this one. There are too many lives at stake.

Should I go to Alastar? I know I'm just one little person, but it seems like, no matter what I choose, many people will die. Please tell me what to do.

I dropped my porridge on the ground next to me and covered my face in my hands while I sobbed. *Please, please, please, help me. Tell me what to do.*

"Is this seat taken?"

I hurried to wipe the tears from my face and collect myself. Sully stood next to me, smiling. Could he see I was crying? "No, it's fine." I picked up my bowl. "You can sit."

"You had the right idea coming up here. It's much too stifling underground." He took a deep breath. "Ahhh." He sat next to me and ate his porridge.

I ate a spoonful. Sully had a calming effect, His presence a soothing force. He even made my gruel taste better.

"I believe it's time for you to meet Alastar."

I nearly choked on my food, then managed to swallow. "Excuse me?"

He wiped his face with his sleeve. "Your brother."

"You know about my brother?" What was I saying? He was the reason we were split up. "I mean, where he is. *What* he is?"

"Aye."

"When you told my parents to give him up and separate us, did you know what he'd become?"

"No. I only did what God instructed."

"Why did God do that to him? He could've had a chance. He

could've been normal." I stirred my porridge. "He liked to cook."

"God's ways are greater. I don't understand. I obey." Sully looked to the sky. "He uses it all for good."

"So God is telling me to go to him? To Alastar?" Had he answered my prayer? There's no way Sully happened to sit down to this conversation with me when I was crying out to God. I'd never understand how all this worked, but it wasn't a coincidence. "Do you know what will happen?"

He pressed his lips together into a thin line and shook his head. "I wish I knew everything, child. I wish I could tell you going to him would save us all. But I don't have the answers. I only know what God reveals. At this moment, it's simply this—your brother has requested your presence, and it's God's will that you go to him."

Well…I wanted an answer. Now I had one. I guess not everything Sully shares becomes a federal case. "So, you'll let me go without telling the others?"

"Not everything is up for debate, Fallon. When God says to go, you go." He closed his eyes and lifted his face toward the sky as if basking in the sun's warmth. "Open her eyes, Lord, so she may see."

The scenery wavered like heat waves rippling off a hot road, but everywhere, not just along the horizon. Thousands of shining forms appeared, like the angel I saw at Turas. A surge of power coursed through me, and I was filled with…hope.

Within seconds, the scenery stilled. Celestial beings dematerialized. The hills and woods seemed lonely. But, though I could no longer see them, they were still there. The feeling of hope lingered.

"Were those—?"

"Angels." Sully nodded. "You have nothing to fear, dear one. God is with you. And with Him, His warriors." He took another bite. "But before you go, enjoy a nice breakfast with me. There's no hurry."

My appetite surged. I scooped another spoonful. It tasted wonderful. And this might be my last meal. Better enjoy it.

A warm sensation emanated from my chest. I glanced down. For the first time since I'd left Ariboslia, an arrow on Drochaid lit up.

Chapter Forty-Four

I FINISHED EATING AND gave my bowl to Sully. We hugged, and I set off in the direction Drochaid pointed, oddly comforted by having a guide. I could do anything if I was sure it was the right thing to do. And, although I was setting off alone, I wasn't alone.

"It might be a quicker, more pleasant journey as a falcon," he suggested.

"I'll need to go back for a sack to carry my things."

He reached into a pocket in his robe. "I've just the thing."

"Of course, you do." I laughed and recalled last year when I flew to Ceas Croi alone. "Will you tie the pouch on my foot, so I don't drop it?"

"It would be my pleasure."

Such calm emanated from him. I soaked it up, allowing it to energize me as I changed into a falcon. I clutched Drochaid in my beak.

Sully gathered my things and stuffed them in the pouch. He held up my shoes. "Better not to take these, I think."

I nodded my little bird head, sending my small body rocking. That had been my decision last time. They'd add too much weight. I'd have to go barefoot. Again.

Sully tied the pouch to my foot. He kissed his hand, then touched my head. "God be with you, little one. You are loved."

If I'd been in human form, I might've teared up. But my bird form didn't feel the need to cry.

He pulled Drochaid from my mouth and slipped it into the pouch.

After another nod, I took to the sky. As usual, peace swept over me. Whether it was the sky, Sully, Drochaid, clear direction from God, or all of the above, I was at peace.

****

Amazing how much quicker it was to fly, to soar above the stumbling blocks. In less than an hour, towers peaked above the tree line. Beyond the trees, the full castle rose from the cliff's edge and sprawled over the hills. Ocean waves crashed, sending up a spray, and seagulls squawked. I was countless miles from home in another realm, yet the familiar sounds of the ocean and gulls eased my mind, as if I were flying home, not to my enemy.

I landed in the woods to change. When I flew to Ceas Croi last year, at least I'd arrived inside. I had smooth ground to step on. Now I was in the woods full of debris. My feet were tough, but shoes helped. I tiptoed out of the woods. Even then, I had to walk with care along the dirt road to the stone road. Each path was easier on my feet, but the closer I got, the larger the castle loomed.

The place was silent. Eerie silent. Like when a fan suddenly shuts off or the power goes out. I neared the castle gates. No guards were present. The gate was wide open. The courtyard should have been bustling. But it was barren. No animals. Nothing. A ghost town. I half-expected a tumbleweed to cross my path.

A slight breeze swept through, but rather than a tumbleweed, it carried the fasgadair's electric scent. I shivered and tiptoed to the castle's grand entryway like someone sneaking in. Alastar probably already knew I was here. I could almost sense his sick enjoyment like he was in my head…or I was in his.

Drochaid pointed to the enormous front entryway. An elaborate chandelier hung from the high ceiling. Straight ahead stood a massive staircase, which split at the landing, then continued upward on either side to their own balconies.

Hallways headed in many directions, but Drochaid pointed to the right where the electric scent grew stronger. Sun streamed through giant stained-glass windows, illuminating the hall in a variety of colors. I followed Drochaid to a throne room. Squat stairs led to a gated platform where a subject likely addressed the king but wouldn't be able to reach him.

The king's throne stood on another platform with two sets of stairs on either side. Behind the throne, four massive windows overlooked the ocean. The sun blasting in shadowed the chair. Was someone there?

I inched toward the throne like a kid turning the crank on a jack-in-the-box, knowing what's coming but pressing on. I steeled myself not to jump. The tile chilled my toes and traveled up my spine as I neared, peering into the darkness until I could make out the outline of a figure. Na'Rycha. Alastar.

"Greetings, Sister." His voice sounded strange, sleepy. With a mixture of hatred, sadness, and glee. I couldn't read his expression. Too much distance and too many shadows concealed the details.

"Where is everyone?" I checked behind me, expecting fasgadair to peel themselves from the shadows and surround me.

"The selkie? Some are dead. Others fled. A large group dove into the ocean and haven't returned." He leaned forward. "What could I do? My men were hungry. We'll search the nearby villages soon. I have many soldiers to feed."

I wanted to see his face—traces of my brother. I edged closer. "Where are your minions now?"

"They don't care for sunlight. They're in the dungeons, resting."

"Aren't you bothered by the sun?" Rays beamed on either side of his throne. Hopefully, they'd keep him right where he was.

"Indeed. But it won't kill me. And I couldn't risk missing an important meeting."

"Why did you want to meet me?" Was there a way to reach the little boy inside him?

"Oh-so-many reasons." He lifted his fingers to count them off. "One, you're my sister. Two, you have some incredible powers. Three, I think we can help each other."

"Help each other." I huffed. "With what?"

"We have common goals. You want Morrigan dead. I want Morrigan dead."

"Isn't Morrigan like an adopted mother to you?"

"Hmph." His fingers curled around the throne's ornate arms like spider legs. "What kind of mother do you suppose the queen of the undead could be?" Bitterness, like venom, dripped from his voice. "Do you think she read me stories at night? Tucked me in? Smothered me in hugs and kisses?"

"So, she wasn't mother of the year. Why do you want her dead?"

"Why do you want her dead?"

"Because I'm supposed to kill her. It's my destiny."

"And I also want her dead. See? Common goals. Let's help each other."

He didn't answer my question. He probably wanted more power. Isn't that what it always came down to with evil creatures? "How do you propose to do that?"

"Well, I'd have to trust you completely. You'd have to become a fasgadair."

"That's not even possible."

"I know what your blood does. But have you tried drinking fasgadair blood? It could work."

"No way." Drink blood. I shuddered. Never going to happen.

"I won't work with anyone who isn't a fasgadair."

"And I won't work *with* a fasgadair."

"So, we're at an impasse," Alastar said.

"It seems so."

He seemed trapped by the sun streaming in around him. With no other fasgadair around and him in his weakened state, it was probably safe to leave. "If that's all, I guess I'll be going." I turned around.

Something clicked. Blinds covered the windows, blocking the light. With imperceptible movements, Na'Rycha materialized and grabbed my neck. "If you won't help me willingly, I'll have to coerce you." He smiled a sick, twisted smile. "And satisfy my curiosity in the meantime."

I struggled to breathe. My fingers couldn't squeeze between his fingers and my neck.

God, help me!

Everything went dark.

CHAPTER FORTY-FIVE

I WOKE IN A dark room. The ropes pinning my arms and legs to the chair burned. I had to loosen them…somehow. Was there anything around that might help? It was a gathering room with couches, chairs, and a fireplace. Paintings of the sea on the wall. Lamps on tables. But nothing to remove the bonds.

Fire.

Duh! I stared at the rope, careful to start a small fire at the outside edge to minimize any burns.

Na'Rycha appeared before me, smothered the flame with his hand, and laughed. "There's no point. Even if you could loose those bonds, you couldn't escape me. I'm much too quick. But if you were a faz-*geh*-deer"—his rising voice drew out the word—"you'd have a fighting chance." Grabbing the chair arms, he leaned in close.

His electrical scent shivered over me. A current I wanted to ignite. His grotesque enlarged irises in my face. I fought the urge to spit in them.

"I miss being in your head"—he trailed an icy finger across my forehead—"reading the thoughts you fought to conceal. No matter." He straightened. "Any time you decide you'd like to join me, let me know, and we'll stop this unnecessary torture."

Torture? My heart sped up, urging me to flee. I fought against the ropes.

He backed away. "Just know…this will hurt me as much as it hurts you, Sister." His sinister laugh rippled the air between us. "Okay. Maybe not quite as much. Bring them in."

The door opened and four fasgadair entered.

"My lord." The vampire in back bowed and left the room.

The remaining three monsters glanced at each other as if one of the others might know what was happening.

"You." Na'Rycha pointed to the closest one. "Bite her."

Confusion remained on his face, but he relaxed, apparently having no issue with being told to feed on someone. He bent over, brushed my hair away, then gripped my neck. Tight. Then he sank his teeth in. I screamed as he pierced my flesh.

God, help me!

The fasgadair released me and stepped back.

Warmth trickled down my neck. I wanted to grab it, to stop the bleeding. But my hands were bound.

Na'Rycha pushed a cloth against my neck as the stumbling fasgadair choked on my blood. The demon fell to the ground, blood spewing from his mouth. His body jerked, then stilled.

The veins in the fasgadair's face grayed. Gray spread throughout his entire face and neck. His skin sifted to dust.

Na'Rycha, still holding the cloth to my neck, nudged the fallen fasgadair dust statue with his foot. The statue crumbled. Its clothes flattened to the ground.

"That was interesting. I thought you made fasgadair return to gachen form."

"Or die." Too bad he wouldn't make that mistake.

"Let's try another, shall we?" He signaled a fasgadair in line. "Next."

The fasgadair shuffled forward at a sloth's pace.

Na'Rycha snapped his fingers at the other fasgadair who stared trance-like at the insanity unfolding before him. "Clean this up, would you?"

The third fasgadair jumped to the ready, picked up the flattened clothes, and headed toward the door.

"Don't think you're getting out of this," Na'Rycha called to him. "Leave the clothes with a guard and return."

The third fasgadair slumped off.

The second fasgadair stood before me, not eagerly awaiting his turn.

"Careful not to bite her in the same place," Na'Rycha motioned the beast forward.

Such a strange thing for him to be concerned about.

The second fasgadair took his sweet time bending over my neck. His moist breath stank like month-old meat in a compost bin. His teeth sank into my skin, and his hesitation ended. Instinct and bloodlust took over as he drank my blood.

I cried out again from the pain. My head swooned as the monster siphoned my blood.

"That's enough." Na'Rycha pulled him away. Blood ran down my neck, wetting my dress.

Na'Rycha returned the cloth, pressing it tight to my neck.

The second fasgadair acted much like the first. He fell to his knees as he choked on my blood. His mouth gaped like a fish out of water, hands clutching his throat, attempting to suck in air. Blood gushed from his mouth, and he fell onto his side. A tremor ran through his body. Another twitch. And done. Wide, lifeless eyes stared. Like the other, his pale face grayed, starting with his veins, then fanning out across his flesh.

Na'Rycha let go of the cloth. He stepped back as if aiming to kick a soccer ball in the goal, ran forward, and booted the dust body. The clothes went soaring. Dust filled the air and settled in a triangular formation.

Na'Rycha returned the cloth to my neck and applied pressure.

What was that about? Was he insane? Angry? Both?

My body weak, tired, my mind couldn't focus. The room swam.

"Next!" Na'Rycha called.

The last fasgadair was still by the door. Like the other, he moved at a snail's pace.

"Now!" Veins sprouted along Na'Rycha's temples and neck. He was coming unhinged. Or was this his normal?

The final fasgadair appeared before me with movements imperceptible to the human eye. One moment he was by the door, the next, standing before me. His gaze downcast, he dared peek at Na'Rycha.

"You know what to do." Impatience or irritation clipped the ends off Na'Rycha's words. I half excepted him to break off the fasgadair's lower jaw and ram his teeth into my neck. But that might make it challenging for him to suck my blood.

The final fasgadair reacted as the others had until he too became dust.

"Aghhhh!" Na'Rycha spun around, veins bulging, and stamped his foot. So, this is what a fasgadair tantrum looked like.

Barely conscious, I let my head loll to the side and my gaze drop, only vaguely aware of the trickle down my neck. Yet I found his response amusing.

I heard faint laughter. Was that from me?

Na'Rycha spun around on me. "You think this is *funny*?"

I tried to shake my head. Perhaps I did. I couldn't tell. The giggling continued, the world growing dark.

"How is it you saved Aodan? Why are these three dead? All three!" His voice rose, on the verge of a pathetic whine. "What is different?"

I shrugged—I think. Then darkness.

Chapter Forty-Six

WHEN I WOKE, THE room was still dark. How long was I out? Minutes? Hours? Days? There were no clocks. Just the dark room with oil lamps lending light to reveal the furniture and paintings.

My head pounded. The room spun.

The door opened.

Had someone peeked in? Or gone out?

A fresh rope replaced the one I'd tried to burn. I tried again, but I had trouble focusing. Pain stung my wrist. "Ow!" Had I missed? I tried again, this time hitting my mark. The rope smoked. A small flame ignited, and the fibers began to unfurl.

Na'Rycha materialized before me and smacked the fire out. "Stop doing that. It won't work. There's no way out. Not in your present, human state. Particularly with so much blood loss." He straightened to his full height. "Since you're awake, let's give this thing another try, shall we?" He pointed to a fasgadair behind him. He bent my head to reveal my neck, the unbitten side. "Bite her."

He'd probably kept the fasgadair deaths a secret. This one didn't hesitate. He leaned in and bit. Blood seeped from my veins as he sucked. I'd never get used to blood rushing from my neck. It made me shiver, but it didn't hurt as it had before.

"That's enough." Na'Rycha pulled him back.

The fasgadair wiped his mouth. Pain filled his eyes. He fell to the ground. His body seized as he moaned. Then he stilled. We waited for his body to turn to dust, but it didn't. Olive skin with a healthy pink tinge swept through his features until no trace of the pale fasgadair existed. He sucked in a deep breath and sat up, gasping as if he'd nearly drowned.

"'Tis true." Na'Rycha sat on a nearby couch, his eyes riveted on the fasgadair who'd returned to whatever he'd been before…gachen, selkie. Whatever he was, he was no longer a fasgadair.

Whoever this was who'd been saved, clutched his heart, then his arms. He studied himself as if he received a new body. Then he jerked his head toward Na'Rycha. "What happened?"

Na'Rycha stood, bent over to the man as if he were about to explain, then twisted his neck. I hadn't even seen his arms move. Before the guy realized anything had happened to him, he fell over, dead.

"Why—?" I couldn't squeak out the rest of the words. But what was the point? My head swam. I wasn't strong enough to lose any more blood. I struggled to remain conscious.

Na'Rycha stood and opened his mouth. His words garbled in my mind. Two of him stood before me. Then three. Then nothing.

****

"Fallon!" Something shook me. "Fallon!" A hushed voice kept calling my name.

I fought to open my eyes. With each blink, a face emerged. Declan's once beautiful face now marred by unnatural pale skin. His once beautiful green eyes. Now eerie green, inhuman irises stared at me. I closed my eyes again. Better than looking at that.

He shook me again.

"What do you want?" I growled.

"'Tis me. I'll get you out of here." He untied my binds.

"No." I tried shaking my head, but I could barely move. Bandages tugged from both sides of my neck. Pain emanated from the wounds. My head hurt. I couldn't think.

Declan paused. "No? You want to stay here?"

"I don't want you to rescue me. You're a–a—"

"Who cares what I am if I can get you to safety?"

"I care." Talking hurt. My throat burned.

He resumed untying my binds. Once free, he pulled at me to pick me up. I fought him with what little energy I had.

"Why are you fighting me? Let me save you."

"Let me save *you*." I didn't have the energy for this. Why was he being so stubborn?

He stared at me, mouth agape. "You can't mean that. You'd want me to risk killing you to save myself? I might die too. Even if I survive, I can't help you in human form. Don't you understand? I need to be this way. I have the strength and power to free you. Without it, I'm nothing."

I shook my head—I think. "You're no good to me as a fasgadair. Only as a gachen."

He continued to stare.

"Please," I begged. "Let me change you back."

"I can't forgive myself if I kill you."

"You won't." I hoped. *Please, God, I know this is what must happen. It must be from You. Please, please, please get through to him.* "I won't go with you as a fasgadair."

Declan peeled back the bandage on the left side of my neck, the side with only one set of bite marks. "Forgive me." I barely noticed his teeth pierce my skin. But that familiar jolt of electricity struck, and shame washed over me. How could I react like this to my brother?

After a small drink, Declan released me and replaced the bandage. He touched my face.

Something should be happening. "Did you drink enough?"

"I—" Pain contorted his eyes. He fell back and twisted on the floor.

Please, please, please let him live.

Declan stopped flailing. As with those who'd been saved before, he sucked in air and breathed heavily until his breathing returned to normal.

Thank You, God!

Like the other guy, Declan inspected his body, then let out a sharp laugh. "I can't believe it."

"Neither can I." Na'Rycha clapped as he closed in on us. "Thank you, Be'Thorr, for playing into my hands. But then, I guess you'll lose your fasgadair name and return to being Declan. For a little while anyway—however long you last in this feeble form. My plan couldn't have gone better. Well...other than losing three of my men first." Anger flashed in his eyes. Then, as if he realized those losses were inconsequential compared to his gain, the evil twinkle returned.

Fear seized my heart. But no. Na'Rycha planned this? He counted on Declan's rescue and my refusal to go with him unless he changed? No way. For what purpose?

Wait. This was *God's* plan too. Perhaps Na'Rycha was playing into *His* hands. *Please, God. Please don't let me have been wrong.*

Declan rose from the floor and stood between Na'Rycha and me, his chest puffed out as if he could protect me.

"You were right, Declan. You can't save her in this form." He waved his hand up and down as if showing the frailty of his new form. "What were you thinking listening to her ravings? Can't you see she's out of her mind?"

Declan didn't speak. He also didn't back down.

"It occurred to me that this is our first—and last—family reunion." Na'Rycha sneered. "Too bad dear ol' mum couldn't join us."

Did Declan know we were his siblings? He didn't seem surprised.

Na'Rycha's gaze switched back and forth between us. Was he hoping for a reaction? I struggled to keep my eyes open, and Declan was probably doing all he could just to stand strong.

Na'Rycha's shoulders relaxed. "Well, dear brother. Now that you're disconnected from Morrigan, no longer a fasgadair, I can eliminate you. Are you ready to meet our father?"

"All this time you planned to kill me?" Declan spoke through clenched teeth. "Why?"

"Why do you think Morrigan kept me around as a child? She knew about us all along. She desired Aodan for his power and each of us for ours. But I won't share it. Once you two are eliminated, I'll kill Morrigan too. I alone will rule Ariboslia." Na'Rycha licked his fangs. "After I have a little fun with my sister's abilities."

"Arrrrrgh!" Declan charged Na'Rycha.

Our evil little brother snatched Declan as if he was a doll, leaned in, and bit his neck.

No! God! How could You allow this to happen? This wasn't part of the plan!

I couldn't move to rescue him.

Declan's eyes bulged. He faltered backward as Na'Rycha drank.

Na'Rycha held him upright until he had his fill, then let go. Declan fell. Na'Rycha stepped back, his eyes bugging. "What's this?" He fell to the ground and thrashed. He screamed, then stilled.

Declan stretched his shirt collar up over the bite marks and held it there. He turned to me, brows raised, then returned to our brother on the floor.

Na'Rycha stilled. Pink fleshed in his pale skin. Like Declan and the other fasgadair, he sucked in air as his life returned. He lay there, breathing heavy, then shimmied across the floor to the couch and dragged himself to a sitting position. "What happened?" He clutched his body, inspecting it as the others had. "How did this happen?"

Declan appeared to be as shocked as Na'Rycha and I were.

Joy filled my heart. This was far better than anything I could have planned. But this wasn't *my* plan. It was God's. Must remember that.

Thank You, God.

CHAPTER FORTY-SEVEN

ALASTAR SCRAMBLED TO STAND. He slipped on the couch a few times before rising. "What have I—This is bad." He paced, head down, chewing on one finger. "How could this happen?"

I shrugged. At least it felt like I shrugged. My head, still foggy and heavy, threatened to shut down again. I had to force myself to stay alert.

"You have her ability?" Alastar waved his pointer finger in my direction. "To–to—change fasgadair?"

Declan rushed Alastar and latched onto his collar. "You tried to kill me!" he screamed in Alastar's face. Declan faltered backward, pulling Alastar with him. They fought to remain upright as if drunk.

Alastar tried peeling Declan's fingers from his collar. "You were a threat to my rule."

"Your rule?" Declan scoffed. "You're Morrigan's lapdog. You were never going to rule…and neither was I. I never wanted to." He pushed Alastar onto the couch.

"Look what you did to Fallon." Declan touched my forehead. "Are you all right?"

I tried to speak, but only a groan leaked out. Any fear I should have was drowned out by Declan's eyes. His old, comforting eyes full of concern. He was back.

"Declan. I—"

Declan cut Alastar off. "As much as I want to resolve our family dysfunction, now's not the time. Is there a way past your army? We have to get her to safety."

Shaking his head, Alastar resumed pacing. "We're weak; they're strong. We're slow; they're fast. And we're outnumbered." He stopped and grabbed Declan's shoulders. "If they figure out what happened, we're dead." He raced to the window and peeked behind the blinds. "Night has fallen. This is bad."

"Are there any weapons in here?" Declan planted his hands on his hips.

"No," Alastar said. "I made sure of that."

"Wait." Declan's hands slipped off, both lifting toward our brother. "What is your totem?"

"Owl."

"We're all birds. Let's change into our totems and fly out the window."

"The windows don't open. I had them checked when we secured this place, this room. The moment we smash it, my soldiers will be on us."

"But there's a chance we could get out first. We have to try."

"There's no way." Alastar motioned toward me. "Look at her. She can't possibly fly." He leaned down, his face before mine. His eyes, like Declan's, but purple like mine. "Can you start a fire?"

"I don..." I mumbled.

"Try." He pointed toward a table. "Try to set that on fire."

I tried to pull myself up. My head spun, and I flopped back. I fought to open my eyes and stare at the table. It moved around, then duplicated. Then split into four. And none of the images sparked. I didn't have it in me. "I can...can't."

Alastar swiveled to Declan. "Do you have Aodan's and Cataleen's gift? Can you start fires?"

Declan shook his head. "You?"

"No."

"How can we get her out of here like this?"

"I don't know."

"Think! Aren't you the leader of an entire fasgadair army? Thousands upon thousands? Did your military strategy die with your fasgadair blood?"

"I knew what to do when I was powerful and heartless. But I'm weak now." He flopped his arms as if to prove his point. "How did you do it? I thought only her blood was special. Is it all of us?" He grasped chunks of hair on either side of his head and resumed pacing. "No. That's not it. The fasgadair who turned you would have died or changed. But there must be another reason." He grasped his head in his hands. "I can't get sidetracked with this now." He paused. "Fasgadair are stationed outside this room at both doors. They're surrounding this castle. And unfortunately, I left my invisibility cloak at home."

"You have those?" I asked.

Declan and Alastar stared at me, then laughed.

Either I was way too out of it or Ariboslian humor was lost on me.

Three sharp knocks rattled on the door. Alastar and Declan jumped. "Master, we have urgent news." The voice came from the other side.

Alastar froze. Then he took a deep breath and steeled himself. "I am not to be disturbed."

All was quiet. Then urgent, hushed voices sounded. "Master, there is movement from the southwest woods. Hundreds are armed and headed this way. We must act. What are your orders?"

"Send our forces outside the castle. Prepare for defensive maneuvers."

Hushed voices heightened from the other side of the door. Then it burst open. Four fasgadair appeared. They surveyed the room and closed in on us.

"What's this? Master?" The one in front sniffed the air like a dog. "You're all gachen."

Their eyes narrowed as they circled. Declan scooped me into his arms, and Alastar stood between us and the approaching vampires.

The fasgadair in front laughed. "I wanted a promotion."

"And what do you think Morrigan would do to you should she learn you killed me, Da'Het? Or Fallon? Morrigan wants her alive." Alastar stared Da'Het down.

"Why would we return to Morrigan?" Another fasgadair held his arms out as if putting the room on display.

"We have a nice lair here." Da'Het closed in on Declan and Alastar. "We'll start our own coven on these virgin lands."

"You think she won't find you? You *actually* think you'd survive this?" Alastar stepped back, his arms splayed, blocking us.

"Aye." The other fasgadair smiled. "I do." He lunged.

I reached out and gripped Alastar's shoulder. A jolt of electricity shot through my arm, and a circle of fire erupted around us. The flame engulfed the fasgadair. He screeched. His cry cut short. His flesh melted, charred, then crumbled in one fluid motion within seconds.

Get out.

Where had those words come from? And what were these flames? They surrounded us, starting at our feet, from nothing, and shot straight up over our heads. The steady fire neither consumed us nor the furniture, only the fasgadair who'd had the misfortune of touching it. I couldn't even feel the heat inches from me.

The other fasgadair stared, slack-jawed.

Alastar strode toward the door. My hand slipped from his shoulder, and the flame disappeared.

"Get them!" Da'Het shouted.

Alastar spun toward us. Just as another fasgadair neared, Alastar wrapped his arms around us to protect us. The fire roared to life. The fasgadair caught in the flame screeched and died as the first had.

Alastar opened his eyes. We each stared at one another in turn, eyes bulging. Without losing contact, Alastar slid his hand down my arm, held my hand, and turned around. He kept a firm grip on my hand over his shoulder. "Don't let go." He shuffled toward the door with me and Declan in tow.

The circle of fire came with us.

Da'Het and the remaining fasgadair bumped into one another as they scrambled out the door before us, keeping their freakish eyes glued on the circle of fire. Once free of the doorjamb, they rushed aside, giving us ample room to pass by.

We continued, surrounded, but not swallowed by, the pillar of flames, through the halls, down the stairs, into the entryway. Da'Het and the other fasgadair followed.

Another vampire at the bottom of the stairs looked at the trailing fasgadair. "What are you doing? Fire won't kill us." He lunged. The moment he touched the flames, he melted, charred, and crumbled. A lesson to those who hadn't seen the others. The witnesses kept their distance.

Alastar pulled the front doors open. The doors erupted in flames.

"Oops," Declan said.

How did that happen?

Two fasgadair attacked from either side. They singed and fizzled to dust. A breeze swept away their remains but didn't disturb the fire. The flames continued straight up, unaffected by the wind.

Mobbing fasgadair circled the flames. They crouched, with their hands up. Like fighters sizing up their opponent before the bell.

We continued forward, and the sea of fasgadair parted.

"Open the gate," Alastar ordered.

The gate squealed and clanged as it rose. On the other side, Sully stood, surrounded by pech and a ragtag group of gachen and selkie armed with swords. They stood there as if they knew the gate would rise. The fasgadairs' gaze jumped between us and the army at the gate as if calculating which threat to eliminate first.

Sully raised his staff, and his army waited like racers at the starting line. Arrows rained from above. I traced their path to our allies in the trees, shooting. Many fasgadair fell.

Sully roared and pitched his staff forward. His army hollered in response and charged under the gate, keeping a safe distance from me and my brothers. They slashed fasgadair with their weapons, pushing them back so others could rush in and behead the felled fasgadair before they removed the arrows and regenerated.

Kai ran up to us, sword drawn, blood splattered across his face and chest. "Fallon! Are you okay?"

"Yes." I tried to sound convincing.

A fasgadair with a readied sword rushed Kai.

"Behind you!" I yelled.

He swung as if hitting a baseball, slicing the fasgadair through the middle. Alastar led us to the body as it fell. It ignited before reaching the ground.

"Be careful," I warned Kai.

He nodded, seeming satisfied I was in good hands, then ran toward another fasgadair.

God, protect him.

I tried following Kai's movements but lost him in the mayhem.

Swords slashed, metal clanged, and cries rang out all. Bloodied faces I recognized were locked in battle. Wolf sliced a fasgadair's neck as Pepin hamstrung it from behind. Cahal brought his battle-axe down on a felled fasgadair. Maili and the other archers had left the trees and lined the wall, sinking arrows into any fasgadair in their line of sight. Sully stood in the middle of the skirmish with his staff in both hands over his head. Not one fasgadair neared him.

Alastar stooped to pick up an abandoned sword. His shoulder slipped from my grasp and the fire vanished. He attacked an oncoming fasgadair.

Declan and I remained unprotected. A fasgadair bulldozed through the throng toward us.

"Alastar!" I cried.

He ran his blade across a fasgadair's neck, grabbed my hand with his left, and swung at the oncoming fasgadair with his right. The fire circle reignited and kindled the fasgadair.

Alastar led us throughout the war zone to unsuspecting fasgadair engaged in combat. The second the fire touched them, they melted.

We continued like that, moving from one to the next and the next, catching as many fasgadair as we could, careful not to come near our own.

A fasgadair knocked the sword out of Pepin's hand and pushed him to the ground. As the fasgadair picked up the sword, we ran up behind him. In one swift movement, the fasgadair sidestepped and shoved Pepin into the fire.

I sucked in my breath. "No!"

Pepin froze as if waiting to melt. But he didn't. The fire didn't harm him. Alastar and Declan took advantage of the fasgadair's shock and ran him through. Dust.

The fasgadairs' numbers thinned, and those who remained knew to keep a safe distance. They dodged our approach. We distracted them, allowing our allies to maim them so we could come up behind and melt them.

We were clumsy but effective. And resulted in a somewhat clean battlefield. Other than our fallen friends.

The clanging metal and shuffling feet slowed. Sully remained in the center of the courtyard with his staff raised. A fasgadair charged him. Valter stepped between them. The fasgadair sliced his sword through Valter's midsection, and he fell. Declan and Alastar rushed to them and caught the fasgadair in the fire.

I dropped from Declan's arms and released Alastar, extinguishing the flames as I knelt by Valter. "You're alive?" I pulled his head onto my lap.

"I won't be…much longer." Blood spurted from his mouth. "I'm sorry. I only want—I only wanted—"

"Shhh…it's okay." I swept his hair from his eyes.

"To—to save us."

"I know, Valter. I forgive you."

"Do—does God?"

"You *want* God to forgive you?" I asked.

Coughing up more blood, he nodded.

"Then, yes. He forgives you." I choked back tears, grateful Valter believed and sought forgiveness.

Thank You, God, for saving him…even in this final hour.

Tears pooled in the corner of Valter's eye. "Tha–thank you." He coughed, and his body convulsed.

"I'll see you in heaven."

"You are loved."

He smiled, revealing bloodstained teeth, and gargled on blood as he sucked in a breath, then stilled. The life left his eyes. I pushed his eyelids down and sobbed.

The fighting had ceased. A bedraggled group collected around us. People sniffed and wiped away tears, I assumed from witnessing a salvation and death within seconds.

Kai helped me stand. I leaned on him. Many rushed about aiding fallen fighters. Others stood with chests heaving, searching in every direction as if waiting for another attack. But nothing came. Only gachen, selkie, or pech remained standing. Not a fasgadair in sight and no electric smell.

Groans rose from maimed bodies. The able-bodied carried them into the castle.

Kai scooped me up.

"I think I can walk now."

"Don't take this moment away from me." His dimples melted my soul.

Kai followed Declan and Alastar to the room we occupied before. Alastar dropped onto the chair he'd tied me to.

Kai placed me on a couch, then sat beside me and snugged an arm around me. "How are you feeling?"

"I'm okay. Just a little dizzy." I coughed.

He closed his eyes and breathed deep. "Why did you take off like that? Do you know how that made me feel…to find out you'd walked into the fasgadairs' camp…without me to protect you? What were you thinking?"

He wanted to protect me? I fought a smile…and the desire to embrace him. "Would you have gone with me?"

"No. I would have kept you from doing something so stupid."

"That's why I didn't tell you."

He narrowed his eyes at me. "So stubborn." He pulled me closer and smoothed my hair.

I breathed in his familiar woodsy scent.

A group of men, selkie by the looks of their dark hair and eyes, entered the room.

"Thank you for helping us reclaim the kingdom," said the man in front with trim black hair and beard speckled with gray. He called to the men behind him. "Please alert the royal court that it's safe to return."

With a nod, one of the men ducked out of the room.

The man in front returned his attention to us. "Please allow me to introduce myself. I'm General Seung." He bowed. "I can't thank you enough for aiding us in securing this kingdom. These shores."

Another man appeared in the entryway. I didn't know who he was, but I recognized him from our ship. One of the crew perhaps? "Na'Rycha?" He spat his name as if it were a curse.

"His name is Alastar," I said.

"Are you going to let him live?" The man waved his arm at Alastar. "He's the reason we're here. He's the reason we don't have a home to go back to. Family." His voice cracked. He cleared his throat and addressed General Seung. "He may have helped us win this battle. But he's the one who brought this evil to your shores."

"Technically, Morrigan is the cause." Alastar crossed his arms.

"If we really want to get technical." I waved my finger. "It was those two women who summoned her through the zpět."

"Actually, it was whoever created the zpět," Declan said. "What difference does it make how we got here? I'm not innocent either. None of us are."

"Well, *I* didn't lead a charge through Ariboslia and kill millions of innocents," the crewman said.

"He's a victim too." I moved to the edge of my seat and braced myself. "He was taken from his family as a child during Aodan's rule.

Morrigan raised him as her child."

Murmurs swept through the room like a cyclone, circling.

"From what I saw, this man is a hero." General Seung bowed toward Alastar. "I'll leave you to handle your own affairs."

"Perhaps you might assist us?" King Aleksander and Abracham came up behind the crewman and sidestepped him.

General Seung inclined his head in a slight bow toward King Aleksander. "How might I be of service?"

"I am King Aleksander of Bandia. This is King Abracham of Diabalta."

"You've never been king of Diabalta," someone said. "Your father died, and the lands were taken by the fasgadair before you could claim the throne. Why do you claim it now?"

"Because now we have hope of reclaiming our lands. We have a way home." Abracham looked at me. "Na'Rycha is dead." He nodded at Alastar. "And, with the selkie and the pech on our side, we have military aid." He turned to General Seung. "That is where I'm hoping you'll step in."

"I will discuss it with the royal council upon their return. But please understand, the fasgadair annihilated our royal family. We'll need to restore the rightful ruler to the crown, then deal with turmoil within our country. Revelation of the selkie-gachen hoax has turned our system upside down," General Seung said. "But many saw your heroism today. I will see what I can do."

EPILOGUE

I FOUND SULLY OUTSIDE the castle on the rocky shore, eyes closed, his face aimed toward the heavens. Gulls squawked as they flittered about from craggy nook to craggy nook.

I sat beside him.

"Well done, lass. Well done." He patted my shoulder and smiled, keeping his face skyward.

I had so many questions. "What happened? How did Declan, Alastar, and I create that fire? Or was it God? But why did it disappear when we weren't connected?"

"You don't yet understand? You haven't figured out by now why we needed to separate you three all those years ago?"

"No."

Sully sighed, pressed both hands on the ground, and shifted his aged form to me, his gray eyes staring as if he could see. "You have your mother's ability to start fires. Declan can control fire. And Alastar can protect you from its sting. And even when you were too weak to start a fire on your own, the moment you three connected, fire erupted. That is why you couldn't be together as small children. You are stronger together, able to use your abilities without awareness of what you're doing. Had you been together when you were young, you could have caused much destruction. And"—he faced the sky—"this was part of God's plan. Had any of these events turned out differently, His plan wouldn't have come to fruition. And His will always plays out according to plan."

"What about Declan?" I tucked my hands under my thighs and leaned closer, inspecting the old man as if his secrets might seep out his pores. "How did he turn Alastar back into a gachen?"

"That is something God has yet to reveal."

I deflated, sagging my shoulders.

"Our fight isn't over."

"I know. I have to deal with Morrigan." My stomach squeezed, pushing up the old fears, squelching the peace of this victory. "How am I supposed to go against someone so powerful? Am I supposed to pick up Cairbre's quest and find the zpĕt?"

"You will need the zpĕt, yes." He patted my shoulder. "For now, remember you have Someone much more powerful on your side. Keep your eyes on Him. He will guide you." Smiling, he stood. Such tender benevolence peered down at me—how could I not trust this man? "You have a visitor."

"Who?" There was no one nearby.

Sully crossed the rocks with the ease of a much younger man with fully functioning eyes.

Waves crashed against the rocks, sending up a spray with each hit.

Kai sat beside me. "I've been looking everywhere for you."

I chuckled. Was this the visitor Sully predicted?

He flashed his dimply smile. "Something funny?"

"No."

"The government will overturn their rule. They'll allow gachen who don't turn into seals to remain. In the future, they will be allowed to keep their lands and titles. The government will work to compensate those who lost their lands and titles and restore them to their communities."

"That's great news." I nudged his shoulder with my elbow. "So, you can return to your family." Why did I feel sad?

Kai nodded. His face serious. Something was off.

"Aren't you happy?"

"I am. But I think I've found something more important to do."

"What?"

He shifted to face me, dark eyes peering into my soul. "To go back with you. To help your people reclaim *their* lands. It's the least I can do after what you've done for us. And I'm not the only one. Others wish to aid the battle. And our government has warships and resources to assist in your quest."

After what we'd accomplished, I felt confident going home and facing the fasgadair. Now we had a weapon. And, thanks to Sully, I had a better understanding of how to use it.

Since I'd fulfilled the quest and removed Na'Rycha from power, I wanted nothing more than to rest. I'd destroyed both Aodan's and Alastar's reign, albeit in unexpected ways. But it wasn't over. This was preparation for what I hoped to be the final battle. It all came down to one thing—Morrigan.

It was time. Time to regroup and focus on this final quest to find the zpĕt and somehow use it to destroy Morrigan.

But how? In traveling through Turas, I'd seen what Morrigan is capable of. The fire my brothers and I could conjure wouldn't take Morrigan out. She was much too quick. And I had no clue how to begin my search for the zpĕt. And, if by some miracle, I found it, I didn't know how to use it to destroy her.

"Are you overthinking again?" Kai pushed my head against his shoulder. "What's that saying your people use?" He grasped my hand. "Ah, yes—you are loved."

I breathed in the mixture of his pine scent and the sea air, and my mind calmed. Why did I worry so much? Hadn't God proven over and over He was in control? He had this. He'd gotten me through two major battles already and countless minor ones.

Thank You, God. Thanks for protecting me. Thanks for bringing people into my life to help. Thank You that I don't need to worry. You've got this. Help me trust You to get me through the next battle. Trust You in the little things too. Trust You more and more.

I'd concern myself with the next steps later. For the moment, I'd bask in victory. Somehow, with God's help, we'd succeed in the next. *Standing on the promises of God…*

The End.

Shameless Request for Reviews

Authors need reviews! They help books get noticed, and I love to know what my readers think of my stories. So, if you enjoyed this book, please consider leaving a review where you purchased this book, Goodreads, BookBub…or anywhere you think a review might be helpful. I'm forever grateful!

You are loved,
J. F. Rogers

More from J. F. Rogers

The Redeemed: Pepin's Tale—A FREE Short Story

J. F. Rogers is working on a collection of short stories from Ariboslia with tales from characters you've met...and some you might not otherwise meet. Though it will take some time to prepare the entire collection of stories, the first, Pepin's Tale, is available now—FREE.

Claim your copy here:
https://jfrogers.com/free-book/

Astray (Ariboslia Book I)

Fallon returns to Ariboslia to save lives. But A mysterious amulet leads Fallon to everything she's ever wanted...and possibly her death.

After a lifetime with no knowledge of her parents, troubled seventeen-year-old Fallon Webb receives a necklace once belonging to her mother. The amulet leads her on a life-changing journey through a portal to a foreign land where she encounters unusual creatures, shape-shifters, and something she's always longed for—family.

In Ariboslia, Fallon learns her mother is alive. Vampire-like creatures have her, and many others, captive. Most distressing is the prophecy that devastated her family. Can she trust it? Because if it's right, Fallon must destroy the vampires' leader—her uncle—to rescue her mother and free her people from the threat.

Unprepared and afraid, Fallon sets out on the journey, with no skills to assist her quest and no other way home. In her travels, she learns about the One True God and how desperately she needs Him. Perhaps, with His help, she'll find a way to fulfill her destiny and stay alive.

Astray is the first book in the Ariboslia Christian fantasy series. If you enjoy visiting alternate worlds that feature fast-paced adventure, supernatural creatures, compelling characters, and exciting plot twists, come to Ariboslia. You'll love this first installment in J. F. Rogers's page-turning series.

Buy Astray to discover this exciting new series today!

Available in paperback and ebook at Amazon and other retailers
(B&N, iTunes, Kobo, GooglePlay, and more!)

Looking for more by J. F. Rogers?
Be among the first to know when new books are released.

Join her clan today at https://jfrogers.com/join/

About the Author

J. F. Rogers lives in southern Maine with her husband and daughter. She has a degree in Behavioral Science and teaches a fifth- and sixth-grade Sunday school class. When she's not visiting Ariboslia, you can find her buried in snow or kayaking, depending on the time of year. Or at church. She's a junk-food junkie turned health nut who believes wholeheartedly in the One True God and can say with certainty—you are loved.

Connect with J F Rogers!
Website: jfrogers.com
Facebook: jfrogerswrites
Google+: +JFRogers
Pinterest: jfrogers925
Twitter: jfrogers925

ACKNOWLEDGMENTS

As always, I must thank God first. He is my Creator, my Inspiration, my All.

Next, my husband, Rick, and daughter, Emily. I don't know where I'd be without you. Thank you for your love and patience. I love you both so much.

Special thanks to:

My critique group: Fantasy for Christ—our gracious leader, Azalea Dabill, Terri Proksch (Terri Luckey), Precarious Yates (aka Sarah Smith), Katie Clark, Tami O'Neal, Phyllis Wheeler, and a special shout out to Jan Davis Warren for seeing it all the way through…even the race to the end.

My editor: Deirdre Lockhart with Brilliant Cut Editing.

My cover artist and formatter: Mark and Lorna Reid at authorpackages.com.

My ARC readers: Jen Tate and Jenny Cardinal.

My friends: So many people showed up to encourage me along the way. Your timing was perfect.

God has blessed me and this novel by surrounding me with so much talent. Adrift wouldn't be the same without you. I can't tell you how much I appreciate you. Thank you! I love you all!